THE HAUNTING OF
OF
SUNSHINE
HOUSE

THE HAUNTING OF SUNSHINE HOUSE

ISBN-13: 978-1949674-02-6
ISBN-10: 1-949674-02-9

www.dominikabest.com

Instagram: @thedominikabest
Twitter: @thedominikabest

Second Edition

Printed in the U.S.A

For Dave

without you, none of this would be possible

The tragedy of old age is not that one is old, but that one is young.

-Oscar Wilde
The Picture of Dorian Gray

1
The Bockerman
FEBRUARY 16, 2005 - DAY 1

Barney Leonard studied the sign flashing "The All-Star Theatre Cafe & Speakeasy" above the entrance to the Sunshine Assisted Living Home cafeteria and wished that the speakeasy part was still true. Instead of delicious mixed cocktails and well-heeled clientele, he and the other residents got a utilitarian buffet of hot and cold breakfast offerings. Scrambled eggs that resembled cardboard, sausage links, wilted fruit and oatmeal that looked like dried concrete. He played with his plain bagel smeared with light cream cheese, the only one they stocked here. What kind of breakfast did Marilyn and Dimaggio eat at this spot, when it was one of the most famous restaurants in Hollywood and not a low-rent cafeteria?

His mind wandered with the possiblities. Bacon. They ate bacon for sure. Marilyn loved bacon, he'd read. Barney missed bacon. It had been years since he'd had a decent slab. At least the company who purchased the place retained the rich dark wood paneling. They made up for that oversight by outfitting the rest of the place with cheap plastic tables and chairs.

He shoved his plate away in revulsion. Where in the hell was Babs? He stared towards the door to the lobby and willed Babs to step inside. The door remained closed.

Mary Ann McClatch, a well-preserved seventy-five, skin stretched and rouged for maximum impact, leaned in closer to him and put her hand on his knee. His head swam with her strong perfume. The woman bathed in it.

"The ghost has to be Irene Lentz, don't you see Barney? She was the lovesick one that plunged out of a window on the eleventh floor?" Her gruff voice whispered in his ear. "Have you ever loved like that?" She pulled back and gave him the look. That look. They had one night together, and he couldn't shake her, however hard he tried. He smiled and lifted her hand off his thigh.

Barney edged away from her and focused on Lauren, a round grandma with twinkling blue eyes who was a dead ringer for Mrs. Claus. She snorted at Mary Ann's failed advance. Barney had struck out with Lauren when he first arrived at Sunshine but didn't hold it against her. The crinkles around her eyes revealed her love of laughter and each time she laughed, he wished his view of the world matched hers better. Babs, in her own way, was doing much to change his outlook on life. She inspired him and he loved her for it.

He recalled the first time he'd spotted Barbara "Babs" Monroe in the lobby and realized she was the one. He never believed himself to be a romantic? Up to that point, he'd been bed hopping for over a year but had grown bored of it and wanted something more substantial. He pursued Babs for several months, and when she turned her charm on him, he was the proudest man at the Sunshine House.

"It's always the lovesick ones," Mary Ann said, glaring at him.

"You should know," Lauren countered, winking at him. He burst out laughing. Mary Ann let go of his arm, ignoring Lauren. He stretched it out to get his blood circulating from her vise-like grip.

"It's not only one ghost. Rudolf Valentino frequented this bar until his death in '26 and Harry Houdini's widow, Bess, held an infamous séance on the roof in '36 on Halloween night." He stopped to Lauren rolling her eyes.

"Do you believe in that stuff, Barney?" Lauren asked.

"It's based on fact, Lauren. I recall reading about Frances Farmer being dragged out of here by the police after skipping parole. She had been a doll on set. This place is our history. I remember going to the silent pictures as a kid, and they're the reason I got into the business. The list of deaths here goes on and on, D.W. Griffith, Irene Lentz, like you said." He nodded to Mary Ann. "And even William Frawley, Fred Mertz from 'I Love Lucy'. I worked with him once. He died at the front entrance. I'm surrounded by old friends and don't fear their nightly wanderings."

"That's eloquent, Barney," Lauren admitted.

"Thank you, Lauren," he said, and observed Mary Ann bristle. Where in the hell was Babs? Everyone in the place knew he and Babs were together, and Mary Ann wouldn't flirt like this if Babs was present.

"But the voice sounded like a woman's," Mary Ann whined. "You've heard the cries, haven't you?"

"No, I haven't," Barney said. However much he felt as though he was home, he still kept a healthy sense of skepticism about actual ghosts. He imagined Frances and William and Valentino hanging here, but they had not appeared to him yet. During his long career as a sound engineer, he created sounds using ordinary objects to make any sound effect a director wanted. Sound was tricky. If a person was primed to hear ghosts, many ordinary sounds masqueraded as ones from the ghostly realm.

"What about James and Judith...the others?" Mary Ann asked. Barney scowled at her question. Five people had died at the Sunshine over a period of two months. Most of the residents panicked thinking they were next, trotting out crazy theories about the reaper walking the halls.

His mind jumped to Babs. She should be here by now. A knot twisted in his stomach, but he reminded himself that she always overslept.

"What if Bess Houdini brought something evil upon us?" Mary Ann whispered, her eyes growing wide. Lauren snorted again.

"You're talking demons now, Mary Ann? As if ghosts weren't crazy enough to entertain?" Lauren asked, squaring off.

"Has anyone seen Babs this morning?" The gnawing pain in his stomach grew bigger as Mary Ann's hand tugged at his arm again.

"She believes in ghosts and demons. Why just two days ago we were fooling around with an Ouija board in her room and I'm positive we made contact. She spoke about black magic and the mirror world." She nodded and scrutinized Barney's face. Babs was kooky, but he loved that about her. Mary Ann scowled at him when he didn't give her the response she was expecting. "What about the séances? On the roof?" Mary Ann struggled to draw his attention back to her, but he shrugged her arm off.

"Something's wrong. I should check on Babs." He stood up and saw Nurse Louise Fairbanks enter. His heart sped up amidst an ominous sense of impending disaster. He faltered as he watched her fill a plate at the buffet and lowered himself back into his seat. She headed right towards their table. Regular angel of death that one, he thought. He was sure she was the one responsible for the most recent deaths here.

He played it cool and forced a smile as Lou, the name all the residents called her by, stepped up to their table.

"Can I join?" Lou asked.

"Good Morning, Lou," Mary Ann said. Lou smiled and sat down, her tray in front of her.

"Maybe you can make sense of all this," Mary Ann said as Lou's fork stopped in midair.

"Not you too? Is this about the noise last night?" Lou asked, stress permeating her voice.

All the residents welcomed Lou and Dads, her dementia afflicted father, when they arrived some months back. Dads kept her busy, his dementia worsening week by week and they rallied to help her in any way they could with him. But then James died, then Judith, and Amy, Nancy, and Regina. Even for an assisted living facility that was a lot of deaths. That quack Dr. Jerris claimed they all died of natural causes and said, 'Well, we all have to die of something. They were old.'

What a bastard, he thought, his eyes narrowing at the memory. Barney didn't have to do too much research before he found doctors and nurses who killed their own patients. The police and media called them angels of death. Lou was a perfect example of one, Barney thought.

"There are no ghosts, Mary Ann. I promise," Lou said, piercing his thoughts as she speared egg on to her fork.

"How can you be sure?" He kept his voice even, but it came out a hiss. Lou smiled at him. He craved to wipe it off her face.

"I'm surprised a scientific man like yourself would believe in such nonsense," Lou said and popped the egg in her mouth. Mary Ann and Lauren leaned in, smelling blood.

"Sound engineer not a scientist," he said, ignoring her tone. "When people die of unnatural causes, such as murder, they hang around seeking vengeance against their killer. What else do you think ghosts hang about for?" He scrutinized her face for any tells but discovered none. She was stone cold.

"No one here died from unnatural causes, Barney. You stir up trouble by scaring the hell out of everyone," Lou said and looked to the women for confirmation. Mary Ann and Lauren avoided her eyes.

"I'm scared," Barney said. "Old people die but how many deaths in a short span of time make you fear for your life?"

Lou pointed her fork in his face. "You don't have a good attitude, Barney. No one should listen to you." She focused back on her eggs, her lips curling until they disappeared. Her expression reminded Barney of a skeletal grimace.

"My age gives me the right to have whatever attitude I want," Barney grunted as he shoved away from the table. "I gotta go find Babs." He stalked to the door, his anger turning to fear. Babs, please be alive.

He fought the urge to run and counted his steps until he stepped over the threshold. The moment the door closed behind him, he broke into a run. Russell Hall, the guard on duty, shouted something as he ran by but he didn't bother slowing down for that asshole.

Barney limped down the hall, wheezing from too much exertion, worry etched on his face. He stopped at Room 837. He breathed in deep, waited a second to get his heart under control then pounded on the door. He hoped Babs would throw it open in annoyance and yell at him for being so obnoxious, but the door stayed closed. He listened for any sound coming from inside. Nothing. He kicked the door one last time, but it remained closed.

"Babs? You there?" He pounded harder and even kicked it again for good measure.

No answer.

With his face pale and sweaty and heart pounding in his chest, he yelled, "Barbara? Are you in there? Can I come in?" He listened, heart thudding in his chest. "Stand away from the door, I'm coming in," he shouted and threw his body against it. The door stood, immovable and solid.

The key. She gave him a key. He had left it in his drawer for safe-keeping. Barney whipped around ready to get it, but stopped himself before racing down the hall. Another thought crossed his mind.

What if?

No, he thought.

She wouldn't have left it open. Babs promised she'd lock the door but what if she forgot?

Cold sweat dripped down his back at the thought. If the door was open...

He squeezed his eyes shut and twisted the doorknob to the right. The lock tumblers disengaged, and the door squeaked open. Jesus, why was her door open?

"Babs? Barbara? You OK? It's Barney," he called out, opening his eyes. Her blackout curtains were open so she couldn't still be asleep. She always complained she couldn't sleep with any light in the room, but there she was still in bed. He took a step inside and smelled it. Decay and death, sickly sweet and familiar. It wafted by him as he threw himself at her bed. "Babs, NO, NO!"

She lay on the bed, her arms at her side and her head on the pillow. He pressed his fingers under her chin searching for a pulse, her skin ice-cold and waxy underneath his touch. She was dead.

2
Zamość, Poland
DECEMBER 19, 1942

Szymon Michalski held onto his mama's hand as they navigated the snow-covered sidewalk. The bad men in the big trucks made the sidewalk shake, and he couldn't help glance their way. One of them saw him look and Szymon turned his face away in fear, hoping he was wrong. His mama told him, right before they left the house, not to look at any faces and keep his eyes on his feet. He obeyed like a good boy but when he felt the rumble, he couldn't help it. The big trucks made a terrible, loud noise and he wanted to cover his ears but mama wouldn't let go of him. She held on so tight that his hand ached in his mittens.

"Pick up your feet, Szymon. It's cold." She dragged him forward, and he followed the best he could. His toes had frozen the moment they stepped outside because the holes in his shoes let in the wet snow. It hurt to walk, but he kept quiet since Mama seemed worried and the grocer's was still several blocks away. Mama gave a small gasp and stopped walking. He peeked up to see what scared her and found a bad man and a woman in a brown uniform blocking the sidewalk. His mama pulled him closer. He tucked his head back down, hoping mama hadn't seen him look up. She'd be so mad.

"Names, please," the man demanded. His mama's arms tightened around him.

"Magdalena Michalski," his mama answered while the woman kneeled in front of him.

"What's your name?" she asked him. Szymon checked with his mama who nodded.

"Szymon," he said.

"How old are you, Szymon?"

"Eight." The woman straightened and pulled off his wooly hat. He shivered as the cold wind hit the back of his damp hair and saw the woman nod at the bad man.

"Szymon, you need to come with us," the woman said, pulling on his arm.

"No! Why do you want my son?" His mama's voice sounded strange to Szymon. Like, when Pani Dudek told them that Papa had gone to heaven.

"He needs to come with us." The woman tugged harder on his arm but Mama wouldn't let go.

"NO!" Mama clutched him to her. The woman took him by both shoulders and pulled harder but Mama kept hold of his arm. "Please don't. I'll do anything. Please," she pleaded with them.

Szymon stared up at the adults as the bad man pulled out a gun and pointed it at Mama's head. His mama sobbed. A bright light blinded him while a big bang hurt his ears. He felt wet on his face as his mama let him go. He clamped his hands over his ears while the woman pulled at him, but he didn't want to go and leave his mama like that. He kneeled down next to her and tried to shake her awake but that just made more blood pour out of her head and onto the dirty, grey snow on the sidewalk. Mama killed a chicken for dinner yesterday and her blood looked the same as the chicken's did. He looked up at the woman.

"MAMA. MAMA. Mama's hurt. You hurt my mama," he yelled at the brown woman because he was too afraid to look at the bad man. She yanked him by the arm, but he fought against her. He had to stay with Mama. He wouldn't leave her here. She needed him.

"MAMA!" He screamed but Mama did nothing. She just lay there, her eyes open. The bad man lifted him up and threw him over his shoulder. Where were they taking him? Why couldn't he stay with Mama?

The woman's face came close to his. "Be a good boy, Szymon. Be a good boy," she said. He whimpered and knew that Mama went to heaven just like Papa had. He was alone now. He fell silent and stopped squirming. The ground moved, and he watched the bad man step into the street. Why did they hurt Mama? Where were they taking him? He had to be a good boy now, or he'd go to heaven too.

3
Grief
DAY 1

Diane Lawrence dreamed of the mid-century modern Vladimir Kagan floating curve sofa for the house she'd selected for purchase after she got her promotion. The sofa's sleek boomerang form fit perfectly into the formal living room with the stunning views of the Pacific Ocean. Matt's tongue traced a wet path along her collarbone and brought her back to her present. He pulled her blouse open.

"I love these girls," he moaned and ducked his head back down. He reminded her of an eager puppy, and she worked hard not to roll her eyes at him. He was a far cry from the producers she'd had to contend with not too long ago. Those assholes were the real predators. She pulled his head out of her chest and gave him a long, hard kiss.

"Matty honey." She put on her sultry voice. "You told me I'd be promoted by now. Can you imagine the fun we'd be having in the same building?" She traced kisses across his cheek and bit his ear lobe playfully.

Matty, or Matt Lacready as he was known at McGregor Holdings, the parent company who owned the Sunshine House, was her direct supervisor. After many months of effort, she'd extricated him away from his wife at the last Christmas party and gave him the ride of his life. He'd been hers ever since. Matty never stood a chance once she'd focused on him. She'd starred in Melrose Place after all.

"Baby, it's not so easy. I have to work through HR. Get support from them and my bosses."

"I've shown a profit for the last couple years, and the company never compensated me for it," she said, pushing him away and buttoning up her blouse.

"Let's not talk business," he said and checked his watch. "I only have another fifteen minutes." He held out his arms, but Diane turned away, disgusted with him. She needed that raise to convince the bank she could afford a 2.4 million dollar home in the Palisades. Between the inheritance she got from her deceased mother and her substantial savings, she had the down-payment, just not the paycheck to make the monthly payment.

"My mind is on business. Maybe we should do this another time," she said and watched Matty's face droop. She wasn't free. He needed to pay for this. She smoothed her shirt and straightened her skirt.

"C'mon, don't be that way." He stepped closer, but she put up her arm to hold him back. He gave her his pouty face, and her demeanor towards him melted just a touch.

Until her eyes wandered around the shabbily furnished office. The Ikea shelves sagged with the weight of patient files, and the two chairs in front of her own desk needed new upholstery. She frowned at all its ugliness and stiffened. This plan needed to move forward and now.

If they found out about the unusual number of deaths, she'd be on the hook. But was it so unusual though? Everyone who lived at the Sunshine was old, and death was an old friend in an assisted living facility.

"Diane, hello? Are you there?" Matty's voice broke through her dark thoughts and she found herself in his arms. She broke away from him as a knocking sounded on her door. Matt's face froze in terror. "I can't be here."

Diane smoothed her long blond hair and took a deep breath. "Pull yourself together and have a seat. You're my supervisor, and you have every right to be here." She knew who it was. Sure enough, Lou stuck her head into the room.

"You have a sec..." Lou trailed off when she saw Matt.

He stood up and shook Diane's hand. "We'll talk more. Call me in a couple of days." Diane pursed her lips as she watched him scurry past Lou and out of the room. Matt was proving more trouble than he was worth. She might need to move to Plan B.

She sat behind her desk. "What can I do for you, Lou?" Diane said as she waved the other woman to the chair Matt just vacated. The residents liked Lou, but Diane found the woman difficult to read.

She only offered Lou the job because of how cheap her salary was. Even giving her and her father free accommodations, she still saved at least twenty percent in wages for a nurse with similar experience.

Lou's ministrations toward her father bordered on the saintly but that didn't prevent Lou from also being a massive pain in the ass. Lou's current demeanor foreshadowed a migraine inducing visit. Her patience for these middling complaints was gone.

"Someone is disturbing the residents," Lou said and waited for Diane's response. "I don't want to point fingers..."

Diane frowned. "But you're going to anyway?"

"The patients are my responsibility," Lou said and shifted forward in her chair. Diane frowned. Nothing she said deterred Lou from going after Barney.

"This isn't a hospice, Lou, and every resident takes care of themselves," Diane said. She glowered at the other woman but Lou plunged ahead.

"Barney Leonard is frightening the residents." Lou said.

"Again with Barney Leonard," Diane snapped. "What is it with you two?" She picked up a Home Decor magazine from her desk in exasperation. They had this conversation every week. "Leave Barney Leonard alone. I've gotten no complaints from anyone else. Everyone loves his stories. Whatever keeps their blood pumping, am I right?" Diane flipped through the magazine, working hard to ignore the fuming woman seated in front of her.

"You're unqualified to say that. Two patients this morning displayed higher than normal blood pressure and no one is sleeping through the night. At their age, that's a serious problem."

Diane slammed the magazine down. "Stop. Just stop talking. You are in here every week complaining about Barney. You need to understand, people moved to the Sunshine because it was the former Bockerman Hotel and they wanted this excitement. We're in the middle of Hollywood. The stories are part of the charm of this place, and YOU need to get used to that," Diane said and watched as Lou's jaw clenched in anger.

They stared at each other across the desk without saying a word. Diane opened her mouth to break the standoff when the door was thrown open. Barney rushed into the room.

"She's dead. Barbara's dead." He skidded to a halt when he saw Lou. "I called 911."

Diane's heart dropped at that. "What? That's not the protocol, Mr. Leonard."

"They should be here any minute," he said through gasps of breath.

As if on cue, sirens sounded in the distance. "Oh, for God's sake, Mr. Leonard. You know the procedure. We always go through Dr. Jerris," Diane said, dread replacing her irritation. The holding company wanted no hiccups in the running of Sunshine. Barney's call created a problem for her promotion, definitely. If any of these deaths turned out as suspicious, she'd have a much bigger problem than lack of advancement. A hundred blowjobs wouldn't fix that mess.

"Why did you do that?" she yelled at him, losing patience.

"Someone murdered her. Murdered!" he screamed, his spittle raining over Diane's desk and magazine. She jumped up from her seat and stood in front of him. Compassion. She needed to show compassion to get control of the situation.

"Mr. Leonard, I'm so sorry for your loss. Barney, can I call you Barney?" She kept her voice soft but business-like. "You cared deeply for each other." She touched his arm, and he jumped back several feet. She held up her hands to calm him and saw his eyes grow wide. He was in shock.

"May I?" She gestured towards him and when he stayed silent, she took him under the arm. "Let's go meet the paramedics." She steered him out the door and away from Lou. She didn't need a fight between them.

Once they were outside her office, she let go of him. "Her death is a shock for all the residents here. Please let me deal with the arrangements for you. I promise I'll take good care of her." Diane said in her most soothing voice. She worried he was about to drop from shock and led him to a sofa near the main elevators.

"Sit here and take deep breaths. If you feel like you will pass out..." she tapered off as Mary Ann materialized next to her.

"Go, I'll take care of Barney," Mary Ann said, sitting next to him.

"Thank you, Mary Ann," Diane said with a grateful smile. She turned to the flashing lights coming in from the street. She steeled herself for the ordeal ahead.

A short time later, Diane stood on the curb of Ivar St. flanked by Lou and two LAPD detectives. She watched Babs and her promotion drive away in the back of an ambulance. The detective to her immediate left, Detective Murphy, was a woman far too young and too attractive to be a cop, but her partner Detective Larson fit everyone's description of a cop: old, grizzled, and wearing a cheap, oversized suit. Detective Larson's look of annoyance did, however, match her own.

"Don't you follow a protocol when a resident dies?" Detective Larson snapped at them, and Diane noticed the female detective shoot him a warning glance.

"What my partner was trying to say was this death appears to be a product of natural causes. We'll wait for the medical examiner to rule on official cause of death but from what the EMT's said, she died of a heart attack. For her age, that isn't surprising," Detective Murphy said.

"We DO have a protocol in place, and I'm sorry for this inconvenience," Diane said. "The resident who found her became distraught over her death and called 911 before contacting me."

Detective Murphy flipped her notepad open. "Barney Leonard, correct? His claim her death was murder is a serious one. Why is he so positive it's murder when the signs point to a heart attack? Did she have any enemies?" Diane felt the heat of the detective's watchful eyes on her face.

"He mentioned other mysterious deaths?" Detective Murphy asked.

Damn Barney and his theories. He spouted off about the other deaths. She frowned and weighed her options. Did she need to start spinning a story? Casting doubt on Barney and the other residents would be easy by pointing out that dementia and paranoia run rampant in assisted living facilities. Who would argue with her? Dr. Jerris ruled the other deaths as due to natural causes resulting from old age, and she was sure the Medical Examiner, Coroner, or whoever examined Barbara's body, would come to a similar conclusion. She was fine, she thought, and kept her mouth shut.

She shook her head in apparent confusion. "Which deaths?" Diane asked. "An assisted living facility has quite a number of passings each year. I'm sure you've seen the statistics on end of life diseases. We have a one in seven chance of dying of heart disease. Most of our residents are upwards of seventy. You both can do the math," she said and paused for effect. "The last seven residents here died of heart failure, half from advanced heart disease. We do all die eventually," she added.

"I see your point," Detective Murphy said. "Did Barbara Monroe have heart disease?"

"I'll ask Dr. Jerris to send you his files," Diane said.

Detective Larson jerked his head towards their cruiser, and Diane caught Detective Murphy's grimace. Apparently, Detective Larson was ready to leave. Good.

"Is there anything else we can help you with?" Diane said. She turned towards the door, hoping she gave them enough impetus to go.

"We've gotten what we need. We'll be in touch," Detective Murphy said and shook Diane's hand as her partner nodded and walked towards their cruiser.

"Thank you for being so thorough, Detective Murphy," Diane said. Detective Murphy nodded and followed her partner without responding.

"Barney's harmless, huh?" Diane jumped at the sound of Lou's voice. She had forgotten about her. Diane turned on her heel without responding and hoped Lou wouldn't follow her. The woman never got a goddamned clue, Diane thought, as Lou followed her inside the lobby, and down the hall to her office.

"I'll talk to him, Lou," Diane said without turning around, worried her professional demeanor would slip this time. She waited for her to leave, but Lou stayed put. She opened her office door and faced Lou, a scowl breaking over her face. "Don't you have patients?"

Lou frowned, crossed her arms in front of her, and stood her ground. "What are you doing about Barney?"

Diane sighed. "Stay away from Barney. He's hurting because he lost someone special to him. You must know how that feels?" Diane gave her a pointed look. "You engaging him in conversation at this moment is a terrible idea."

She closed the door firmly on her without waiting for an answer. Locking the door crossed her mind, but she decided Lou wasn't crazy enough to pursue it any further.

Anxiety rose in her chest. Diane quashed it. She wouldn't let this derail her plans. This was a hiccup. She was fine. It would be fine. She settled in behind her desk to check her day's schedule.

The phone rang and her heart sank. How could corporate know so quickly, she wondered? Her bravado melted away.

"Hello?"

"Matt, here. What's this I hear about the police over there?"

Nurse Lou Fairbanks glowered at Diane's nameplate. How dare she speak to her that way? Her anger turned to panic as her heart raced in her chest. Lou stumbled into the door, reaching her hand out to stop herself. As the heart palpitations and the shakes cascaded over her, she dragged herself towards the lobby. A sudden bout of vertigo made her stumble and clutch at the nearest column. She couldn't let anyone see her like this. She focused on the elevator, her beacon. In her deteriorating state, the stairs were too far away.

After what felt like hours, she reached the elevator doors and burst into tears of relief when she found it already on the ground level. Lou jabbed the up button, and the doors opened with a familiar ding. A small laugh erupted out of her. You did it, she said to herself and slid down to the floor, regulating her breathing so she wouldn't hyperventilate. The elevator lurched to life and rose with a creak.

Her brewing panic attack kept her claustrophobia at bay. As her vertigo subsided, Lou grabbed the handrail, and pulled herself back to standing, focusing her attention on the numbers of the floors flashing by.

Four.

Five.

Six.

Seven.

Eight. The eighth floor flashed brighter than the rest and the elevator ground to a halt. Lou stood taller, clutching the handrail for support, and forced a smile. If any of her patients saw her like this, she would lose her job. Be normal, she hissed to the empty elevator as the doors squeaked open.

The hallway beyond stood empty.

A light flickered.

The elevator car trembled.

Lou staggered out keeping one hand on the door to keep it open. Footsteps sounded in the hall to her right.

Lou bolted back inside. A sob gurgled in her throat as she punched the button for the tenth floor.

The doors stayed open.

Weeping, she stabbed the button again. The elevator stayed still. The doors didn't budge. She jabbed the Close Door button.

Ding, Ding.

The elevator protested but still didn't move. The sound of the footsteps grew closer, and a sob choked out of her. This contraption had to move. Whatever was out there came closer.

Her heart palpations clawed inside her chest as she hit every button on the panel. Please God, take pity on me for once, she blubbered.

The doors whirred closed.

Lou flopped against the elevator wall, tears flowing down her cheeks.

Ding.
Ding.
The doors slid open.
"No! NO!" She screamed, punching buttons for every floor, the open and close buttons, even the emergency button.
The doors closed. Then opened.
Lou made a break for it, stumbling out of the elevator and sprinting down the hall, away from whatever was in that hall.
Her body hit the exit door hard. Grunting, she yanked the door open and threw herself into the stairwell, the darkness coming at her from the edges of her vision.
The blackout, she thought. It finally came for her. She'd been careful for so long and now, when her life depended on it, her mind handicapped her further. Lou pitched herself at the wall and hoped that she wouldn't fall down the stairs to her death.

Barney opened his eyes to find his head in Mary Ann's lap. He had no idea how long he'd been out for and didn't even remember falling asleep. He sat up and gave her a crooked smile. "I didn't expect to fall asleep like that," he said.
Mary Ann patted his knee. "Grief hits us in different ways. Babs was an amazing spirit."
He nodded. "I should have forced her to put on that lock. She laughed at me, but I should have made her."
"It's not your fault. The killer did this. Put the blame on him."

"We need to stop this, and I need your help," Barney said and took her hand. "Will you help me?"

She nodded. "Anything." Mary Ann helped him get to his feet. "I'll take you back to your room."

4
Creeps
DAY 1

Sara Caine pulled her cap down to shield her green eyes from the harsh midday sun glaring off the concrete of 5th and Main Street. The corner was home of numerous crack dealers, and famous for nickel and dime bags strewed like confetti on the sidewalks. The march towards respectability and development failed at this particular intersection of Los Angeles, with dealers haunting each of the four corners and skid row sitting two blocks away.

Even in its heyday in the 1940s, Main Street resisted a good reputation and now, as developers bought up many of the grand old buildings and priced out the artists, the place was filled with a strange mix of wealthy, young professionals and the destitute.

Sara was headed toward the first of these new developments, the Old Bank District. In the 1980s, no one in their right mind ventured downtown past nightfall. Numerous people had died on this street over the years, their ghosts hanging around to this day. Sara fixed her gaze straight ahead and pretended she didn't see them. The moment the ghosts ascertained what she was, they'd be all over her.

Sara slowed her pace as she reached the San Fernando Building on the corner of Main and 4th Street. Her client lived on the top floor.

She took a deep breath and prepared herself for the encounter. Ghosts extracted much of her personal energy to present themselves when she called for them, and it felt like getting mononucleosis times a thousand. She meditated to build walls of protection around herself most of the time, but dropping them was, unfortunately, a necessary part of her job.

The lobby of the San Fernando was eerily silent and was, at first glance, part of a deserted building, the only clue of occupation was the stack of LA Weekly's next to the double bronze doors. She dialed the client's apartment number into the call box, and the buzzer sounded within moments. Sara passed through the interior lobby and called the elevator down, spreading her attention ahead for any signs of activity. Finding nothing extraordinary, she stepped into the elevator and pressed the client's floor. The elevator shook once and began its slow ascent. Maybe she should have taken the stairs, she thought, and grabbed the handrail. Sara pulled her hand away in disgust. The sticky rail hadn't been repaired in years.

"I'm so glad you came on such short notice," Mr. Delancy said as he opened the door to her knocking. He was a large man well into middle age with a round belly, and dandruff sprinkled onto his shoulders. She followed him inside the loft, a strong smell of whiskey wafting after him. He cleared his throat.

"So, uh, how does this work? I've never done this sort of thing before."

"It's pretty simple. Nice view, by the way," Sara said as she gazed west to the Continental building, an architectural gem and, formerly, the tallest building in Los Angeles. Usually, her cases consisted of bad plumbing, rodents, and ever shifting foundations, but her cases at the Continental tended to be real hauntings and she had a fondness for the place.

"Do you know the top floors of this building were a gambling and gin joint," Sara asked him as she touched the exposed brick wall to her left. In some cases, her touch alone called up the spirits of the dwelling and played their story in her head as if she was watching a movie. It didn't happen often, but once in a while she got lucky. She preferred this touch technique over others since buildings and objects didn't sap her energy as dead people did.

"Really?" he asked. He didn't sound convinced.

"Run by the LAPD and the mob," Sara added and took her hands off the brick. He perked up at that.

"That's so cool. Could that be my problem?" He smiled wide. "So did anyone die in here? Can you feel anything? How does it work? Oh and my girlfriend wanted to know, how do you become a paranormal investigator anyway?"

Sara took a deep breath and gave herself a moment before she spoke. She'd been asked this question multiple times, and she still hadn't come up with a smooth enough answer to satisfy clients. Today, she wasn't in the mood to be clever and decided to just tell the truth.

"Your building is a historical one, so yes that could definitely be the problem. I can't entirely explain to you how it works. I see ghosts or apparitions in front of me, and sometimes I feel their thoughts in my mind. On some rare occasions, I can touch a wall or an object and the story that the ghost wants to tell comes flooding in." She stopped and checked her client's expression. He was still with her and looked more interested than he had the entire visit. She continued, "My parents died in the same car crash I was in when I was in high school, and when I woke up, I just had this new ability."

"In high school?" he said, looking aghast. "That sounds horrible. I mean, high school is painful just being high school. I can't imagine what that must have been like to lose your parents and start seeing ghosts."

"Thank you for saying that. High school was tough, but I figured out a way to help people with this new skill. I try my best." She shrugged. "As far as how today goes, I'll do a preliminary analysis of paranormal phenomena in your residence. If you do have a paranormal problem then I'll call in my cleaner, and we'll get rid of whatever is plaguing you."

"What a trip it must be to see ghosts?" he asked, shaking his head. "I still can't believe what I saw with my own eyes."

The first impulse of many of her clients was to state their disbelief. It was a protection against them sounding mentally disturbed. They state the obvious, then get into the ghost hunting. Sara longed to transition into a more mainstream profession, mainly a regular investigator.

As a PI, she wouldn't need to expose her odd abilities daily. Odd abilities. Her cleaner Johan coined that term when she kept calling herself a freak. Johan strongly disapproved of that description, but most people looked at her differently when they witnessed her abilities in action. Even with all the ghost hunting shows on TV making the supernatural world no longer so taboo, the general population thought she was a charlatan and even worse, a grifter. The new wave of paranormal shows did make talking to her clients easier, however.

"What's the most haunted building in Los Angeles? Is it my building?" He stepped in too close to her and she moved back to get away from him.

"No. No, it isn't." Was this just another creep? Her hand traveled down to the place in her bag where she kept her pepper spray. One more move buddy, she thought. "Supposedly it's the Bockerman Hotel. Or rather former. It's an assisted living facility now called Sunshine House."

"Oh yeah," he said, his eyes already drifting. "Have you been?"

"No. They won't, uh, let paranormal investigators in." Sara stumbled over the words.

"I see. So how does this work again?" He scratched the back of his head, and Sara watched the white flakes accumulate on his collar. Didn't she explain this already? He had to be drunk, she thought.

"Like I said before, I open my mind..." She trailed off as his eyes glazed over. "I see them. Ghosts, I mean. I see dead people." She imitated that small kid from that movie, The Sixth Sense. Mr. Delancy cracked a smile and focused back on her. "So tell me about this couple," Sara said.

Mr. Delancy rubbed his face with his hands and sat down on a green, leather couch, the stuffing coming out in two different places.

"My girlfriend and I were eating dinner one night last week, and we heard these voices that sounded as if they were in the room with us. They sounded as if they were coming closer and closer to us, and we freaked. Then, a couple appeared right in front of us, just like that." He snapped his fingers. "The man, wearing a suit and fedora, pushed the woman, wearing a blue dress, out the window." His hands gestured towards the window. "She screamed, and they both disappeared."

Sara closed her eyes and opened up her mind. She slowed her breathing and brought one of her walls down. Jazz music filtered into her consciousness. The sounds of clinking glasses, laughter and voices undulated in and out of the fabric of sound. She smelled the cigarette smoke but felt no specific presence.

"Have you experienced any other phenomena since living here? Noises, cold drafts, nightmares?" she asked. She built her walls back up, and the music and sounds faded away behind it.

She opened her eyes and looked around the loft one last time.

"No, I haven't experienced anything like that," Mr. Delancy said. "But I'm afraid to sleep in here which is why I called you."

"No need to fear anything. You experienced an echo and not a presence. Since this building has such a unique history, both the happy and the dark emotions of its former inhabitants exist as echoes in the space, in the very walls. Human emotion has energy, like an electric current, and these walls are like sponges." She stopped and waited for this to sink in. Mr. Delancy just stared back.

"An echo?" he asked.

"Echoes but no ghosts." Sara stood up. It was time to go. "I'm a cash kind of girl," she said in a rush. "That'll be fifty dollars." She hated her bluntness in discussing money, but clients felt foolish when no ghosts were found and grew stingy with the payment. She was still chasing after five clients for that damn fifty-dollar fee.

Mr. Delancy lifted his butt off the couch and took a money clip from his back jean pocket. He counted out two twenty-dollar bills and a ten. Sara's body relaxed as he handed her the cash.

"Thank you very much, Mr. Delancy." Her cell phone buzzed in her back pocket. She pulled it out and checked the caller id. It was Fredrick and his ghost hunters. "I have to take this." Thankful for the interruption, she rushed out the door and breathed a sigh of relief at the sound of the click of the lock behind her.

"Hi, Fredrick? A call from the Sunshine..." she paused. "Really? The Bockerman, right? Wow, I was recently talking about it with a client. I definitely want to be there for that!" She took the stairs fast, wanting to put as much distance between her and Delancy as she could. "What time do you want me there?" She stopped. "Wait, a ghost murdered someone? That's not...oh, ok. I'll wait for your call." Sara ended the call, excitement building. No one in the paranormal world had ghost-hunted inside the infamous Bockerman. Until now. She wondered who had precipitated such a change in policy AND held such crazy ideas as ghosts could kill. Ghost couldn't kill, could they?

5
Midnight Wanderings
FEBRUARY 17, 2005 - DAY 2

Barney Leonard sat hunched over his desk dismantling a short wave radio. Using his hands kept his grief at bay and let his mind wander towards more useful emotions. Like revenge and murder and ways he could get away with it. He lifted his head and glared at his shabby apartment where he crammed his entire life into a ten by ten room. Memorabilia lined the walls: rock posters of the bands he toured with, covers of record albums he worked on tiled in a grid pattern over an entire wall, and even a gold record in a place of prominence. His life's achievements.

A gentle knock sounded on the door.

"Come in," he said, not turning around.

"You awake?" Mary Ann asked as soon as she walked through the door. She never disappointed him with her reliability.

"What do you think," he said and put his screwdriver down. He swiveled his chair around to see her, and she sauntered over to him with a come hither smile. He couldn't believe she would try. "I'm busy. What do you need?" he said and watched her deflate. He got no pleasure from being mean to her and felt bad for being such an ass. "Sorry, it's been a long night," he said. No one ever mentioned how lonely being old was, and he knew the need she was throwing his way. But his need was to avenge Babs' death.

"You're taking it apart again," she said when she saw what he was doing.

He shifted his body to hide the radio from her view. "It keeps me occupied," he muttered.

"I'll keep you occupied," she whispered in his ear but he disentangled himself out of her arms. "What do you need, Mary Ann?"

She stuck her bottom lip out in a pout. "I'm scared, and I want to start."

"Let's get started then."

Lou Fairbanks' eyes opened to complete darkness. An unseen force pinned her body to the bed. She craned her head around to see what sat on her chest, but she had no control over her body. The fear paralyzed her. A woman's giggle came from somewhere to her right and then the click clack of heels rushed toward her.

She choked on her own spit, trying to scream. A gargle was all that came out. Lou strained as hard as she could to turn her head, but her body would not obey. A pathetic scream finally wheezed out of her as tears streamed down her cheeks.

The footsteps closed in, and the evil leaned over her. Her time had come. Death grasped her throat and forced her mouth open. She screamed.

Lou woke up to the sound of her screams, her body sprawled on the landing of the staircase. The harsh light from the wall sconce drove daggers into her eyes, and she closed them against the pain. The back of her head throbbed. Another concussion but not the worst she'd had. No one had found her passed out and she picked the right direction for her fall. Winning at life, she thought with a small smile. If she had chosen her left, she would have fallen headfirst down the stairs to her death. Her secret was safe, for now.

Barney precipitated this latest anxiety attack with his nonsense, she thought and her rage bloomed. He dismantled her calm with his undermining comments and she'd gotten lucky this time.

Lou groaned with effort as she lifted herself up to standing and waited for the nausea to pass. Her head throbbed and her vision swam. Definitely a mild concussion, she thought, as she gripped the balustrade for balance. She took her time going up the remaining two flights of stairs to the tenth floor and expelled her breath when she saw the door marked number 10. Lou pushed through the exit door and ran her fingers along the wall as she walked to her and Dads apartment. She fumbled her keys, almost dropping them. With a shaky hand, she opened the door.

Dads sat in the exact same spot she left him in earlier, still staring out towards the Hollywood sign. She was passed out for hours, she thought and he never got to eat lunch or dinner. "Dads, I'm so sorry. I passed out again, and I came to several minutes ago. You must be starved," she said. He didn't respond.

Lou shuffled across the small room, and lowered herself down next to him. Her hand fluttered to the back of her head. The last concussion she had, she'd been puking for days. This one felt different, and she hoped it wasn't as severe. The experts said not to sleep for several hours after the incident and to wake up every couple of hours through the first night. She'd set her alarm accordingly and hoped Dads wouldn't awaken with her.

"I hurt myself, Dads and I'm setting the alarm to go off throughout the night," she said. His blank stare never wavered. How was she going to get him to eat tonight with her as incapacitated as she was? Standing up made her too dizzy to fix him anything. She tried anyway. Her vision distorted as blood rushed into her face.

Lou grabbed the table for support. Dads paid her no mind. "We should get ready for bed," she said instead.

Lou woke up to the beeping of her alarm, confused why the room was moonlit. Why did the alarm go off in the middle of the night? The pain in her head reminded her why. At least, she heard the beeping and woke up. You're going to be OK, she thought, as she turned the alarm off and rubbed her eyes with her fists. It was 3am now. She set the alarm for her next wake-up at 5am. The morning would be an ugly one and she was not looking forward to it at all.

She lay her head down on the pillow and closed her eyes. The bump on the back of her head pounded with pain. Tylenol, she needed more Tylenol. Lou threw her covers off and sat up. A wave of dizziness hit her again. As she waited for it to pass, she checked on Dads. His mouth hung open and as he inhaled, a soft snore came whistling out of him.

Until several weeks ago, Dads often woke in the middle of the night but with the new Ambien dosage he slept all the way through. Thank God for small miracles, she thought as she shuffled to the bathroom.

She swallowed two Tylenol dry and turned back towards her bed.

A woman wept somewhere in the darkness of their room. She held her breath and listened for the direction the sound came from. The weeping changed into a loud sobbing. It came from beneath her feet, but no one lived in the apartment down below.

The crying faded into silence. Lou swayed in place for a moment, listening to the creaks and groans the building made. Concussions caused visual and auditory issues. The crying had to be a hallucination. Anything else was too crazy to contemplate.

She crawled into bed and lay back down.

A distant faucet squeaked open, and water gushed into a sink. Her sink. Her heart beat faster.

NO.

She was a professional nurse. She didn't believe in ghosts. But what if the old pipes were acting up and, if she didn't turn off the water, the whole bathroom flooded? Lou slid out of bed and padded to the bathroom.

The sink was empty, the faucet off.

She checked their kitchenette and that faucet was not running either. The mystery faucet squeaked again, and the gushing water turned off. Maybe her concussion was worse than she thought. She vowed to call Dr. Jerris in the morning to get herself checked out.

The crying crescendoed to the most anguished sobbing Lou had ever heard. It was no longer coming from the floor but from all around her.

Lou spun to see whether there was anything behind her, but the room was empty. She ran back into her bed and pulled the covers above her head like she used to do when she had nightmares as a child. This was all in her head, she thought. The sobbing subsided.

A window creaked open, and the sound of wind came whooshing around her.

Lou wheezed in terror. She didn't want to look, couldn't look. With a small cry, she pulled the covers down to face whatever was climbing through their window.

The window was still closed. "This is just a hallucination," she whispered to the room and willed it to go silent again.

The sobs grew to a howling scream. Lou screamed along with it.

Dads sat up in bed, awake and disoriented. The ghostly scream subsided abruptly. Lou choked back her own scream and scrambled over her bedsheets to him. He couldn't get out of bed.

"It's OK, Dads. It was me. I had a nightmare," she said, stubbing her toe on the chair as she crossed the room. "Damnit," she cried as the pain shot up her leg. She grabbed at it and fell onto Dads' bed. "It's me, Dads. It's Lou."

She put one arm around his shoulder as the other massaged her toe.

"Did you hear her scream?" Dads asked.

"That was me. I had a nightmare," Lou said.

"No, the other scream. I heard it," he mumbled. "Who is she?" Lou stopped massaging her toe and stared back at him.

"You heard it too, Dads?" He turned his head towards the window, his eyes blank again. If he heard the sobbing, did that mean it was real? She bit her lip as another thought invaded her mind. Even through all that noise, how did Dads wake up through that heavy dose of Ambien?

"Will you lay back down, Dads? We should both get back to sleep," she said and he did as she requested. She tucked him in, humming to herself to keep both of them calm.

Lou waited until Dads' first snore before climbing back into her own bed. She lay on her back, covers pulled up all the way to her chin. How had Dads woken up? The dosage was so high she didn't think it safe to up it anymore. Could he have been sleepwalking? Really asleep but eyes open? Or was he not taking the medication properly? She couldn't just stick fingers into his mouth to check, could she? No, he'd bite. She was sure of it. Whatever thoughts of sleep she had were long gone. She stared up at the ceiling, chewing on her bottom lip, fear of screams and running water plunging her thoughts into darkness.

Sara Caine's parents barreled down a dark road in the silver Jaguar with the rich, red leather seats. She listened from the backseat as her father pumped hard on the brakes.

"Shit," he said, fear permeating his voice.

"What's wrong, James?" Her mother leaned her body towards him. She touched his arm.

"The brakes, they're gone," he whispered back and pulled hard on the hand brake. His knuckles turned whiter with effort, she noted and mentally catalogued the observation so she wouldn't forget it. She didn't remember that detail from the other nightmares. Nothingness seeped all around the edges of the dream, and she knew the end was coming. She memorized the other new details like her mother's pearl earrings, her father's watch and the briefcase sandwiched between them. The scene went black. The sound of twisting metal, the crackle of fire, and the explosion took over all her senses. Her mother's anguished screams faded with the dream.

Sara Caine sat up in bed shrieking, the nightly dream never loosening its grip on her. Johan warned her about accessing the last moments of her parents' lives, but she forged on, ignoring his advice. She needed to know who killed them and knew the clues were in the dream. Why else would she have it every night since they died nine years ago?

She grabbed the small notebook and pen she kept on her bedside table, and wrote down the new details: pearl earrings, the watch, the briefcase, and her father's fear. A drop of sweat plunked down on top of the word briefcase and caught the ink in its salty water. Sara smudged it into a black blob. She wrote briefcase underneath and placed the notebook back onto her nightstand. She wiped the sweat off her face with the sleeve of her T-shirt and lay back down.

The orange light from the outdoor sodium lamps gave her small studio apartment an otherworldly glow. Of all the ghosts she interacted with in the nine years since she discovered her gift, the only ghosts she wanted to speak with never surfaced. She watched the headlights from the cars outside create patterns on her ceiling and debated whether to get up. The dream visited her only once a night and she never fell back asleep after it. She preferred it coming towards dawn since she was an early bird anyway and didn't mind getting her day started so early.

She groaned when she saw it was only 2:30 am and hoped that maybe tonight the sandman would come and knock her out.

Sara got out of bed when the sky took on the golden hues of a Los Angeles dawn. She ground her single source coffee beans and scooped two heaped spoonfuls into her French press while the water boiled. Her father loved coffee and when she kicked her alcohol habit, instead of switching to cigarettes like everyone else she knew, she chose caffeine as her new go to. She poured the boiling water in and watched as the grounds swirled and stained the water. Each time she made a cup, she thought of him and smiled. He'd been particular with his coffee, and Sara took up his routine by researching and finding single source beans from an outfit called Marty's Coffee, switching to drinking it black and having at least five cups a day.

She sat at her small kitchen table gazing at the sky smudging brighter and brighter. The coffee awakened her senses. The quiet of the morning washed away the stress and sadness of her night. Los Angeles didn't wake up before 9am since many people here didn't work typical 9-5 jobs. Whenever Sara was out working a case, she marveled at the amount of people out and about during the day. How they all lived in such a wealthy city as Los Angeles she'd never understand. She took another sip of coffee and checked in on her mental walls. Even with such a rough night, she'd learned her lessons well enough for them to be strong. They were all up, and she felt safe. Almost.

Sara swigged down the last of her coffee and washed her favorite coffee cup, red with a white snowman on two sides, formerly her Dad's prized possession.

She crossed her small living room and stood in front of the door. She paused before grasping the doorknob, and closed her eyes in preparation to clear her mind. She attempted to see the evidence from a new angle every time she walked in. Ready, she pulled the door open and stepped across the threshold. Sara flicked on the lights, her eyes focusing and unfocusing. She let them wander through the familiar landscape of files. Evidence of the fatal car wreck and subsequent investigation into her parent's death filled every inch of wall. Her eyes stopped on the composite drawing of the suspect or witness. The police were never sure which.

Did he make those phone calls that terrified her father so much? As a prosecuting attorney, her father was used to threats but these calls affected him differently. Even at thirteen years old, she knew fear when she witnessed it. It was the first and last time she saw that on her father's face. Well, until her dream last night. He was dead five weeks later. Sara went through her mental list of questions.

Where were her dad's files from his last case?

What were her parents arguing about that night?

Who made the strange skid marks on the road? Were they from another car?

Who was the man running from the scene?

The questions haunted her the same way the dream did and after so many years, she wasn't any closer to the answers. She tracked down every possible lead but that only uncovered more questions. Her eyes flew over the images of the twisted metal and the few visible blood droplets on the pavement. If she could just get admitted to the police academy, she'd have access to more advanced investigative classes. As the sole survivor, the LAPD granted her several meetings to view the investigative files but she figured she was missing something because of her lack of schooling. Or, the files weren't complete.

Her phone rang. Sara ran to get it. It had to be Johan as he was the only one who called this early in the morning.

"Hello?" she said, slightly out of breath.

"You awake?" Johan asked.

"Been up for hours."

"Can I come up? I think I've made a breakthrough," Johan said. The excitement in his voice had to be about Luther, the demon he'd been hunting since she'd met him.

"Of course," she said and left her evidence room, making sure the door was firmly closed. He must have been standing right outside her door because the knocking started immediately,

"You were already here," she said as she opened the door to Johan Luken, looking as though he hadn't slept in weeks. His ever present six o'clock shadow had grown into a short beard, and his hair was sticking every which way as if he'd slept in his car. Even with all that, he was still handsome enough to make her heart leap.

He jumped inside, energy crackling all around him. "Asmodeus is back. I saw his symbol burned into the side of a building in Koreatown. I knew I was feeling him close by. He's come back to Los Angeles after all this time," he said, his blue eyes alive with what Sara recognized as the fever. She'd looked like that on more than one occasion when she went down a new rabbit hole, chasing some previously unknown clue.

"Are you sure? When was the last time you slept? Do you want something to eat?" she asked as she led him to the couch. His clothes hung loosely on his usually built frame. She'd never seen him in this shape before. "How can I help?"

The moment he hit the couch, his eyes closed and he began to snore. Sara went and poured herself another cup of coffee and got herself comfortable across from him on her easy chair. Even if she had to wait all morning, she'd get the full story out of him. He'd only mentioned Asmodeus, or Luther as he sometimes referred to him, twice to her before and both times he was at the point of exhaustion. This time he looked even worse.

6

Retellings
DAY 2

ou Fairbanks glared at the sign flashing "The
All-Star Theatre Cafe & Speakeasy" above
her head as she shuffled into the cafeteria,
eyes glazed and burning. All the unnecessary
throwbacks to old Hollywood reminded her of
Barney Leonard and made her scowl in irritation.
His stupid stories were making her doubt her
sanity. And if last night was any indication, a
patient here needed help and right away.

The tenth floor was only partially occupied and
Lou hadn't recognized the voice of the anguished
crier. Could crying travel so far? The very idea of so
many people hearing it made the whole situation
even worse. It was a disgrace for so many to hear
someone's private moments like that.

She went over to the buffet and loaded her
plate with eggs and bacon. Though the smell of
the breakfast churned her stomach, she needed
the protein to make it through her day . Not really

wanting to interact with anyone, she sat at an empty table nearest the door and focused on her food. She steeled herself and speared a piece of dry, scrambled egg on her fork and shoved it in her mouth. As she chewed, she overheard the conversation happening right behind her.

"There were footsteps..." She heard another resident named Doreen say but couldn't hear the whispered response.

"I know I heard..." Barney's voice came to her in snatches. The anger from yesterday rose up, and she had to spit out the bacon she was chewing to prevent herself from choking on it. He was at it again, she thought. Disturbing everyone with his crazy stories of ghosts. She leaned back to better hear him.

"Sobbing...water running..." Barney said, his voice rising. His description of the running water made her swivel in her seat.

Doreen, a robust workhorse of a woman in her early eighties, Barney, and Mary Ann were gathered at the table behind her, all of them sleep deprived with dark circles under their eyes. Mary Ann shuddered at whatever Barney whispered to her.

"Did you hear the water too? And the sobbing?" Lou asked and scraped her chair closer to their table. "Do any of you know who it was? I was going to complain to Diane right after breakfast. The privacy issues in this place are too numerous to count. The fact that we all heard such a private moment because of the pipes..." She paused, her body trembling from the imagined embarrassment. "Someone in this facility is in a lot of pain and needs professional help." They all stopped talking, and three pairs of eyes found hers.

"Why are you so sure that it was one of the residents?" Barney asked as Mary Ann and Doreen exchanged knowing glances.

"Well, who else could it have been? I heard her sobbing, and the pipes are so faulty that I could even hear when she turned on the water," Lou explained, trying to cut off the ridiculous idea it was a ghost.

"So it was a woman?" Barney asked.

"Absolutely," Lou said. "My floor is pretty sparse so I'm thinking it could be one of the residents on the ninth or the eleventh floor. The sound was so loud that I can't imagine her being further way. I was racking my brain about whom it could be, but every one of the women on those floors said they were fine. Do any of you have any ideas or heard any relevant gossip?" she asked, her worry over the poor woman making her ask such an unprofessional request. Barney turned and nodded to Mary Ann in an 'I told you so' sort of way.

"It's Irene—it has to be Irene," Barney said to the table.

"Irene? Who's Irene? I don't know of a resident here by that name?" Lou said.

"Could it be Barbara?" Doreen whispered, eyes wide.

Barney shot her a look.

"Barbara supposedly died of natural causes. Ghosts don't die of natural causes, do they?" Doreen said.

Lou glared at him. "Who said anything about ghosts? I heard the poor woman. So did Dads. She was real," she insisted.

Barney ignored Lou's outburst and shot Doreen a nasty look. "We don't know whether she died of natural causes, do we?" he said and stabbed at his cold eggs. Mary Ann squeezed his shoulder in support as Lou scowled, her anger building.

"Did you hear what I said? There are no ghosts," she reiterated.

"What makes you the expert, Nurse Lou?" Mary Ann piped up, massaging Barney's shoulder. He shrugged her off, and Lou felt his full attention on her.

"Did you know that Irene Lentz stayed right above you on the eleventh floor? She checked into Room 1129, went to the bathroom, opened up the window, and jumped to her death."

"What does that have anything to do with a sobbing resident in the middle of the night?" Lou demanded. Keeping her stress level at a minimum was shot to hell, but Lou suppressed her anger anyway.

"Because that is probably who you heard last night," Barney shot back.

"Why did she kill herself?" Doreen asked. Lou didn't think Doreen should step into the middle of her and Barney's argument. Barney agreed with her, she noticed.

"She loved Gary Cooper. They had an affair and when he died, she came here to kill herself," Barney explained, never taking his eyes off Lou. His eyes filled with hate. She'd seen that look before. "It has to be her. Suicide is violent. Her excruciating pain imprisoned her in that room," Barney finished. He'd thrown down the challenge.

"You," jabbing her finger at him, "and your

stories are going to hurt people. You watch and see." Lou pointed at Mary Ann and Doreen. "And you both are his accomplices."

"People are dying here, Nurse Fairbanks," Doreen said, catching her off guard. Doreen had flights of fancy here and there, but Lou never believed she was on Barney's side.

"So, all three of you believe I heard a ghost last night?" she said, the cafeteria lights pulsing around her. The headache she'd had all morning was in danger of turning into a migraine. Why was she even arguing with her patients, she wondered?

All the fight evaporated from her, leaving her spent and shaky. "There must... has to be another explanation," was all Lou said. Mary Ann fell back into her chair, crossing her arms against her chest.

"Why don't you prove us wrong?" Mary Ann said.

"How do you propose I do that?" Lou asked, wishing she had never turned around.

"Talk to all the residents on the ninth and eleventh floors. I bet you that you won't find anyone who was even awake last night," Mary Ann said.

"I've already spoken to most of them. No one will admit they were sobbing all night long," Lou said.

"Aren't you a nurse? Shouldn't you be able to see signs of depression and crying? Puffy, red rimmed eyes, swollen face?" Barney asked.

"Fine. I'll do exactly that and prove to all of you that ghosts don't exist," Lou said, taking up their challenge.

"You know we're right, Lou. But go ahead and get your proof. You'll be back asking us about ghosts in no time," Barney said and the women at the table nodded in agreement.

"And what about what I heard last night? And the night before? The whispering and the screaming? You know I'm not a superstitious woman, Lou. Explain why I heard what I heard. It was another night of no sleep," Doreen said.

"I don't know what you're hearing, but I do not believe in ghosts. I can give you a sleeping aid for tonight. It's not healthy for you to lose this much sleep," Lou said in her nurse tone. "And anyway, aren't ghosts governed by rules? They stay put in the place they died? Why would Irene Lentz be traveling down to the sixth floor or to the eighth floor?" she asked, directing the last part to Barney.

"You've seen too many movies, Lou," Barney said.

"Maybe we have multiple ghosts. Maybe it was Houdini," Doreen piped up, nodding to Barney. "You said they held those séances on the roof every Halloween trying to contact him."

"What about Frances Farmer? Or DW Griffith?" Mary Ann jumped in.

"You really believe that? That we have multiple ghosts?" Lou said, rotating her neck to help relieve the tension in her head. "I'm done with this conversation. There are no ghosts. People are filled with loneliness and sadness as their time of death nears. I've seen it over and over again," she said.

"Are you speaking about anyone in particular?" Barney interjected. When Lou didn't answer, he continued. "We all heard something. A presence, or rather several presences, ARE here. It's frightening. Who are you to say what is real or imagined?" He put his arm around Mary Ann.

"Could the ghost be killing us?" Doreen said as she leaned in. "Maybe it killed Babs. And the others?" she added.

Lou had heard enough. She stood up and put her hands on her hips. She didn't care if she looked like a schoolmarm about to scold a table full of schoolchildren. "No one is killing anyone, Doreen," she said. "I'm very sorry about Babs, Barney. I really am. She was a wonderful woman and her death was unexpected and unsettling. Her passing upsets us all. However, grief causes insomnia as well and is a more viable explanation." she said, her voice coming out more curt than she wanted. She modulated it to be more caring before she continued. "This building has a fascinating history, I'll give you that, and I'm sure it's thrilling thinking about all that happened between these walls. But ghosts don't exist. If any of you find yourselves unable to sleep another night, please come to me. I'll dispense sleeping aids." Barney scowled back at her as the women looked away, not wanting to meet her eyes.

"You are wrong. It's not our fault you aren't more in touch with your senses. Believe what you need to believe to sleep tonight. We will go into the night with our eyes open," he said and turned his back on her. The women followed his lead.

"I'm sorry to hear that. I hope you all change your minds on seeking help," she said and stomped away, leaving her unfinished food behind her.

Detective Eva Murphy hated going to the morgue and Larson knew it. He sent her off alone each time they had to deal with the Coroner, explaining that the more she went, the more desensitized she'd be to it. She credited him with helping her get to the point of no longer passing out the moment the smell of death, sweet and rotten simultaneously, assaulted her nose. That was a huge step forward.

Each time her olfactory sense caught that specific smell, she flashed back to the first day at the Body Farm and the embarrassment she saw on the faces of her Behavioral Science Unit seminar classmates. She considered herself a strong, not easily frightened woman, but her fainting spell surprised even her with its intensity. After that first time, each subsequent whiff of death caused the same embarrassing fainting spell and she took great pains to hide the affliction from her colleagues.

The weakness invaded her dreams late at night. She would wake up, shivering and covered in a cold sweat, from dreams where she passed out in front of her colleagues. She'd hidden her phobia through most of her time in Patrol. Luckily, she hadn't come across a single dead body. Dead bodies were the job of the murder squad, however.

Her first case with Larson was a home invasion, and she had unexpectedly walked in on two dead victims. Larson caught her before she hit the floor and after that, he made it his mission to have her overcome the phobia. He never spoke of his intentions but instead made an excuse not to go to the morgue each time they called.

Murphy took a deep breath before opening the door to Autopsy Room #1 of the LA County City Morgue. She nodded to the coroner, Dr. Leann Grimley and held her breath as long as she could.

"Hello there, Detective Murphy. Come on closer, you don't need to be shy," Dr. Grimley said as Murphy let out her breath in a whoosh. She held onto the edge of the table for support as the smell hit her nostrils. She might not pass out now, but that didn't mean it didn't torture her all the same. She breathed the smell deep into her lungs and reminded herself that this was the squad she chose.

Dr. Grimley touched her on the shoulder. "You're getting better."

Murphy nodded. "I'll get there. So, what do you think?"

"We're lucky this woman's friend dialed 911 instead of just calling in the doctor." She pointed to a small puncture in the crook of her arm. "See this?"

Murphy glanced at it and nodded. "I'm looking at a puncture wound, correct? Could it have been made by her doctor at the nursing home?"

"Her medical files showed she had no appointments in the last month. This is fresh and was made less than 24 hours before her death. The tox screen came back clean so I'm postulating an air bubble in the vein."

"How does that kill someone?" Murphy asked.

"It's called murder by embolism, and it was first used by the Nazi's at the Meseritz-Obrawalde hospital," Dr. Grimley said.

"That's a piece of history right there. How do you know that?" Murphy asked.

"World War II fascinates me. This method killed in minutes. The nurses would inject about 100 milliliters of air into their victim's veins creating an air bubble. The bubble then traversed to the heart where it got stuck in the chambers causing the blood to stop flowing. The victim would go into cardiac arrest in seconds. With an older woman like Barbara, well, not many doctors would check for a syringe mark."

"Outside of the Nazi's, has anyone else used this method in the last, I don't know, twenty years?" Murphy asked.

"There have been numerous cases of this type of murder. The media dubbed past killers using this technique Angels of Death. A nurse in Germany killed fifteen patients using this method and there have been several pretty famous murder cases here in the States and in England," Dr. Grimley said.

"Are they always medical professionals?" Murphy asked.

"Typically yes," Dr. Grimley said as she put the sheet back over Barbara's body. Murphy nodded, the smell scrambling her thoughts.

"Thank you for putting her ahead of the others on such short notice," Murphy said as she walked quickly to the door. She couldn't take it much longer.

"You're welcome, Detective. I hope you find whoever is doing this. We all took an oath to do no harm," Dr. Grimley called out after her.

Murphy nodded back at her. She pushed the door open, and as soon as the door slammed shut behind her, she broke into a run down the hall, sprinted up the two flights of stairs and blasted through the exit doors. Sunshine warmed her face. She soaked it in as she slowed to a fast walk, gulping in the hot, smog-filled LA air.

She'd made it through without embarrassing

herself. It was the fourth visit in a row to the morgue without incident, and she'd gotten a new break in the case.

Murphy dialed Larson. "Grimley is calling it a suspicious death. You ever heard of Angels of Death? Doctors and nurses killing their patients?" Murphy asked.

"Angel of Death? Was she poisoned?" Larson sounded as excited as she felt.

"No. Embolism. Perp injected air into the vein. Dr. Grimley found a needle puncture in the crook of the victim's elbow," Murphy said as she clicked her door open. "You have Dr. Jerris' address?"

She heard Larson flipping through the files. "He works at Cedar's. I'd imagine we'd find him there."

"Meet you there," Murphy said and clicked off. They had a case. Her heart beat faster, the thrill of the chase beginning. Dr. Jerris and Nurse Louise were the most obvious suspects but were there others? Her mind filling with "What if?" questions.

Who had the motive? Opportunity? What were the unique properties of the weapon? How hard was it to find a vein, use a syringe? A diabetic would know as would medical professionals.

And did an Angel of Death need to be a medical professional? Any history buff who had an interest in the Nazi's could track down the method, or an interest in serial killers come to think of it. She started up the car and bet that Larson had already made up his mind on the nurse.

Murphy and Larson finally found Dr. Tom Jerris in the commissary of the Cedars Sinai Medical

Center. The place resembled a labyrinth. After a half hour search, they found him seated at a corner table reading a Scientific American and eating a yogurt.

"Dr. Tom Jerris?" Larson flashed his badge at the doctor.

"What can I do for you, Officer?" Dr. Jerris gestured to the seats around him without looking up from the magazine. Murphy and Larson sat on either side of him. "We'd like to ask you some questions about Barbara Monroe, a resident of the Sunshine House, an assisted living facility."

"She died of heart failure, didn't she?" he asked. Murphy stared hard at his Scientific American until he got a clue and put the magazine down.

"The coroner deemed hers a suspicious death," Larson said.

Dr. Jerris shook his head in confusion. "She was 75."

"What does that have to do with anything? The coroner found a puncture in her arm. You didn't take her blood two days prior to her death, did you?" Murphy asked.

"No, I didn't take her blood. She stopped seeing me some months ago," Dr. Jerris said, all business like.

"When was the last time you saw Ms. Monroe then?" Murphy asked, penetrating his personal space.

"Let's see." Dr. Jerris closed his eyes. "I'd say last May. When it rained that one week." He opened his eyes, his lips forming a thin line. "I remember it vividly. I was none too pleased to have to go over there. You know how the roads get. No one knows how to drive in LA when it rains."

"And that was to see Ms. Monroe specifically?" Larson asked as Murphy wrote down the date.

"Yes. She wanted me to check a mole, thought it was cancerous or something. I checked it, cut it off, and took it for biopsy." He paused and scowled. "When I called her with the negative results, she told me I had a terrible bedside manner and she had found a private doctor." Dr. Jerris stared pointedly at Larson. "I sat in two hours of traffic to get to that woman. Good riddance, I say."

"How was her heart?" Murphy cut in.

"Great. Normal blood pressure for her age. I'd say she was healthy. A bit of a hypochondriac but aren't they all." He rolled up the magazine and stood. "That's all I have for you. Gotta get back to it." Murphy and Larson followed suit.

"We might need to speak again," Murphy said.

"Not a problem, just call my office," he said on his way out the door.

"Eager to leave us," Larson said to Murphy. She stared at the Doctor's receding back. He was definitely guilty of something, she thought. They followed him out.

"Think he's our perp?" Murphy fished.

"He didn't show surprise about the coroner's report."

"Aren't doctors trained not to show emotions?" Murphy asked as they walked towards the parking garage. Dr. Jerris could easily have done it, she thought, and he was definitely on the potential perp list.

Lou Fairbanks set soup and a sandwich in front of Dads and plopped in the chair across from him. She had taken up Barney's challenge with a fury and neglected all her other tasks to talk to each and every resident on the ninth and eleventh floors in search of the mysterious, crying woman. There were six women in total on both floors and none of them looked as though they had spent the entire night crying. She had done her due diligence and administered depression questionnaires to each of them to be absolutely sure they weren't suffering in silence, but all of them reported as normal. Every one of them tested neutral for depression and all were well-adjusted.

Almost too well adjusted, she muttered angrily to herself. The effort had taken an enormous toll on her and the migraine that started after her conversation with Barney and his gang in the cafeteria had dogged her the entire morning. She needed to call Dr. Jerris, she thought, and gingerly touched the bump on the back of her head. On second thought, she would wait. What could he say to do that she hadn't already done herself? She was a nurse after all.

She noticed Dads ignoring his lunch and pushed the sandwich plate closer to him.

"Eat, Dads. Lunch." She tapped him on the hand to get his attention. His gaze never shifted from the window. "I can't handle you doing this today. Please."

Dad turned to her as his eyes focused. "You look tired," he said.

"I am tired. Very tired. Eat."

Dads picked up his sandwich and took a bite. The tension released out of Lou's shoulders, and she sat back in the chair. "Thank you, Dads," she said.

He nodded and mumbled, "Good. It's good." She softened a touch and smiled. He had these kinds of lucid moments several times a week, but they were getting to be spread further and further apart.

Dads took another bite, his eyes sliding down to the soup.

"How was your day?" she prodded, attempting to engage him.

He nodded on command. "Fine," he mumbled back.

"What? I didn't hear you," Lou explained. His eyes unfocused and he said nothing more. He dropped the sandwich onto the plate and pushed both it and the bowl away from him. It was only a matter of time now, she thought and hoped it was true.

"You need to eat, Dads." She hated how her voice turned into a whine. "Please. For me?" His face stayed blank.

She wished for the millionth time she had more friends. Or even one friend. Just someone else to talk to besides Dads. Like Lindsey. She hadn't found anyone to replace her yet. In one of his more lucid moments, Dads claimed her caustic character kept everyone away. Who wanted to be friends with someone like her, he reasoned.

She pushed that nasty thought away. "Do you want some tea? I can make us some tea," she said instead and heaved herself out of the chair with a considerable amount of effort. She went to the kitchenette, filled the tea kettle with water and set it onto the hot plate.

"Unfortunately, I still have my afternoon rounds left," she said, and kneaded her forehead. "I'm so tired, Dads. I'm just so very tired. My patients demand so much of me," she said, setting two Lipton tea bags into chipped coffee cups. The kettle whistled, and she filled the cups to the brim. She added a touch of white powder from a vial to Dads' cup and made sure to stir it well, hiding all trace of it.

"We need a good night's sleep. That's all. A good night's sleep," Lou mumbled to herself. She wasn't well enough to do the rounds. They could wait til tomorrow.

A dark fog swirled around her as Lou fought to wake up.

Thump! Thump!

Someone was in their room, and she had to stop them from hurting her.

Thump! Thump!

She struggled towards the surface of consciousness, fear pushing her forward.

Thump.

Lou woke with a gasp and sat up in bed, disoriented. She rubbed the sleep out of her eyes and strained to see what was making such a noise.

Thump!

The sound came from the window, but she didn't see anything or anyone there. She scrubbed her face with her hands. Could she still be sleeping? She pinched her arm.

"Ouch," she muttered as she rubbed the spot until the pain went away. She was definitely awake. Lou rose up from the bed for a closer look and gasped in horror.

The yellow light from the streetlights streamed through the window and, at her current angle, revealed two handprints in the middle of the pane of glass. When Lou sat back down on the bed, they disappeared. Standing up, they appeared again. Lou rubbed her eyes once more and stepped closer, never taking her eyes off the prints. She had to angle her head several times to make them out, but the prints were definitely still there.

Lou leaned into the window pane and ran her finger over the edge of one of the handprints. Her hand recoiled in shock when she left her own smudged fingerprint on the inside. Ice-cold fear invaded her body and dumped adrenaline into her blood stream.

The handprints were made on the outside of the window. Not the inside like she had previously thought.

Her hand matched in size to the ghostly imprint. A woman's imprint then, she thought. She undid the lock on the latch with shaking hands and threw the window open, sticking her head out. Lou stared up at the sky and then back down to the street below. She didn't know whether she was expecting some sort of Spiderwoman hanging off the side of the building, or a ghost floating in the air. Either way, the side of the building was empty.

"Get a hold of yourself, Lou," she said and pulled herself back into the room, closing the window behind her. Dads' snores were the only normal thing about the room.

She sat back on her bed, both scared and perplexed. How in the world could anyone leave those handprints? And if it was the ghost of Irene Lentz like Barney claimed it was, then why was she leaving handprints on HER window? Someone who didn't believe in her very existence. She crawled under the covers, wanting to stay under them forever.

A sob broke the silence in the room, the same sob she heard last night. Lou bit the blanket as the sobs picked up in volume. The grief spilling from the woman overwhelmed her. The woman wailed into her ear. Lou threw herself off the bed and fell into a heap on the floor, blankets tangling around her.

It got louder, and Lou could swear the sobbing was coming from inside her own room. Lou pressed her hands over her ears.

"Please, leave me alone," she cried to the empty room. The sobbing grew fainter, the ghost listening to her pleas. Or so she thought.

A faucet turned with a squeak, and the sound of water filled the room like the night before.

Lou crawled over to Dads. He was still asleep, thank god.

Thump. Thump.

The sound reverberated around the room. She pulled the covers over her head, her eyes wide with terror. Why was the ghost scaring her like this?

THUMP.

She flinched and cowered against Dads' bed, positive that the ceiling would fall in on them.

Dads shifted in his bed. Had he woken up again? She peeked out from under her covers. He sat on his bed wide-awake, his head cocked to the sounds swirling all around him.

"Dads. Dads, it's all OK. Just the old hotel making noise. Go back to sleep," she said, her voice cracking. He looked down at her. All she could see were the whites of his eyes.

"Are you awake? Can you hear me?" she asked. He stayed silent, his eyes never wavering from hers. Chills ran down her body as she struggled to get up. Lou kicked off the blankets. The thumps ended. She froze. Holding her breath in anticipation of the ghost, she waited for any sound. The room stayed silent.

She hurried to his side. "Let's go back to sleep," she said and he obeyed without comment. Lou lay down next to him and hummed an off-tune version of Imagine, the only thing that consistently calmed him. Dads closed his eyes. She kept singing until he snored. Confident he was asleep, she tiptoed back to her own bed, exhausted. Tomorrow would be different.

7
Sleeplessness
FEBRUARY 18, 2005 - DAY 3

Lou Fairbanks' hand shook as she pulled it through her disheveled hair and wondered if she'd made a mistake by coming here. As she'd lain in bed unable to sleep, she convinced herself Barney was right and that the ghost of Irene Lentz was haunting her and Dads. When she woke up this morning, reality set in. The pipes were bad. A resident somewhere in the Sunshine desperately needed help.

She blinked against the light that filtered through the blinds behind Diane and tried to come up with the best way of broaching the subject with her. The glare prevented her from thinking straight. She shifted her gaze to the Home Decor magazine in Diane's hand instead. Finally able to think, Lou took a deep breath and plunged forward.

"There's something wrong with the pipes on my floor. More importantly, however, a resident needs our attention," Lou said and watched Diane's expression change from annoyance to confusion.

"What's wrong with the pipes? Are they backed up?" Diane said putting the Home Decor down.

"No, nothing like that. Sound travels through them and threatens our resident's privacy. For the last two nights, a woman sobbed the entire night. The sound traveled through the pipes. I've checked the ninth floor and eleventh floor residents to find the woman needing our support, but I've been unable to locate her. I wanted to broaden my search to more floors," Lou explained. "But we should fix these pipes. Residents shouldn't have to fear that their private moments are broadcast to everyone else."

Diane shook her head. "Let me get this straight. You've been kept awake by a woman's crying, and you think that it's coming through your pipes? What pipes exactly?"

"Maybe the vents then? Or the water pipes?" Lou said. When said out loud, her theory sounded farfetched. Lou's face heated unbidden. Diane's eyes narrowed.

"I'm beginning to worry about you, Lou. When was the last time you slept through the night? You look positively exhausted. How can you be doing your job properly when you're running on fumes?"

Diane's questioning of her ability to do her job shook Lou's resolve. She needed this job. Lou sank lower in her seat, wishing she'd never come. She hadn't realized her frayed nerves showed on her face.

"This depressed patient needs our help," Lou said. "The sobbing is so raw, I'm worried this woman is suicidal."

"Have any of your patients exhibited signs of depression?" Diane asked.

Lou shifted in her seat, ready to leave. "No, just the usual phobias. I gave the residents on the two floors around me psych eval tests to make sure. Everyone appears normal," Lou said and stood up. "I'll keep searching for the woman. I just wanted to bring this to your attention."

"I really don't think it's pipes, Lou, but if this keeps happening please come back and talk to me," Diane said with such concern in her voice that Lou took a step back. Did she know about her anxiety? Had someone seen her passed out in the staircase after all? She'd done everything to keep it out of her medical records and if Diane knew, then everyone in this place would too. She blanched at the thought and backed out to the hallway.

"I should go do my rounds. Thanks again, Diane," she said and got out of there as fast as she could. She hurried down the hall unsure of what to do next. She agreed with Diane on one point, she needed to get a good night's sleep. She couldn't take sleeping pills because of Dads, which left the plan of getting to the bottom of who the crying woman was. She didn't see another way of getting her sleep back.

What if Barney was right, though, and it was a ghost? After saying her theory out loud to Diane and realizing how nuts she sounded, admitting she might be haunted by a ghost wasn't as farfetched as she first thought. She changed course and made her way to the cafeteria instead.

Sure enough, Lou found Barney, Mary Ann, and Doreen back at their usual table, deep in conversation while Lauren gestured with excitement to some residents, several tables away from the main group. No one paid any attention to her as she made her way over to their table.

"Hi," she said with a mix of trepidation and excitement, "May I join you?" she asked, and waited until Doreen nodded before sitting down at the last remaining chair.

Barney stopped talking to Mary Ann and turned to her. "You haven't slept either, have you?"

"No, I haven't," she admitted and gulped down the lump that hadn't been there a second ago. "So if it is the ghost of Irene Lentz, what do we do about it?"

"None of us slept a wink either," Mary Ann confirmed what Lou could plainly see on all their faces. "I can't keep going like this. I need my beauty rest," she whispered and stole a glance at Barney.

"Is it the same ghost then? Are you all hearing the sobbing?" Lou asked. Mary Ann nodded.

"What we need to do is find out what she wants. I've called in some people I know," Barney said. "It's the only way."

"People?" Lou asked.

"Ghost hunters. If we can make contact, we stand a chance of allowing her to pass and leave us in peace," Barney explained.

"Maybe we'll stop dying in droves as well," Doreen added with a raised eyebrow.

"I can't believe you'd say that, Doreen," Mary Ann said, glancing over at Barney to check in on him.

Doreen scowled. "Well, it's what we're all thinking, isn't it?" she said in a huff as Lauren appeared at her elbow.

"What are we all thinking?" Lauren asked and pulled a chair up to sit with them. Doreen scooted over, giving her some room.

"That maybe these ghosts are the ones that are taking us all out," she said and Lauren looked confused.

"Take us out? I thought Babs was ruled a heart attack, like the others?" She looked around the table. "Wasn't she? I've heard the rumors, but you can't really believe them, can you?"

"I highly doubt a ghost could muster up enough energy to kill someone," Barney said dryly.

Doreen banged her hand on the table. "What about this? The ghost appears to them, and they die of fright? That would cause a heart attack, wouldn't it Lou?" She turned to Lou, expecting her to agree with her.

"I'm sorry, Doreen but that condition is really rare. I don't think that's what is happening. Getting back to Barney's point," Lou said, "Who did you call? What kind of ghost hunters? Do mediums or psychics really exist? I thought all those people were charlatans?"

"My friends know a legitimate medium," Barney said, nonplussed. Lou tried to keep her mind open. First, ghosts and now mediums? She'd landed in the twilight zone. A flash of the woman's pain reminded Lou of why she'd come to the cafeteria in the first place. She'd see this through and if it was just a hoax, well, they'd all know and at least it would get Barney to finally shut up.

"Would Diane have to give us permission for that?" Lou asked Barney. By the look on his face, she'd asked the wrong thing.

Barney bristled. "We pay to live here. We don't have to ask permission for every little thing," he said, pushing back his chair.

"I didn't mean anything by—" Barney cut her off. Her anger rising, she hid her clenched fists under the table. He drove her crazy like no one else did.

"I'm making the call. You can go tell Diane whatever you want," he said and stomped out of the cafe.

Mary Ann pushed back her chair with a screech. "He shouldn't get upset like that...his heart," she admonished all of them and bustled after him. Lou turned to Doreen and Lauren.

"We're all crazy right?" she asked, still trying to process what she'd just got herself into. The women stayed silent. "I mean, this can't possibly work," she added.

"Not in the least bit crazy, Lou," Doreen said with a gleam in her eye. "Whatever will bring us back our sleep, I say. Plus this is more excitement then we've had in weeks. Better than dwelling on all the death going around."

"What's the harm?" Lauren added.

"I suppose there isn't any harm in it," Lou said, unconvinced. What was the worst that could happen? Most likely, this medium was a sham and they would all have a good laugh. Maybe with the commotion of the ghost hunters, whoever was crying would come forward to get help. Lou smiled for the first time today. "Well, we'll see what happens. I should go check on Dads."

"We will definitely stir something up, won't we?" Lauren asked and gave Doreen a pointed look. Doreen made another sign of the cross and sighed. Lou got up to go.

"Will you get me when they arrive?" Lou asked them.

"You think they'll come today?" Lauren's eyes grew large as she checked in with Doreen.

"Who wants to miss another night's sleep? I sure don't," Doreen said in her matter-of-fact voice.

Detective Eva Murphy pulled up to the Bockerman Hotel and thought it remarkable that she'd already forgotten the assisted living facility's actual name. It didn't help matters that its name was nowhere to be found on the outside of the building and that the massive vintage sign, spanning the width of the roof, proclaimed it The Bockerman. The city probably wouldn't allow the owners to take the sign down as it was a fixture in the Hollywood skyline, she thought as she parked her unmarked car in the unloading zone. Murphy checked herself out in the rearview mirror and got out, her mind churning the facts of the case.

When she stepped into the lobby, the first person she encountered was the security guard at the front desk, a man in his early thirties that had the shifty eyes of a teenager, close-cropped hair, and a skinny build hidden by his ill-fitting suit. After seeing their security setup, Murphy ruled out the possibility that a stranger to the facility was their perp. She pulled out her badge and checked the man's name tag. Hall, no first name. He didn't make such a bad suspect himself though, she thought.

"Detective Murphy," she said and held out her hand. He took it limply in his own.

Keeping his eyes averted, he said, "Russell Hall. Everyone calls me Russ." Murphy found his not meeting her eyes suspicious, like he'd had problems with the law in the past.

"I need the security tapes for February 13 through last night, February 18. Diane Lawrence told me you'd be able to get them for me," Murphy said.

Russell nodded. "They're in the room next to her office. Could you follow me please?" He turned on his heel.

"Great," Murphy said to his back and followed him into the darkened hallway. She didn't think anything would go sideways, but she put her hand on her pepper spray all the same. She wondered what in the world Diane Lawrence was thinking when she hired this man in the first place. He didn't instill confidence, and he wasn't imposing enough to stop an intruder. He was your garden-variety creep.

She doubted the residents came to him with security issues. Could Diane Lawrence have hired him on purpose to help her cover up these murders? He wouldn't be someone to raise flags to the owners on the goings on in the place.

Russell opened a door and stood aside to let her pass. She entered a room containing two tables with four monitors sitting on top of them and three whirring computer towers below. A stack of DVD's filled the room's only shelf. Each monitor showed a view of four cameras covering the front and back entrances, the main staircase and main elevator.

"Does each DVD contain all four camera angles?" Murphy asked.

"Yup. I've already made the first three. Diane, um, I mean Ms. Lawrence, asked me to. I just need to do the last night for you. It shouldn't take too long," he said and sat at the lone chair in the room.

Murphy leaned against the door. "Great, mind if I ask you whether you were on duty the night of February 15?"

"I was," he mumbled.

"All night?"

"My typical shift is from 6pm to 6am."

Murphy closed the distance between them. "Do you do rounds on the floors or do you stay down in the lobby the entire time?" She kept her tone conversational.

"I stay down in the lobby, keep my eyes on all the cameras and make sure none of the residents wander out overnight."

"Are they not allowed to leave the premises after a certain time?" Murphy asked, surprised.

"They need to sign in and sign out. People can come and go, but they need to be lucid. No wandering off."

"I see. Did anyone leave that night?"

"I need to check the log but I don't think so." Russell put in another DVD. "This is the last one," he said over his shoulder.

"Did you see anyone after 10pm?" Murphy prodded, and edged even closer to him.

"This place is usually quiet at that time. I saw Ms. Lawrence leave around 8pm but..." He paused. "I don't remember anyone else. Do you have any suspects yet?" he asked, and swiveled his chair around handing her four DVDs. She took them with a small smile.

You're on my perp list, she thought. "Beginning days yet. We're still gathering evidence," she said. "How long have you worked here?"

"Three years this April," he said.

"We'll need a statement from you regarding your movements on February 18. I'm sure you understand how important the information is, Mr. Hall." She smiled. "I mean, Russ."

He nodded.

She left him sitting in front of the monitors. She couldn't wait to find out what that guy's deal was. He was hiding something. Murphy called Larson when she got back into the car. "Russell Hall, the security guard. My gut says he must have a record," she said. "I'll be there in fifteen."

By the time she got back to the station, Larson's smile was as big as hers. "We have a live one. A good, ole Orange County family, Neo-Nazi style," Larson started. Murphy flopped into her desk chair and grabbed the long printout from his desk.

"Mr. Gerard Hall, Daddy Hall, that's his record." He motioned to the printout in her hand. "Lots of assault charges for the old man but nothing yet on Russell. He's come close, but Daddy always steps in, and nothing has stuck."

"Was Barbara Monroe Jewish?" asked Murphy.

"I have a call into the family. We could check some of the other mysteriously deceased patients' families as well," Larson offered.

"I thought you weren't behind the theory that the other deaths are connected?"

"Better to cover all our bases," Larson said.

"How can we talk to Daddy Hall about Junior?"

"He's in lock-up at County awaiting his trial date. Know anyone at the Sheriff's department?"

Murphy nodded and picked up the phone. "Larry, hey, it's Murphy over at Hollywood."

Murphy and Larson sat across from a hulking skinhead, tats covering ninety percent of his body including his skull, in a barren interrogation room. I would not want to meet the likes of Daddy Hall in a dark alley, Murphy thought.

"Why am I here?" Daddy Hall rumbled.

"We want to talk to you about your son, Russell Hall," Larson started.

"Is he OK?" The hulk leaned forward, his eyes filled with worry.

"He's fine. Is he part of your gang?" Murphy asked.

"He has nothing to do with my gang. He's straight," Daddy Hall said, crossing his arms over his massive chest.

"What about the assault in Fullerton in 2000?" Larson asked.

"That was me and some of my boys. Russ wasn't even there." Daddy Hall stood up. "I don't need to talk to you."

Murphy looked up at the hulking man and put on her best smile. "There have been murders at the Bockerm— I mean, at the Sunshine House, the facility he works at. We just want to make sure he wasn't involved."

"My son is no murderer. He's a security guard there for chrissake. He was always too weak for our kind of life. He is NOT your guy. Guard, we're done!" he yelled over his shoulder. The interview was over.

Sara Caine parked her car in front of the Bockerman Hotel and marveled at the dusky light that washed all of Hollywood in a pinkish, purple glow. She loved the contradictions that Los Angeles possessed. The atmosphere now made the city soft and romantic compared to the usual harsh, bright light of day that called to mind The Day of the Locust or something written by Raymond Chandler.

She had arrived on time but knowing the boys, they would be late. She got out of her car and paid the meter. Should she wait out front or... she looked up and down the street, unsure. She lucked out meeting Fredrick on a job a couple of years back and although the job turned out to be a hoax, they had kept in touch over the years. Every ghost hunter wanted access to the once world-renowned Bockerman Hotel and she had no idea how Fredrick finally got permission to go inside from the company that ran the place.

Famous for the movie stars that stayed at the hotel in its prime, the Bockerman stayed famous for the supposed ghosts that haunted it. Sara doubted that she'd see Marilyn Monroe or Rudolf Valentino today, but she was thrilled Fredrick invited her along for the ride. She smiled when she saw the white van pulling up to the curb with Fredrick behind the wheel, and waved hello. The van door slid open and William, a scruffy cameraman wearing a photographer's vest filled with all sorts of electronic equipment, jumped out of the passenger's seat.

"Hey Sara," he said and headed to the back of the van. Fredrick joined Sara on the sidewalk as a younger man, Jerry, dressed like a surfer and pumped on Red Bull, scrambled over the seat and jumped to the curb. He rubbed his hands together.

"I can't believe we're finally getting to go inside this place." Jerry jumped in glee. He grabbed her hand and pumped it up and down in greeting. "I've heard so much about you. It's such a pleasure to meet you and that you're here." He reminded her of an undisciplined puppy. "A real medium. Awesome!" He grinned at Fredrick. "So cool, Bro."

"We should unload. We only have another half hour before sunset," Fredrick reminded him. Sara flashed him a grin and felt her own excitement rise. The gang tended to have that effect on her.

"Yes, boss." Jerry joined William at the back of the van.

Fredrick hugged her hello. "How're you doin, kid?"

Sara gave him a squeeze back. "Day by day, Fred. Day by day," she said. "Thank you for inviting me along. I'll do my best to stay out of your way, but you know how it goes," she said with a wink and bumped his fist with hers in solidarity. It'd been awhile since she'd seen him.

"No way, we want you in on this. If we capture any of the famous ghosts on tape, we'll be famous ourselves. Or at least get our own reality show."

"Who called you in?" Sara asked.

"An old friend of my father's," Fredrick said. "I'm not sure I believe his story, but no way was I going to pass up the opportunity. We've tried to get in here before, but the manager Diane is a real hard ass. She said no the last four times we've asked. Don't even get me started on the sharks who run this place." His grimace turned to wonder as he scanned the facade. "Wow, man. Can you believe we're here? The Bockerman. You ready for this?"

"Am I ever," she said as they headed back to the others and the growing amount of video and sound equipment on the pavement.

Sara wandered through the two-story lobby as the team set up their gear on a makeshift table next to the entrance to the once famous "The All-Star Theatre Cafe & Speakeasy." The cafe opened in the early '90s as a retro coffeehouse frequented by celebrities like Leonardo DiCaprio and Sandra Bullock. It didn't last long.

The doors leading to the elevators and hallways matched the window arches that looked out over Ivar Avenue, and she would call the style 'Mission'. The walls rose to a wooden beamed ceiling and, although the paintings on the beams had long ago faded, she imagined they must have been stunning. Couches lined the walls, and cheap rugs obscured the colorful Moroccan tiles under her feet. The shabbiness of its present reincarnation could not mar the old splendor of the former hotel from peeking out among the present detritus.

She touched the nearest column and didn't have to wait long to hear the big band music all around her, laughter, and footsteps on tile. She caught the scent of freshly picked roses and perfume. A breeze caught several strands of her hair, and she lifted her hand to brush them away when a shimmering started in the center of a beam of light streaming in from one of the large windows.

This effect always reminded her of heat waves coming off the concrete in the middle of the summer, and she wondered yet again what the significance of ghosts appearing within light was. It never mattered whether the light was sunlight or lamplight. It just needed to be light. Johan had spoken of things coming out of the shadows, the darkness, but she had been lucky never to experience that particular phenomena. The shimmer, as she called it, made for quite a beautiful effect.

An older, thin-faced man, wearing a shabby suit, and bow tie, smoking cigarette in hand, materialized out of the shimmer, his fierce gaze catching hers. He knew she could see him.

"Have you seen my film?" he whispered to her. She leaned in to hear him better as her eyes scanned the lobby. The gang had finished setting up the equipment, and a small group of residents clustered around the video screens in anticipation. No one paid her much attention.

"Which film?" She kept her voice low.

"Have you heard of Birth of a Nation?" His raspy voice held traces of sadness.

"You're D.W. Griffith," she said with a sparkle in her eye. He gave her a small bow.

"I am he." His eyes took in the scene in front of him. "There are many of us here."

"I'd heard you might be here," Sara said.

A delighted smile spread across his face. "You're too kind." A chair leg scraped across the tile and set Sara's teeth on edge. Griffith's smile faded.

"There are bad things here, and you need to be careful. Death surrounds us," he whispered. "Tired. Must. Go." He flickered and disappeared. Sara's ears popped with the change in pressure. She wondered what bad things he was talking about. Like ghosts killing people?

She crossed the lobby just as Jerry turned on all the computers. The screens sprang to life and showed eight views of three different hallways.

"This is cutting edge surveillance technology," Fredrick said and gestured to the impressive array of equipment. "With the help of our medium, Sara Caine, we will find whatever ghosts you have," he said as he pulled her into the middle of the small crowd. "Sara, may I introduce you to Nurse Lou, Barney, Mary Ann, and Lauren. Barney was the one who called us in." He pointed to a Hollywood blond. "This is Diane, the manager here, and Doreen." Sara fought the urge to take a small bow and managed to nod and give them a smile.

"Wait, so as a medium, you see ghosts?" The middle-aged nurse in scrubs named Lou asked her. Sara heard the familiar incredulity in her voice.

"Lou," Barney warned her making Lou purse her lips into a thin, bloodless line. She didn't utter another word and, instead, crossed her arms and pushed to the back of the crowd. Obviously, those two didn't get along.

Sara took note of everyone's dark under-eye smudges and general fear and figured no one was sleeping much. The blond named Diane, attractive enough to be an actress and, knowing LA, most likely one, looked well rested but Sara doubted she lived on the premises. Sara noticed the other women kept close to Barney, leaving Lou, and Diane as the outsiders of the group.

"Have any of you been physically attacked?" Sara asked.

"If by physically attacked you mean tortured by sound, then yes, we have been. The screams, whispers and knocking have become too much to bear," Mary Ann replied.

"And the thumps. Someone was at my window last night and tried to get in," Lou called out from the back. Her eyes grew wide with the memory.

"But nothing physical?" Sara prodded.

"What do you mean?" Sara couldn't make out who called that out.

"Like killing us? That physical enough?" Mary Ann said. Sara saw Barney elbow her in the ribs, and the woman clamped her mouth shut. Fredrick shot Sara a warning look and she held up her hands with an implied sorry.

"So these are live?" Doreen asked, pointing to the monitors.

Jerry nodded. "I don't know how much ya'll know about hauntings but ghosts—or how we like to call them, dead guys." Jerry cracked a smile. "The dead guys, typically present themselves through sounds. All this equipment is trying to catch those sounds."

Fredrick jumped in. "I'll be carrying what's called a spirit box. It uses AM and FM frequencies to generate white noise. Ghosts get energy from that noise and talk within it." Sara heard this spiel the last time she joined their hunt and took the opportunity to study the riveted audience.

"I'll be using this EVP." He held up a small box. "It's a very sensitive recording device. If there are ghosts, we'll hear them." He finished and checked his watch. It was time. He and William plugged in their receivers, and William switched the camera on and lifted it to his shoulders. Fredrick turned to Barney.

"We'll start with the tenth floor. You can all watch on the monitors. Jerry will man our station here." Barney nodded.

"Let's roll," William said.

8

Ghost Hunting
DAY 3

Lou Fairbanks hung over Jerry's shoulder and stared at the screens so intently her eyes began to water. She felt Barney, Mary Ann, and the rest of the group pressing against her back and it was comforting to know she wasn't the only one mesmerized. On the uppermost left screen, the two main ghost hunters, Fredrick and William, walked down the hall with those things they called EVPs held out in front of them with the medium trailing some distance behind them.

What was the medium's name again, Lou thought, and ran through a list of names until her memory spit out the correct one. Sara, Sara Caine. She'd heard of psychics on the daytime talk shows and wondered if mediums were the same thing. She'd even thought, in her darkest of moments, to contact that Sylvia Browne woman who frequented the Sally Jessy Raphael show, but came to her senses before she picked up the phone. That was a long time ago and, over the years, lots of stories came out claiming her a fraud, which cemented Lou's belief that none of that stuff was real. But, here she was now, excited to see what they would find.

The crackling of white noise penetrated her thoughts and brought her back to the hallway. On the monitor, Fredrick dialed a knob on the EVP until he found a constant white noise that was free from any static.

A flash of movement caught her eye at the edge of the screen. "Did you see that?" She pointed at the general location, and Jerry flipped the monitor to the same camera, searching around for any sign of movement.

"I'm not seeing anything. Could you describe it? Where was it exactly?" Jerry asked her as William and Fredrick appeared on both screens. Jerry flipped one of them back to the other angle for a better view.

"Did you hear that?" William's voice blared out of the computer speakers making Mary Ann gasp and push past Lou to get a better look. Lauren and Barney were not far behind her. They watched Fredrick hold up his monitor to William.

A gentle sobbing came through the static of the receiver.

"That's the woman. That's what I keep hearing every night," Lou said and nudged Jerry in the ribs. "Can you turn it up? Or clean it up?"

"Who are you?" Fredrick's voice crackled through the speakers and made everyone jump. Jerry turned the sound down a notch as the two men turned round and round. The medium frowned.

The sobbing grew louder as Fredrick and William ran down the corridor, the medium trailing after them. Lou cocked her head at another sound and got closer to the monitor.

"Help, help," came through so faintly that at first Lou thought she was imagining it.

"Do you hear that?" she asked Jerry and he nodded, playing with the sound knobs to isolate it better. Lou paled as the voice became clearer. That wasn't a woman's voice, that was Dads' voice.

She pushed past the others and sprinted through the lobby. She'd given him several Ambien earlier to keep him asleep, but he must have woken up and found himself alone with the apartment empty. What if...she stopped the thought from forming. She had to get to him first.

Lou came to a halt in front of the elevator, hyperventilating, the familiar panic welling up inside. She glanced over to the stairs and vetoed the idea immediately. She couldn't risk passing out. Her secret would be out.

She steeled herself and punched the up button. To her relief, the elevator doors opened. Lou rushed inside before anyone else could join her. She didn't need an audience for her insanity and jabbed the button for the tenth floor.

She closed her eyes as the floors dinged by, her heart in her throat and her mind fixated on Dads. Lou stayed that way until the elevators doors slid open. She covered the distance to her door quickly, and as she slid the key into the lock, the ghost hunters appeared to her left, flushed with excitement over the new voice.

"Is it in there? That's where the voice is coming from," Fredrick said never taking his eyes off the EVP.

"It's my father, not a ghost," she yelled at them as she opened the door and found Dads sitting on the edge of his bed, staring out to the Hollywood sign and cradling his arm.

His bleeding arm.

She rushed to his side. "Dads, you're bleeding. Let me see," she said and gently extricated his right arm from his side and straightened it out. She stared down in horror at what she was seeing. How could anyone do this to an old man, she thought.

Someone, or something, had carved HELP ME in crude letters into his forearm. The cuts weren't deep, but the wound bled plenty, staining both his pajama pants and the carpet underneath him. She hurried to the bathroom and grabbed the first aid kit, relieved the cuts hadn't hit any major arteries and weren't too severe. But, the intent to harm was evident, she thought as she came out of the bathroom and noticed the ghost hunters crammed into the doorway.

"Dads, who did this to you? Was it the crying woman? Did you see her?" she whispered and kneeled down in front of him. He never broke his gaze from the window. She opened up the kit and tore open one of the alcohol towelette packs.

"Are you getting this?" She heard someone exclaim and shifted her body to shield Dads' arm from them.

"DON'T tape this. Can't you see he's hurt! Leave us alone," she yelled behind her. They were disgusting vultures. Her hands trembled, and she found it hard to clean up the scratches properly. She took a deep breath and tried again.

"Sorry, I know this stings," she said but got nothing out of Dads. He didn't flinch nor pull his arm away and when she looked into his eyes, they stayed empty. The camera clicked behind her. They were still there. Her rage burst through her fear.

"I asked for you not to tape this. Get out!" She barreled at them, her arms reaching for their camera lenses. "Can't you see he's hurt? What's wrong with you people?"

"We'll call 911," Fredrick said before Sara Caine pulled him away from the door. Lou pulled herself together.

"No police," she said too sharply. Fredrick sent Sara Caine a surprised look.

Lou cleared her throat. "Thank you though. These aren't deep, and he appears fine. What would the police think about a ghost hurting him? We'd all look like a bunch of loons," she said, reminding everyone of the craziness they were partaking in. With some satisfaction, Lou saw that it did the trick. Fredrick flushed while William nodded in agreement.

"I'm sorry I yelled at you, but I lost it when I saw him. I'm relieved they are very shallow," she explained to them.

"That's understandable," Sara Caine cut in as the men took cover behind her.

"Thank you for that," Lou said, returning to Dads side.

"We'll get Diane for you, if you'd like," Sara said and closed the door.

"Find out who did this to him. If it's a ghost, find it. Get rid of it. That's what you can do," Lou urged her, surprising even herself. Sara nodded and closed the door, leaving Lou alone with Dads.

"Did Irene really do this to you, Dads? The woman who sobs every night?" Lou asked him as she perched back on his bed. He didn't give any indication that he heard her. She checked his bandage one last time.

"This should be good enough for the night. Can I tuck you in?" she asked. Lou gently helped him lie back down. "Can you get under the covers?" He did as she requested without saying a word.

She pulled them up to his chin. He turned to her. They stared at each other for a moment before she broke away, the guilt of what she had done to him eating her up inside.

Sara Caine took her arm off Fredrick as soon as Lou's door closed. Something about that woman didn't sit well with her. Fredrick nodded at William and they both turned off the EVP's and made their way to the elevator.

"How did you know?"

"Know what?" Sara said.

"Someone would get attacked?" Fredrick's eyes bore into her as the elevator doors opened.

"I didn't know, Fredrick. It's a standard question I ask. Also, I didn't pick up any ghosts in that room or on this floor," Sara said and held him back, letting the elevator doors close in front of them.

"Why did you rig this floor?" Sara asked. "This floor is devoid of activity unlike some of the other floors. The lobby had more ghost activity then here." She shot him a knowing look. "What are you not telling me?"

"Let it go, Sara." Before he could say anything else, a furious Diane Lawrence stormed out of the elevator and stopped right in front of them.

"I think it's time you all packed up and left," Diane said, and stomped down the hall to Lou's door.

"What about the Cafe?" William called after her. Diane shot him a nasty look and opened up Lou's door without saying a word. Sara watched the angry woman disappear inside.

"Damn it. Can we sneak in another way?" William whispered to Fredrick.

"Not gonna happen," Fredrick said. "Did you see the 'Help me' carved into his arm? Could a ghost get enough energy to do that?

"Not that I've ever encountered. He'd have to be held down first and then cut. That would take more than one ghost."

"What about a demon?" Fredrick asked.

"That's a question for Johan Luken, not me. But, he's always told me that when you are in the presence of that kind of entity you will feel it down to your bones. I've felt nothing here like that," Sara said.

"Who in the hell did that to the poor guy then?" William asked, staring back at the door. They stood silent for a moment.

Sara let down one of her walls to make sure nothing was there and was hit with the stench of sweat. Before she could drag her wall back up into place, she was hit by a force. Her mind spun in circles, and dizziness slammed into her. She grabbed onto Fredrick for support.

"You OK?" Fredrick asked. All she could do was nod as she fought to get back her equilibrium.

"Sara?" he asked again. His voice came to her as if through a fog. The smell of death was all around them, and it was fresh and filled with fear. This feeling wasn't coming from the old Hollywood ghosts. She took several gulps of air and made sure all her walls were back up. When she was sure she was safe, she opened her eyes to see Fredrick and William staring at her, concern all over their faces.

"I'm fine. Really, I am." The blood rushed through her body and knew that to be true.

"What did you see?" William asked. "Was it a demon?"

"No. A ghost slammed into me, and it's death was recent," she said. Something was really wrong with this place. The old man's bloody arm flashed in her mind. Could a recent ghost hurt him like that, she wondered? Ghosts rarely maintained enough power to complete that kind of task. Could her senses have missed something? Was the stench of death coming from the elevator? She had no way of answering those questions positively.

Neither Fredrick or William moved to get into the elevator. Fredrick glanced down the dreary hall and scowled. "We should get in." He gestured to the elevator. In response, the doors started sliding closed. Fredrick grabbed onto one of the doors to keep it open. The elevator protested by dinging.

Some unseen force tugged on Sara's elbow. She jumped away in surprise. Ghosts had pulled at her clothing before, but she never got used to it. It pulled at her again. This time toward her left. Then it tugged again. Sara guessed it wanted her to go left.

"I think I'm going to take the stairs," Sara said and stepped away from the doors.

"Why? Is there something wrong with the elevator?" William squeaked. "The smell of death isn't coming from the elevator. You should be fine." Sara said. William was jumpy even on the quiet ghost hunts, and this was not one of them. William's face paled.

"The smell of death?" Fredrick asked.

"It was a whiff in the hall," Sara explained. The elevator protested again. "It's safe," Sara reiterated again.

The crew finally got in with their equipment. The doors closed on their grim looks. Sara hoped she'd made the right decision by not telling the boys about the ghost tugging on her. As if it heard her thoughts, it tugged at her arm again. She turned towards it's pull, her heart beating faster. The ghost led her to the last door on the left, a gold placard with STAIRS written on it.

Sara entered a staircase straight out of a Hitchcock film and hoped that she hadn't just become the stupid girl that the audience yelled at. The wooden balustrade snaked around in an endless spiral. The marble stairs held indents from decades of feet that had traveled on them, and single sconces on each landing emitted a murky yellow light that barely reached past several feet. Shadows controlled this place.

She stepped off the landing, allowing her senses to wander ahead of her. A wall of sound roared in her ears as voices from the last century fought to be heard. No distinctive voice emerged as the winner, however. Sara erected all but one of her mind's walls, and the roar transformed into a hissing whisper. That was better.

She checked what floor she was on and stared at one of Fredrick's cameras. He'd made no mention of rigging the eighth floor. Fredrick prided himself on keeping his team well-informed during a hunt.

He'd never kept vital information from them before. Her skin prickled and the hairs on her back stood on end. She froze. A sobbing overtook the rest of the voices. She yanked the door open and a shockwave slammed into her. It threw her into the doorjamb and she grunted in pain. God, that hurt. Sara picked herself up and limped away from the staircase, the sobbing following her.

Someone had been murdered here and very recently. A metallic taste bloomed in her mouth. She'd bitten her tongue.

The sickly, sweet smell of decay assaulted her nose and made her want to vomit. Keeping her hand on the wall to steady herself, she searched for Fredrick's cameras. The team had placed six of them along the ceiling, spread evenly down the corridor for maximum coverage. The red lights were still blinking on all of them. Good, she thought. The cameras would catch whatever phenomena presented itself to her.

"Where do you want me to go?" Sara whispered. The entity pulled her arm towards the right. She followed its lead to Door 837.

The temperature dropped in the hallway making her teeth chatter. Her breath came out in small puffs as she pushed the door open, gritting her teeth as the hinge squeaked. Sara walked into an emptied studio with a brand-new mattress on top of a metal frame, the only piece of furniture in the room. She flipped the light switch. The lights stayed off. The air inside was frigid. The door slammed closed behind her. She rubbed her hands against her jeans as her eyes adjusted to the dark.

A scene revealed itself to her. Sara stood in a fully furnished room, a stream of moonlight breaking through the blinds on one of the windows. The entity pushed her deeper into the ghostly echo. Stumbling, over a pair of shoes, Sara grabbed the wooden baseboard of the bed to steady herself.

An old, frail woman, flowered scarf covering her hair and in the throes of a nightmare, lay among several pillows. The woman's eyes shifted back and forth beneath her lids. She whimpered.

An unseen force pinned the woman's arm down to the mattress and pulled her shirt sleeve up. A small red dot appeared on the crook of her arm. The woman's eyes opened, her face registering shock then fear. She thrashed against the invisible murderer for mere seconds before all the fight went out of her. Whatever the murderer had injected into her was fast acting. Her eyes grew wide and became blank.

Sara sucked in her breath. She'd watched someone murder a woman. The unseen murderer pulled her shirtsleeve down and placed the victim's arm next to her body. The comforter lifted and the murderer tucked it in and around the body. That act of tenderness made the echo even more obscene.

The tableau vanished, and a gust of wind lifted Sara's hair from the back of her neck. She strained her ears to receive the ghost's message. Terror swept over her, instead.

Sara whimpered, desperately wanting to run but her feet staying rooted in place. The presence of the dead still scared the hell out of her. She swallowed the lump in her throat and touched her neck to feel her pulse, something she did to calm herself down.

"Murder." A gentle hiss caressed her ear. "Barbara. I...Murdered. Help usssss." The hiss turned into an almost indiscernible whisper. Sara nodded to show her understanding.

"I hear you, Barbara. I'm here." She waited for more but was met with silence. She was left in the empty room with the new mattress. Barbara had left. Sara sighed in relief.

It was time to call Johan. He could help Barbara's ghost pass, but he wouldn't be able to help the old man. That horror was perpetrated by a human on the living plane. She was sure of it.

Sara sent a tendril of consciousness out to the far corners of the room searching for any other type of darkness. The room held no echoes of other supernatural entities. The murderer of Barbara had been human.

She built the last of her walls back up as Johan had taught her all those years ago. She went back into the hall and made sure the red light of Fredrick's camera still blinked. The cameras were sensitive enough to pick up a ghostly entity entering the room. Fredrick would know she'd made some sort of contact. She felt an information swap was in order: a ghost for the real reason they were at the Bockerman.

When Sara joined the rest of the gang in the lobby, the group of senior citizens that she met earlier had dispersed save one, Barney Leonard. Fredrick and Barney spoke in whispers off to the side as Jerry and William broke down the rest of their equipment. Fredrick glanced over to where she stood several times and gave her the distinct impression that they spoke of her.

Fredrick motioned to her to wait for him. She nodded and watched the two men shake hands before Fredrick walked over. Barney was definitely behind whatever Fredrick was hiding, she thought. No doubt about it.

"You going to tell me what's happening, Fredrick?" Sara asked before Fredrick had a chance to say a word. She kept her voice low, not wanting his boys to hear. "I experienced a ghost on the eighth floor but not on the tenth floor. I thought that we were just investigating the tenth floor, but you wired up the eighth just the same. And not for nothing but I think you know the tenth floor had no ghost but..." She let the sentence hang and watched his face for clues. His eye twitched. She plowed on. "Her name was Barbara. I watched her get murdered. Was she the real reason we came here?" Fredrick paled at the name.

"You saw her get killed?" he asked. Sara nodded. Fredrick took her under the elbow and headed for the elevator. "Barney called me about the ghost activity here several days ago. He knew all about the Bockerman and how hard I've tried to get our equipment in here for the last five years. He didn't mention anything about a murder, but he did ask us to hook up the eighth floor," he said and frowned.

"But he didn't ask us to investigate the eighth floor, did he?" she asked. He nodded. "Did he just want the footage then?"

"That's right," Fredrick said. "He didn't want the focus to be on the eighth floor, but he made sure we wired it up to record. He only wanted the footage from the eighth floor which I found odd."

"You find this all strange as well, right?" Sara asked.

"Well, now that we know a woman was murdered, then yes. A resounding yes. We should contact the police," he said. "When did the murder happen?

"Very recently. Within the last month at least. Barney didn't say anything about her? Why all the secrecy between you both then?" Instead of answering her, Fredrick stared at the boys finishing up with the packing.

"You don't really think that Barney killed this woman?" he whispered.

"No... Well, I don't know. He wouldn't have called you in if he killed her. But someone did. Killed her, I mean," she said and bit her lip. "This place smells of recent fear and death. Not the old Hollywood variety," she said. "Did the tapes pick up anyone going into Room 837, the murdered woman's room?"

"I haven't checked the tapes yet for that."

"What about the room where that man was attacked?"

"No. Nothing showed in the videos. The crying began when we were in that hall as everyone down here watched. Jerry alerted us to the specific cry for help since we didn't hear that up there. When we rewound the tapes, we didn't see any type of entity come in or out of the room," he added, brow furrowed. "Getting back to what the ghost said to you. Did she actually tell you there have been other murders?" he asked, doubt in his voice.

"Not specifically. But she said us. Not just I," Sara said as she looked around the empty lobby.

"I don't want any part of this. We must call the police," Fredrick said, concern crossing his face.

"We can't contact them. Who is going to believe us? A ghost told us? C'mon Fredrick, you know how that goes."

"There's an active killer in here, Sara." Fredrick said.

"Someone needs to help her. I'll call in Johan. He'll help me."

"I don't know, Sara. Maybe she didn't mean anything by saying us."

"That still leaves her. She's stranded, Fredrick."

"I prefer ghosts, preferably ones from long ago. That's why I'm a ghost hunter. I don't do active killers." he said and scratched his head. He was rightly disturbed, but there wasn't anything she could say. He focused on William, surrounded by silver cases. The elevator arrived and Jerry stepped out carrying the rest of the cameras.

"Looks like it's time to go. I don't know, Sara. If what you're saying is true, then this is really a matter for the police," he said.

"I hear you, but you know what I think about the police."

"What's this about police?" Jerry asked.

"I'll explain everything in the van." Fredrick turned back to Sara. "I don't think you should go looking for trouble here but knowing you—" His lips formed a thin line. "I know that's exactly what you're about to do. For once, please heed my warning." Fredrick heaved a silver case up off the ground.

"Thanks for calling me, Fredrick." She gave him a crooked smile.

"Be careful, Sara," he said, giving her shoulder a squeeze. "Seriously. I know you hate to hear that, but there are people out there who care about what happens to you. I happen to be one of them."

Lou Fairbanks paced up and down the hallway trying to clear her head. The movement helped her feel as though she wasn't completely losing her mind. Diane pulled her back into the apartment, and Lou realized that all she wanted was someone to tell her everything would turn out fine. But, she knew better. No one could do that for her.

"We watched all the footage, several times. No one came in or out of your apartment, Lou. NO ONE," she added for emphasis.

"Someone did that to his arm. Are we saying a ghost did it? Are we seriously saying that? He's too catatonic to have done that himself. He barely registers my presence in the room," Lou said, so quietly that Diane had to lean in to hear her.

"There's no evidence someone broke into that room. It's on camera," Diane said in the gentlest tone Lou had ever heard her use.

"I sound nuts. I get that. But, who hurt him? How and why?" She fell silent not knowing what else to say.

"I don't know, Lou. I really don't know," Diane said. Lou headed back to Dads. She lifted the covers and checked on the bandage.

Another thought struck her. "What if someone is in the walls?" Lou asked. This new theory made as much sense as a ghost. If a woman were stuck in the walls, she'd have a reason to be sobbing.

"Lou, I realize you're under a lot of stress. What, with Dads' condition..."

Lou interrupted her. "Who makes all the noise at night? I'm not imagining those sounds. Did you hear the tapes? There WAS something in that hall."

Diane sank into the chair nearest the door and tucked her hair behind her ears, deep in thought. "I don't know what to say. I'll understand completely if you want to move on," Diane said and tears welled up in Lou's eyes. Here she thought Diane was being kind to her, when in reality, Diane wanted to get rid of them.

Embarrassed by her tears, she faced the wall behind Dads and wiped her face with a furtive move of her hand. She didn't have the money to go anywhere else, and it had been hard enough to come to the generous terms that she had here. She complained enough about the place being a dump but knew that it was one of the reasons they'd gotten the deal they had. Who else would let them live for free and allow her to spend at least half of her time taking care of Dads? And between her anxiety and her credentials only going back so far, she'd gotten extremely lucky. "I can't leave here. Dads is settled, and Dr. Jerris said it's not good to uproot him," Lou said, hoping Diane didn't hear the desperation in her voice.

"What about his arm?" Diane reminded her.

Lou cursed herself for not thinking far enough ahead. She should have seen this situation coming. "They aren't deep. We can't afford to..." Lou blushed. "I'll make it work." Diane nodded but looked unconvinced.

"Is there anything I can do?" Diane asked.

"Better security. We need better security. I'll be extra vigilant as well. With ALL the residents." Lou closed her eyes and rubbed her forehead. "And if it was a ghost, we need to figure out what it wants. All the books on the paranormal say that," Lou said and grimaced. She snuck a peek at Diane but she was busy scrutinizing a cuticle.

"You really believe it's a ghost?" was all Diane said.

"You said yourself, no one came in or out of the room. What else could it be if it's not someone in the walls?" Lou asked as Diane got to her feet.

"I find this conversation absurd, Lou. Ghosts? I expected more of you." Diane shook her head. "If you need anything, please let me know." And with that, Diane left. She couldn't trust that woman, Lou thought.

Diane was clever and had been around the block. She survived Hollywood and even got herself a supporting role on a sitcom, as she reminded everyone at least once a month. Lou needed to remember that Diane was never kind to be kind. She always had ulterior motives, and Lou, in her need to talk to someone, had forgotten, much to her detriment.

She couldn't kick her out. She just couldn't.

Diane Lawrence unbuttoned the two top buttons on her blouse and checked herself out in the mirror in the elevator. Good enough for him, she thought, and sauntered out. She stopped at the front desk and put her best smile on for Russ.

"Good evening, Russ." Diane melted into him. Russ looked at her cleavage in appreciation just as she expected him to. The best way to get men to do what she wanted was to give them some sugar, and this technique hadn't failed her yet. "I have a big favor to ask," she said as she perched on the edge of the desk.

"Anything, Diane," he said like the whipped pup he was. She was sure if she asked him to commit murder he'd do it in a heartbeat. Not that she would ever suggest such a thing, but it was nice to know that she still had it.

"Could you please speak with Barney Leonard? He's always so disagreeable with me, and I really need to get a key for those new deadbolts he put on his door. He's not allowed to make alterations per his agreement, but he did it anyway. Do you think you could get a copy of the keys?" she asked and smiled again.

"Don't you worry. I'm not afraid of a little old man. Consider it done," he said and touched her arm gently. She fought the urge to move her arm away and leaned in closer instead, proving to herself she could do anything if she put her mind to it. She knew of his family past and figured he'd be good to have around in case she ever needed anything shady done. She had anticipated her need for him correctly. But, if she were really honest with herself, the man scared her just a bit.

"Have the police spoken with you yet?" Diane asked.

"I gave them the surveillance footage for the nights they asked for. Do you really think there is someone killing our residents?" he asked, reddening. Diane shrugged.

"Maybe someone had it in for Babs. Nevertheless, people come here to die. That's why they're here. I told the police the same thing, and I seriously doubt we have a killer on the loose, if that's what you're implying."

"No, no. I didn't mean that. I mean, I don't know what I mean," Russ said and smiled sheepishly at her. "I just want to make sure I'm doing a good job, that's all."

"Oh, you are," she said and patted him on the hand. "No one has been coming in and out of the place without your knowledge, right?"

"Nope."

She touched his hand. "That's your job. So good job," she said, got up and smoothed down her pencil skirt. "Thank you again for your help, Russ. I so appreciate it," she said. Diane wiggled her fingers in a goodbye and sashayed across the lobby.

Diane settled into Lauren's armchair, took a sip of coffee and sighed. Lauren had the best coffee she'd ever tasted. "This is delicious, L. Thank you."

Lauren nodded as her needles clicked. Diane had never seen her without her knitting and that made her think of her Grandma Genny, long deceased. Visiting her made Diane feel at peace, and her place felt like the home she wished she had, all warm and cozy.

"What do you think of Babs' death?" Diane asked.

Lauren clucked her tongue. "You sure you want to talk about that Di?"

"I'm afraid I'm going to be in trouble with corporate."

"That's all you're ever worried about? What about the mutiny brewing here? Everyone thinks ghosts are killing our residents. Can you believe that nonsense? I mean, I love the history here just like anyone but I don't think Marilyn Monroe's ghost is wandering the halls." Lauren clucked her tongue again. "You need to get to the bottom of this, Diane. Get ahead of this. It's the only way. Were there any mysterious deaths before Babs? Anything out of the ordinary?" Lauren pressed. Her needles stopped clicking. Diane put her cup down.

"I swear to you, Lauren, they all died of heart attacks. If Dr. Jerris had flagged anything, I would have reported it to the police and to corporate."

"I know, honey. I know. You are many things, but I know you aren't cruel. No, not cruel." The needles began clicking again and Diane picked up her coffee mug, reveling in its warmth. She hoped Lauren was right about her not being cruel, and that she hadn't made the most terrible mistake of her life. She had already kissed her promotion goodbye and knew there was no way Matt would help her out now, even if she were the best lay he'd ever had. Just her luck.

9
Cattle Car, Poland
DECEMBER 18, 1942

Szymon crouched in the dark train car and was proud of his efforts to be small and quiet. He kept silent the entire walk to the station. The bad man deposited him with the other children near a train. Szymon didn't wait long before other bad men packed him and the other children so tightly into the train car that Szymon couldn't lift his arms up. The wind howled outside as the temperature dropped down to frigid.

Night came on stealthy feet. He heard some girls crying behind him, but the car was dark enough that he couldn't see anyone's faces. His stomach grumbled as his mama only gave him a piece of bread and a small bit of cheese for breakfast.

He shifted to his left. The other children's bodies helped him stay warm and made his eyes want to close. He wanted to sleep, but Papa said sleeping was very bad when it was so cold outside and warned him that if he ever got lost out in the forest behind their house that he should never sleep. He forced his eyes open. He had to stay awake.

He shifted his weight from foot to foot. He could only move several inches back and forth before his neighbors complained or jabbed him in the ribs. He hummed the song his mama sang him every night. It was the only one he remembered.

Despite his best efforts, Szymon felt his eyelids grow even heavier. He struggled to keep them open and shifted from one foot to another again. If he could just push the boy next to him, he thought, he could get more room. Syzmon tried a gentle nudge, but the boy next to him didn't react at all.

The car lurched forward, and he heard a small cheer come from somewhere in the darkness in front of him. They were moving.

He had to pee so badly. He'd heard somebody pee some distance away and could smell the pee everywhere in the car now. Maybe the bad men would let them out soon, Szymon thought, and his stomach grumbled in response. He was so hungry and cold. Maybe he could close his eyes for just one minute. His mama always said that sleep made the next day better.

10

Night Terrors

FEBRUARY 19,2005 - 2AM - DAY 4

The first place Sara Caine checked when searching for recent deaths was the Los Angeles County Public Health Office. Every death in Los Angeles needed to be registered with them, and she had a friend who could access their files. She took the ramp onto the 101 freeway, the lights of downtown Los Angeles on the horizon. Midnight on a Tuesday and the 101 had enough cars on it for traffic to bog down to a crawl. Her contact, a computer whiz named Ritchie, would be just getting going.

Sara and Ritchie crossed paths numerous times at local waterholes downtown. The community was a small one. When she heard how good he was on computers, she approached him to work on a job with her.

She drove onto the Spring Street exit and headed for the Arts District. At this hour, downtown LA sat empty, and the only people on the streets were cops and the homeless taking shelter in the empty doorways.

She turned left on Second Street and passed both police headquarters and Little Tokyo. She slammed on her brakes as some night owls suddenly stepped into the street from one of the late night noodle joints. They waved their apologies, and Sara smiled back, giving them a small nod. Thank God she wasn't driving too fast, she thought as she took her foot off the brake and cruised forward.

Ritchie lived in an industrial area that was collectively known as the Arts District. It started the moment she crossed Alameda Street from Little Tokyo. She loved this area herself, but rents had already gone way past her budget. She turned right onto Alameda Street and then onto Fourth Street. New graffiti flashed in her headlights and she marveled at its artistry.

The Arts District consisted of former factories redeveloped into million dollar lofts and was home to the prestigious Southern California Institute of Architecture. Strange sculptures sat on most corners and every building was a canvas for colorful paintings, graffiti, and political posters. None of the owners minded the art that turned up overnight on their buildings' walls. Rather, they welcomed it.

The art provided a stark contrast to the trash filled streets and homeless encampments. Many factories were still in use, adding a raw flavor to the neighborhood. The price hikes didn't make much sense to her with the smaller version of skid row existing alongside the front doors of the converted lofts. But that's how things stood. She turned onto

Molino Street, found street parking and dialed Ritchie.

He picked up on the first ring. "Hey Sara, how's the ghosting business?" She smiled at the sound of his voice. He was good people.

"I happened to be in the neighborhood. Wanna help me with something?" she asked as she got out of the car and walked to his loft. "I'm right outside your building."

"Code is 4698. Let me get decent, doll," he said. Sara punched in the numbers he gave her and got buzzed in right away.

She stepped into a small vestibule containing a bank of mailboxes and a metal staircase leading to the upper levels. She went up to the second floor and took the corridor to the right. The olive green walls and dim wall sconces made the halls gloomy and, although she felt no ghosts here, there were plenty of nooks and crannies where a human predator could easily be hiding. Her pace quickened.

She found 1168 in one of the numerous miniature hallways and knocked on the door. The door swung open immediately and Ritchie, his blond curly hair still dripping from the shower, grinned.

"Sorry I showed up unannounced," she said and eyed his body beneath the blue chambray shirt and jeans. The man was built like that English soccer player that everyone was in love with, Beckwith, or was it Beckham? She had written him off as a pretty boy, but then he told her about the darknet one drunken night, and they became friends. His computer skills came in handy during a case involving a missing girl, and she was able to pick up a few non-paranormal clients after that, off book. She might not have found a private investigator to take her on as a mentee, but she'd logged in some investigative hours. She gave him a percentage of her fee, if the client paid, although he never asked for money in exchange for his help.

"Another case?" He gestured her inside, his voice rising in excitement. She walked into his ultra-modern loft and noted nothing had changed since the last time she was there. Ritchie's was a consummate bachelor's pad filled with dark wood, black leather, and treated metal furnishings, the only light coming from four monitors and various computers. The flickering blue and red glow made the shadows come alive.

"I think so, but I don't have a client yet," she said and perched on his black, leather sofa. His furniture might be beautiful, but it was also seriously uncomfortable. "Fredrick got us into what used to be the Bockerman Hotel. It's an assisted living facility now."

"Is it as haunted as they say it is? I never thought Marilyn walked those halls but Valentino surely must have. What about D.W. Griffith? Fanny Farmer?" He knew the history of Los Angeles better than she did, she thought as he sat down next to her. They'd spent many nights bonding over LA history and scotch.

"I saw Griffith in the lobby. He's a real character," she said and smiled. "That was the fun part. I then watched a woman get murdered." She rubbed her face. "She'd intimated she wasn't the first."

He got up and crossed over to his setup. "That must have been beyond intense. You OK?" he asked, his face grim. Sara nodded. "So I'm thinking you want me to get you some death certificates," Ritchie said. He opened up a terminal shell and started typing. "This might take a while."

Sara assumed as much and settled into the uncomfortable couch for the long wait. Feeling safe there, her lids soon got heavy and she fell asleep to the sound of his typing.

Barney Leonard stepped out of the elevator and into the path of Russell Hall, Sunshine's security guard and its preeminent creep. He attempted to push past him, but the man grabbed him by the arm.

"You put your deadbolts on without permission. Diane sent me up here to either get them off your door or get a copy of the keys. It's in your lease to give the management all keys so we can get into your apartment in case of an emergency," Russ explained.

"I'm not doing either. This is my apartment, and I will not be the next victim," Barney spat out. "If Diane has a problem with that, you tell her she can come up here and tell me herself. We can work it out on our own. I don't appreciate her sending you to intimidate me. It's not going to work," Barney said and shoved past him. Russ threw his hands up.

"Fine! I'm just trying to do my job. You don't have to be such an asshole about it," he said. Barney spun around, rage coursing through him. He stalked to Russ, finger pointed at him.

"YOU are the security guard. YOU are supposed to be protecting us. Someone is KILLING US and you are worried about the locks. Thank God for my locks. I'd be dead by now if it weren't for those locks. Babs would still be alive if she had put hers on as I urged her too," he said, jabbing his finger into Russ' chest. "Maybe YOU should do your job and protect us," he spat out.

Russ, his face a deep shade of red, stared at him. Barney, furious at himself over his outburst, turned away and stalked back to his apartment without saying another word. He shouldn't have lost his temper like that. Russ was just a big oaf, and this wasn't his fault. He slammed the door shut behind him.

Barney shifted in his bed and stared up at the ceiling. A decent night's sleep had eluded him ever since Babs died. A ticker tape with the words MY FAULT ran through his head in a continuous stream. He should have convinced her to put that damn deadbolt on her door, should've installed it himself. The guilt squirmed in response and tightened its grip on his stomach. The acid bubbled up, and he sat up in bed before it journeyed up his pipes. He'd gone through several bottles of Tums in the last week, but the chalky tablets were not working.

His stomach problems, especially when he felt guilt, dated back to childhood. His mother, a practitioner of basic village homeopathic remedies, had always made him a concoction of cheese and radish. She grew the black radish in their small back garden and made the cheese herself from the two cows the Nazi's had allowed them to keep. The rest of the cows had been confiscated by the Blue police, Granatowa policja, on the order of Krimanlpolizei Braun, the German officer who ruled over their town of Szczebrzeszyn.

He thought back to that time more and more, especially since Barbara's death. The past seemed more real to him than yesterday's dinner. His mother's face had become more vivid then it had been in years. But, that was another life, another land.

Barney rubbed his face and returned to the present. He looked to the pieces of short-wave radio scattered all over the top of the desk. Taking the short-wave radio apart and putting it back together gave him something to do with his hands. It was the closest he came to relief. He'd told Babs that, and she understood. She was good like that. Babs listened to him when he talked. Most people waited to say their piece and never truly listened. She reminded him of his mother, or the few memories of her that he still had. Another reason he fell so head over heels in love with her.

Time to do something useful, he thought, his workaholic tendencies taking over. He padded over to his worktable. Denny, his former boss, forced him into retirement when he discovered his partial hearing loss. He couldn't be a sound engineer when his right ear couldn't recognize mid-tones. Barney understood, but retirement slowed down the time to a crawl.

His mind wandered back to that night as he picked up his screwdriver. What if he'd stayed the night? Babs wanted him to, but he told her it wasn't his thing. If he had, she'd be alive or they'd both be dead. That would have been preferable to this hell.

Barney pushed that painful thought away and let himself wander back to the past. War twisted people. Some people forgot the horrors while others buried it deep. Barney never spoke of those times with anyone, but the nothingness followed him nonetheless. He'd kept it at bay for most of his life but now, in the middle of the night, it crawled to him from the shadows. Tightening one of the screws, he closed his mind to everything but the work.

The door handle shifted back and forth with a grating sound. Barney stopped his work to listen. Someone was trying to get into his apartment. Tough luck, killer, he thought. The deadbolt was doing its job.

The handle stopped moving.

Barney tiptoed to the door as fast as he could. He wanted to see Lou's face as she attempted to kill him. He peeked into the keyhole as his hands ran over his four locks and deadbolt making sure they were locked.

All sound stopped as if even the building held its breath and waited for Barney to unmask the killer. But, the hallway beyond stood empty. The killer moved on. Barney feared the other residents hadn't taken the same precautions he had.

Mary Ann McClatch tossed and turned in her bed. Her feet were cold but when she used her extra blankets, they got too hot. Her studio felt drafty, and her preference would have been Barney's bed. It had been several days already, and it wasn't as though they had all the time in the world. She didn't go in for all this guilt and regret. It was a huge waste of time.

Who knew how long any of them had? Get busy living or get busy dying, Morgan Freeman said in that Shawshank Redemption movie. She teared up each time she heard it. Barney could use some cues from that movie.

God, her mouth was parched, she thought as she smacked her lips together. Mary Ann slid her slippers on and padded over to her kitchenette, filling a glass with water. She brought it to her lips when she heard the sound.

Click.

Click.

Click.

She turned to her door and stared at the moonlight glinting off the three locks, one of them a deadbolt. No way was anyone getting in here. Thank you, Barney.

She gawked at her door handle as it rotated left to right, her adrenaline kicking into action. Something shoved hard against the door, but the door held. The footsteps receded into the distance. Mary Ann let out her breath, not realizing she'd been holding it in.

She finished off the glass of water and climbed back into bed. She lay down and stared up at the ceiling.

The footsteps sounded different than the last one's she'd heard. They were muffled like footsteps on carpet. She frowned. A ghost would walk through the door, not use the door handle. The killer was a human being after all.

Lou Fairbanks's eyes flew open, panic stuck in her throat. The black void stretched into her. She wanted to look away, but she was paralyzed.

Evil was in the room, somewhere in the corner near the door. She used every ounce of effort to try to turn her head, but her body wouldn't obey. The evil shifted. Lou struggled to open her mouth and scream. Her mouth opened a crack and the pressure on her chest increased. Her breath came out in short gasps. She'd pass out if this kept up.

Whoever was in the room would kill her and she wouldn't be able to do anything about it. If she could just make a sound, Dads would wake up and scare them off. Lou choked on a cry and tried to scream. All that came out was a gurgle.

One horrible gurgle.

A sound came from around the door, and she waited to die. The evil slithered closer and she was helpless against it. Lou squeezed her eyes shut, tears rolling down her cheeks. After all that she'd done, she deserved this. She deserved all of it.

Sara Caine woke to a steaming cup of coffee under her nose. She had slept through the night. Tossing off the blanket Ritchie had covered her with, she sat up, her entire body screaming in pain. "Why didn't you wake me?"

"You looked like you needed sleep, girl," he said and handed her the cup.

"Thank you so much, Ritchie, and thank you for letting me stay here last night." She noticed the bags under his eyes. "Did you sleep at all?" He shook his head as he handed her a sheet of paper with a list of names and dates.

"These are the deaths recorded at the Bockerman, actually called the Sunshine House - An Assisted Living Home, going back five years. If you look at the dates—" He pointed at the first couple. "—they have a death maybe once a month. Sometimes twice. That goes on for about three years and then the rate of death jumps to about three a month." He points to the bottom of the page. "This is the last four months. The death rate has jumped significantly to about five a month. Isn't that weird?"

Sara sipped the coffee and scanned the list. The last six months had been deadly for the Sunshine House, especially the last month. Six deaths in the last three weeks alone with the last victim being named Barbara Monroe. She pointed to her name. "I bet you that's the ghost that contacted me last night. She said Barbara and it's the only Barbara on the list. If she was murdered, then we should assume some of these deaths were murders as well. If we take into consideration the previous data on natural death at the facility, I'm thinking three or four of these deaths are murders."

"That sounds about right. All the causes were listed as cardiac arrest and heart failure. Not sure how to figure out which death is which."

Sara finished up her coffee, thinking of what the next step could be and came up with a blank.

"Do you think the killer is supernatural?" he asked, breaking the silence.

"No, I didn't feel anything like that. This one is human. I'm sure of it." She thought back to the pulling feeling she had on the eighth floor. "She needs me. Everyone is so scared there." She took another sip of coffee.

"Why do they stay?" Ritchie wondered.

"Where would they go?" Sara countered.

11

Another Death
Day 4

Barney Leonard marched down the hall to Babs' room. He wanted to be near her, to remember the good times they had there, that good did exist in the world.

He tried the knob and found it open. The door open like that meant the police still didn't take his accusations seriously.

Barney snorted. They would find out soon enough. Babs was killed, just like the others were. He stepped into her apartment and took in the faint smell of her perfume. She'd once told him she wore a mixture of Chanel No. 5 and Chanel's Mademoiselle. Obsessed with having a signature scent, Babs mixed perfumes so no one else would smell like her. Her particular application style consisted of walking into the perfumes' mist, and he imagined her spritzing the two perfumes into the air.

The memory made him sigh. Even though Diane cleared out Babs' things, he still felt her presence in the room.

Barney closed his eyes and imagined what it used to look like, but his mind lost many of the details. His legs wobbled beneath him, and Barney lay down on the new mattress. "Babs, I wish you were here."

The former hotel whispered back with its own secrets and painful memories. It shifted and groaned and trembled. And that's when he heard her.

The footsteps stopped in front of him. His eyes flew open, and there she was, standing in front of him, wearing her pink hair curlers and flowered bathrobe.

"Babs." His voice quivered as he got up off the bed. "Is that you?" She nodded at him. "I'm sorry I didn't protect you. I should have...I failed you." He sobbed out that last part. She shook her head at him and motioned to the window. "Who killed you? Was it Lou? Did she get in here through the window?"

Babs shook her head and motioned to him again.

"Here," she whispered. She lifted her arm and pointed at the window. Then she disappeared.

Barney drew closer to where she'd pointed. He dared not touch the window and its components in fear of destroying evidence. So instead, he studied it as he would a new piece of music gear, trying to figure out its secrets. Both the jamb and the windowsill looked normal.

Could she have meant the view, Barney thought as he stared out onto Hollywood and the Roosevelt

Hotel sign. "I'm not seeing it, Babs? Is it the view or the window?" he asked to the empty room in the hope she came back to him.

"Bre.....athe."

He whipped around to see her once again, but the room stayed empty.

Breathe. What did that mean? He inhaled and filled his lungs with air. Here went nothing. Barney expelled all the breath in his lungs and created a circle of dew on the windowpane.

Wait, what was that? As the dew faded from the surface, he caught the edge of something.

Something hand drawn. He sucked more breath into his lungs and exhaled up and down the window where he thought the drawing started.

And there it was. A drawing of something that looked like a trident. Three diagonal prongs coming from a vertical line.

He stood back, his mind racing. What the hell was going on? He'd seen this mark before in the old country on Nazi gravestones. He scratched his head, perplexed.

Why would a Nazi symbol be drawn on a window of a murder victim in Los Angeles in 2005? He mentally did the math. If anyone here at the home were a Nazi, they'd be in their 80's now. He couldn't imagine someone that old being able to overpower Babs.

What was the sign doing on her window if it wasn't made by the killer? He stood and stared as it disappeared in front of him, just as Babs had. She wanted him to know this was here. Her killer had to have put it there.

Diane Lawrence knocked on Lauren's door and checked her watch one more time. She'd never known her to be late, and it was already 11:30am. She knocked harder and checked the knob. The door creaked open, and her heart dropped. Please God, no, not Lauren. She stuck her head through the door, the blood pounding in her ears.

"I thought we were meeting for lunch. Lauren? Are you awake?" She walked further into the room and saw Lauren in bed, sleeping. "Take a sleeping pill or something?"

She sat on the bed and nudged Lauren.

Lauren didn't move.

She pulled the covers down and saw the blue tone of Lauren's skin. And she knew. "Oh my God, Lauren. Please wake up." She touched her face and checked the pulse on her neck. "Fuck. FUCK. FUCK." She jumped up, thoughts rushing through her head.

She had to call Dr. Jerris.

My God, Lauren. Not her dear Lauren.

"Please Dads. Help me," Lou Fairbanks begged as she tried to get the sweater over his head. He had allowed her to put his pants on but decided to fight her on the rest. She tugged the sweater down, and he shoved her away, almost knocking her over.

"Jesus, Dads," she said, surprised by his strength. He plopped down on his bed and turned back to the window. Exhaustion hit her hard enough to make her grab for the bedpost. She could barely stand up, she thought, and checked the time. It was only 11:30.

She sat next to him and put her hand on his shoulder. He stayed absent.

"I'm so tired, Dads. Really tired." Her bottom lip trembled, and she fought back tears. "She came back last night," she said, but was interrupted by frantic knocking. She stared at the door a moment before heaving herself off the bed. She opened the door to find a distraught Diane. One look on her face told her all she needed to know. Someone else had died.

"Who?" Lou asked.

"It's Lauren," was all Diane said.

"Give me a sec. Have you called Dr. Jerris yet?" Diane nodded and hung back as Lou guided Dads from the bed to the dining chair and got him seated. She took a sandwich and a bag of chips out of the small fridge and put them on the table in front of him.

"Be right back, Dads," she said, patting him on the back and grabbing her medical bag from under the bed. She turned back to Diane and found her staring off into space. "Diane?" Lou prodded.

Diane's eyes focused back. "Sorry, I need to plan my course of action," she said more to herself than to Lou. "Sorry, I mean..." She stepped back into the hall. "I'm in shock. Pardon me for whatever I say. Lauren was a friend."

Lou nodded and followed her out.

Lou examined Lauren's body as Diane hovered behind her. She marked down lividity, temperature, and time in her file and straightened when she heard the knock at the door. Dr. Jerris, a man with snow white hair and an orange tan, walked in carrying his own medical case under his arm. How a doctor still used tanning beds in 2005 was beyond her. He flicked his eyes over to her and nodded. Did he think that look worked for him, Lou couldn't help thinking?

"Good Morning, Diane," he said in a strong, booming baritone.

"Dr. Jerris," Diane said and sank into the nearest chair.

"And how are you today, Nurse Louise?" Dr. Jerris pulled the sheets down from Lauren's body, "Have you notated time of death?"

"I guessed between 2-4am. Rigor is still set," Lou replied.

"Good. Good. And this woman? What was her health like?" Dr. Jerris asked.

"Shouldn't you know that, Doctor?" Diane asked, an uncharacteristic sharpness creeping into her voice.

"No, I wouldn't. Lauren Dolmar decided to go with another doctor some months back. I haven't seen her since that time," Dr. Jerris said.

Diane frowned. "I'm calling the police. She told me last week she had the heart of a fifty year old per her last physical and even spoke of moving out of here. This scenario reminds me too much of Babs' death." She got up from the chair. "I'm going to call them."

"What about Corporate?" Dr. Jerris asked her.

"What about Corporate? I'm not covering for them anymore. This is wrong. Everything's wrong," Diane said and left them.

Lou froze.

"What other deaths?" she asked.

"She must be talking about the recent spate of heart attacks," Dr. Jerris said as he bent over Lauren's body.

"Didn't you rule them as natural causes?"

"I did," he said, and opened Lauren's right eye with a thumb. "She didn't die in her sleep," he said.

"What do you mean?"

"I don't know, Nurse," he said and straightened. "If what Diane says is true and the woman was in perfect health...she should call the police. She was over seventy-five. That's a long life," he said and tried to laugh. It died somewhere in his throat. Lou glared back at him.

Diane Lawrence stood next to Detective Murphy and Detective Larson and watched as the paramedics wheeled Lauren's body out of the room.

"I'm glad you called 911 this time." Diane jumped at Lou's whisper. She shot her a nasty look to quiet her down and hoped the detectives hadn't heard her. Diane inched closer to the detectives.

"Don't mention the ghost. They'll think we're nuts," Lou hissed at her back and Diane pretended not to hear her. Did the woman really think she was stupid?

"The Doc and the paramedics say heart attack. Is there any reason you think otherwise? She was seventy five, wasn't she?" Detective Larson asked as he jotted down notes in his logbook.

"She got a clean bill of health just last week,

Detective Larson. I also saw her last night, and she was not exhibiting any symptoms of stroke or heart attack," Diane said through gritted teeth. "Check with her doctor, you'll see. There was nothing wrong with her. She was killed in the same way as Barbara Monroe," she said with as much emphasis as she could muster. Lauren deserved much better than these two, Diane thought, and if she needed to go above them she would.

"We've had other deaths before these last two," Diane snapped.

"What kind of deaths?" Murphy flipped open a little notebook.

"Well, heart attacks—some of them unexplained. The resident didn't have heart problems, but they died," Diane said.

"Is that unusual for an assisted living facility?" Larson asked, clearly not buying what she was trying to tell him.

"It is unusual. Some deaths are expected every month, but this is definitely out of the norm," she said and crossed her arms.

"How do we contact..." Murphy noted something in her notebook.

Diane picked up on her thought. "Family? She didn't have any..." Murphy looked up at that and Diane gave her a small smile. "That's not so rare, unfortunately," she said.

"Have you changed your security since Barbara Monroe's death?" Larson cut in.

She pulled back on her aggressiveness when she saw she had gotten his attention. "No, we have the same security as before. Cameras at all the entrances and a night security guard, Russell Hall," Diane said.

"Yes, we've already spoken with him about Barbara Monroe's death. Anything strange or unusual happen in the last couple of weeks?" Murphy asked. Diane knew this was her opportunity to come clean about the ghost hunters, but she wasn't about to lose their interest with that story. She decided to keep her mouth shut.

Larson stuck out his hand and she took it. He pumped her arm up and down.

"We'll be in touch after we speak with the coroner," Larson said. Murphy handed her card to Diane.

"If there IS anything else you want to tell us or, God forbid, another incident happens, call us directly," Murphy said and Diane nodded, her mind already rushing forward to all the things that could go wrong. "Oh, and could you supply us with the names of the recently deceased. The ones you think were suspicious," Murphy added.

"Of course," Diane said without any hesitation.

Barney Leonard paced outside Mary Ann's door, trying to decide whether he should knock. Screw it, he decided, and banged on her door. Mary Ann opened up after several seconds and the look on her face told him all he needed to know.

"How are you doing?" She started first.

"I don't know. You?"

Mary Ann avoided his gaze. "Do you want to come in?" she asked and stepped aside to let him pass. He didn't move.

"We should probably stay away from each other," he said.

"So what are you doing here?"

"I wanted to tell you that," he said, his guilt making him stare at her feet instead of her eyes. He should never have gotten her involved in any of this, he thought. Her thin pale legs stuck out of pink leopard skin slippers and the thought that Babs wouldn't have been caught dead in those popped into his head. He had done all this for her and had gotten Lauren killed in the process.

Mary Ann sagged against the doorframe, all pretense gone. "Won't people notice that?" she asked, and Barney shrugged. What did it matter now?

"We aren't responsible..." She began, but he jerked his head up and stared into her eyes.

"It's our fault, Mary Ann, and don't you go believing otherwise. We knew the danger... We poked at the pile of snakes, sat back and watched. Our irresponsibility killed her as sure as that monster did," Barney choked out.

Mary Ann held up her hand. "NO. NO. I won't allow us..." she started but Barney couldn't take anymore. He ran away from her.

"Barney! Barney Leonard. Talk to me!" Mary Ann yelled after him, but he didn't slow down. Instead, he kept his eyes focused on the elevator bay. Acid sloshed around in his stomach as he came to a halt and hit the button. Damn old elevator, it never came when he needed it, he thought.

He checked behind him and saw Mary Ann coming after him, waving her arms to get his attention. He should never have come to talk to her, and ran to the staircase instead. He doubted she'd follow him in there. He pushed the door and stepped onto the landing of the staircase. He took a step down and heard the whisper. Barney stepped back onto the landing and cocked his head to listen. Could it be her?

"Heeellooo." The word swirled around him, and he welcomed it. He welcomed her.

"Barney." The voice whispered in his ear. "B...a....r..ney." It was a woman's voice. It was her voice. The air got cold enough to make his fingers freeze and his breath came out in small puffs, just as it did in the dead of winter in the old country. He leaned against the wall, surrendering himself to her, to the haunting, to whatever would happen.

"I'm sorry. I wanted to help you, prove that you were killed," he cried as he felt his legs give out beneath him. He sank to the ground and covered his face with his hands. For the first time in years, hard sobs shook him. Frustration, guilt, and rage poured out of him and he could do nothing to stop himself.

"Take me with you," he sobbed to Babs. He felt her near him, heard her breath and he wanted to hold her desperately. The air began to warm up, and he felt her dissipate. The feeling of her standing right next to him was gone.

"Come back, Babs, please," he whispered to the empty stairwell. Pull yourself together, he thought, and used the wall to get himself back on his feet. Babs came back to tell him what happened, and he needed a way to hear her.

Although he had called the ghost hunters under false pretenses, they had introduced him to Sara Caine. She would be the one to help him find out what had really happened.

12

Sèance
FEBRUARY 20, 2005 - Day 5

Bright morning light forced its way through the feeble curtains and blinded Lou Fairbanks as she re-dressed Dads' wound. The paralysis from last night haunted her into the morning and made every piece of her body ache. She regained control of her body later that night, but the nightmares terrorized her into the morning.

Each time she woke up from yet another night terror, she checked for the evil presence. It didn't return. That was no comfort to her though. After her 4am wake-up, she couldn't sleep and waited for the glare of the Los Angeles sun to chase away all the shadows.

Lou finished with his arm and placed it down on his lap. She checked the time. Twenty more minutes until her morning rounds. Dads' wounds had scabbed over nicely, and infection wasn't likely. Thank goodness for small miracles, she thought as she rubbed her sore, red eyes and wished she could call in sick. Her fight against anxiety was constant, and she was exhausted. So what if everyone knew she had an anxiety disorder? What was the worst they could do? She glared at Dads and wished he would just die already.

"You must be as scared as I am," Lou said. He stared straight ahead. "Did you feel the evil presence here last night in our room? That thing paralyzed me, Dads" He was the only one she had left to talk to. Barney's plan had worked.

Lou pulled out his pill box. She'd forgotten to give him his morning dosage yesterday and rushed back, missing her first afternoon appointment. He never remembered to take them on his own.

She poured two into the palm of her hand and held them out to him. Dads swallowed them obediently and took a sip of water. If she was going to make it to Doreen on time, she needed to hurry up. A knocking interrupted her progress to the bathroom. Who could it be at this hour, she wondered and prayed it wasn't Diane with another death.

When she saw Barney standing in the hallway, she smiled at him. However much she disliked the man, he was much better than the alternative. She liked the plan he had outlined for her the night before. At least, he wanted to find out who had done that to Dads.

"Is she available?" Lou asked him before he said anything.

"She said she could do it tonight," Barney said, looking past her at Dads.

"How's his arm doing?"

"It's healing nicely, thank you for asking."

"Has he said…" He trailed off when she shook her head.

"That's why we need her," Lou said. "Thank you for arranging this."

Barney stepped back a step. "We need to do it in Barbara Monroe's room," he said.

Lou exploded. "NO! We need to do it in here. Dads was attacked here, not in her room. I thought you said we were dealing with Irene Lentz."

"Babs was murdered and she's our ghost. Her death is more recent and I think we'll have an easier time contacting her," he said. Lou couldn't believe his nerve. Barney had been in love with the woman and she understood his pain, but Babs was dead. Something attacked Dads.

"If you're so afraid, why don't you leave? Move out. You don't have to be here like we do," Barney said, sensing weakness.

Her hands balled up into fists. "I can't move. I WON'T. I'm going to get to the bottom of what's going on here. We're doing it in my room." She widened her stance and stood taller. He wouldn't bully her into an unwanted decision.

"What if Sara doesn't make contact?"

"Then maybe we don't have a ghost."

"Someone or something is killing everyone," Barney said.

"It didn't kill Dads and if you're speaking of Barbara, there is still no indication that her death was anything but a heart attack, unless you know something I don't."

"I don't know why Dads was spared, but I don't believe any of the others died from natural causes," he said and looked past her at Dads. "He must have a strong heart."

"What time is she coming tonight?" she asked. Why was he studying Dads? Lou closed the door a crack to hide Dads from Barney's prying eyes.

"Nine o'clock tonight in Barbara Monroe's room," Barney said.

"No. Here," she said. The back and forth was getting ridiculous.

Barney sighed. "Fine. What about this? We start here, and then we go to Babs', I mean Barbara's room. I'm sure Sara wouldn't mind," he said.

"That will work for me," Lou said.

"What about Dads?"

"What about him?" Lou kept her voice neutral.

"You think he should be there tonight?"

"I want him there." Lou said.

"Why?" Barney asked and stood on his tiptoes to see past her. She pressed her body into the crack and blocked his view.

"He's central in this," she said, her frustration growing.

"He shouldn't be there, Lou," Barney said, as she pushed the door closed.

"Asshole," Lou muttered to herself.

After the disastrous ending of their ghost hunt at the Sunshine House, Sara Caine, Fredrick and the boys were sure they'd never be let into the the building again. To everyone's surprise, Barney contacted Sara to perform a séance and, just like that, they were back in.

Fredrick and Sara agreed someone else had to have been attacked because of the unusual nature of the call. According to Fredrick, Barney Leonard was the last person to participate in a seance.

Now, Sara needed to convince Johan Luken to join them. She'd never performed a séance before and worried she'd somehow do it wrong. Johan was an expert on all matters of the occult, but more importantly he was her rock. If he was by her side, she could do anything. He wouldn't be happy about the murder taking place so recently, with the potential of an active killer still on the premises but she'd face that hurdle when it came. She wished she could explain the entire situation to Johan face to face. Unfortunately, he'd left her apartment without telling her where he was headed, or when he'd be back. Sara called him, nervously pacing.

"Sara."

"Johan, how are you?" She did her best to keep her voice neutral. "I'm on a case with some real spirits. One of my—" She paused. What was Barney? A client? "Um, one of my clients called me requesting a séance."

"You don't do séances?" Johan interjected.

"I know, but it's at the Bockerman."

"Wait? The Bockerman? The place none of us can step foot into? How did this happen?"

"The job came from Fredrick. Fredrick's father knows the client. Anyway, we went there, and the initial places we investigated were not haunted. I saw DW Griffith in the lobby, but Fredrick was called in for someone more recent. The client wanted us to rig the place for a more recent haunting. So, we did. At first, we didn't get anything in the areas that caused the residents problems. But, then I got that special pull. The disturbing one that only happened that one time at the high school."

"The one that makes you go places you shouldn't?" There was no amusement in his voice.

"If you say so. The entity pulled me to a room on the eighth floor where a woman was murdered."

"Did you see her get killed?" Johan asked, his voice all business.

"I did. The event left an echo. At least, that's what I think it was." Sara said, feeling decidedly defensive.

"When did this murder take place?"

"From the records Ritchie found for me, a week ago. He also found a number of unexplained deaths at the home." She paused.

Johan cut in before she continued. "So this séance is to contact the murdered woman?"

"I think so. Although, Fredrick believes someone else has been attacked. The client isn't one to call for a séance."

"I don't want you to go, Sara," Johan stated. Sara's heart dropped.

"I thought you'd say that. Please, hear me out. It's only a séance, and Barbara contacted me already. She wants to tell us what she knows. If you are so concerned, why don't you join us?"

"Call the police, Sara," he said. "How many deaths did Ritchie discover?"

"About ten to twelve deaths above the norm."

"Wait, how many?" he asked.

"Ten to twelve," she said more loudly. "But that's just the deaths above the statistical norm. Ritchie reiterated that. We don't know if those are all murders per se."

"Police, Sara. Call the police. That's way too many deaths, whether they're statistically accurate or not. How long ago did the uptick of deaths start?"

"About 4 months."

"That's a very active killer, Sara. If you don't call, I will," he said.

"May I remind you that you got me into this business? I could be working in film production, but YOU convinced me to use my talents to help people. You remember that, right?"

"Not when there are so many murders, Sara. Use your head. This is way too big for you. You can't protect yourself from someone like that."

"This is a séance not an investigation, Johan. If Barbara gives me something I can give to the police, they'll be the first phone call I make. I want my PI license. This case will get me in the door of most PI agencies in town. They won't take my phone calls right now, as you well know," she said.

"Why this one Sara?" was all he said.

"Because it's here, in front of us. We have a chance to help through the tools we have at our disposal." Her words came out in a rush. She didn't want to give him a chance to interrupt. "All they have is us right now. The woman who runs the place doesn't want this trouble in her facility. She's swept all of this under the rug."

"If even half of what you say is true, this is a very active serial killer, Sara, and we should let the police deal with it," he said.

"But, you hate the police?" she asked, confused by the whole conversation. "Why should I call them with the little info I have from a ghost? You know how I will be treated."

"This isn't a missing girl or someone who died years ago and came to you to help find his body. This is an active predator who is smart enough to have gotten away with it. I'm scared this is something neither of us can handle."

"I'm going, Johan," she said.

"I can't change your mind?"

"No, you can't." They sat on the phone in silence for what felt like ages. Sara's pacing had become frenetic.

Johan broke the silence. "What time should I come get you?" he asked, and Sara frowned.

"Why?"

"You aren't going to listen to me. I can hear it in your voice. I might as well be there to help in whatever way I can."

"Pick me up at eight o'clock tonight," Sara said. "We're supposed to meet Fredrick there at nine."

"See you then," he said.

She hung up before he could say anything else, and pressed her palms to her flushed cheeks. He'd been her partner for the last four years, and he'd never questioned a case like this before. That alone gave her pause. What if he was right and she was putting all of them in danger? She shook the thought off. They were just going to do a séance, she thought. They would be fine.

Nervous energy sizzled through the air as all the members of the group settled in place. Lou Fairbanks had pulled the small, round table out into the center of the living space and had borrowed chairs from some of her neighbors. Dads sat on her left, and Sara Caine, the medium, was on her right.

Johan Luken, Sara Caine's friend, sat on the other side of her. Pitch-black hair and a permanent six o'clock shadow made the man look dangerous, even though he dressed and carried himself like a Venice Beach surfer. Lou saw through the surfer getup though. The man was something else entirely, she thought, as his intense eyes flicked from face to face, studying them all. Fredrick, the lead ghost hunter, was seated next to Mr. Luken and then came Barney, Mary Ann, and Doreen.

"I don't always work like this," Sara explained to the table. "I'm a medium, but I can't just call ghosts up at will. If the ghost or ghosts want to contact me, they will show themselves. I wasn't expecting so many people..." She trailed off as the dark man squeezed her hand. Interesting, Lou thought and a pang of jealousy hit her out of nowhere. That touch was gentle and reassuring. It'd been so long. She cut that thought off. Now wasn't the time.

Sara closed her eyes, took a deep breath and became still. Lou held her breath with everyone else and waited. No one made a sound.

Sara emitted a small sound, and Barney stared at the medium with a fierce intensity. Sweat ran down his face, and he shifted back and forth in his chair. Maybe they should have done the séance in Babs' room first, Lou thought, concerned the man might keel over at any moment.

Sara opened her eyes. "I'm not getting anything from this room," she said and gave a small nod to Fredrick. "That doesn't mean the ghosts aren't here. They are not choosing to make contact right now."

"Was the attack on Dads some sort of message? What do you want from us?" Lou spoke out into the room, hoping the ghost responded.

"Everyone waited. They all focused on Sara to see if anyone responded to her. Sara glanced at Johan, and gave him a small shake of her head.

"Im not getting anything. If a ghost attacked Dads, she doesn't want to make contact right now."

"What else could it be?" Barney asked.

"A demon." Johan Luken spoke for the first time. His baritone voice was gruff.

"You can't be serious?" Barney asked.

"Very. Demons are more powerful than ghosts. I find it implausible that a ghost caused Mr. Fairbanks' wounds. A demon is more likely to cause such bodily harm."

No one spoke. The room grew hot and uncomfortable.

Barney cleared his throat. "Are you out of your mind?" he asked. Doreen and Mary Ann nodded in agreement. Lou had to agree with him as well. She was not a religious person. If evil existed in the world, it did so in human form. Who needed to make up demons?

Johan Luken's words really disturbed the ladies, both of whom looked as though they had just sucked on sour lemons. "What kind of cockamamie people are you?" Mary Ann sputtered.

Sara held up her hand. How was she going to explain this? "Wait. I think..." She cocked her head. "I feel something. I feel..." The woman's eyes closed. No one present was entirely buying her act. Except for her. Lou was mesmerized.

In her excitement, she touched Sara's arm. "Is it her, is it Irene?" Sara Caine convulsed at her touch as if electrocuted. She grasped Lou's wrist as her eyes flew open and rolled into the back of her head. She turned to Lou, and the world around them disappeared. Sara Caine's blank eyes stared directly into Lou's soul.

Lou tried to loosen Sara's fingers from her wrist, but the medium held fast. Lou felt the woman inside her head and screamed.

Someone pried Sara's fingers off her wrist, and Lou shuddered as their connection was broken. She was only vaguely aware of Sara slumping away from her. The room spun in circles. Chaos broke out all around her.

"Call 911," Johan yelled to Fredrick who sprang into action. Lou grabbed the table for support. "I have a pulse, but it's faint," Johan said as Fredrick dialed 911. Lou's senses returned. The medium was still unconscious.

"A woman, my friend, passed out at the Sunshine House on Ivar. It's the assisted living facility," Fredrick yelled into the phone as Mary Ann began to cry. He listened for a moment. "That's correct. On Ivar, the former Bockerman Hotel. Big sign on top of the building. She has a pulse but won't wake up."

Fredrick hung up the phone and joined Johan at Sara's side. "Paramedics should be here in less than five," he said as Johan cradled Sara in his arms, his eyes focused on her face. Lou heard him whispering her name. When he looked up at Lou, his eyes were no longer brilliant blue but black. Lou shivered in fear.

Sara Caine woke up to Johan's concerned face hovering above hers. Her surroundings swam in and out of focus, and her head hurt like the day after a weeklong bender. She attempted to lift herself up, but sparks of pain shot through her eyes and forced her back down to the pillow.

"Sara? Sara? Can you hear me?" Johan's voice faded into the distance as the darkness swallowed her back up.

Sara opened her eyes. She was in the back of an ambulance, Johan holding her hand, as an orderly took her blood pressure. "Johan?"

"I'm right here, Sara," Johan said and squeezed her hand. Her eyelids drooped. She yearned for the quiet. Johan's voice pulled her back into the ambulance. Sara used every ounce of strength she had to open her eyes for him.

"Sara, Sara?" Johan said, shaking her arm.

"What happened?" she croaked through her parched lips. She felt his breath on her cheek as he leaned in to hear her over the whine of the ambulance sirens.

"You lost consciousness and were out for way too long, fifteen minutes or so," he said. "Has this ever happened before?"

"Never that long," she confessed. She'd never noticed the yellow flecks in his blue eyes before and, despite her current condition, she basked in his closeness. She turned to him and noticed her vision dimming. "I'm going back under, Johan.

Don't leave me." She clutched at him. "I don't understand what's happening..."

A hand pushed a door open onto a bright, sunny apartment. A blond, laughing woman stood in front of her and held up a letter. It flapped in the breeze as the woman said something Sara couldn't hear. The woman pushed the letter into her hand, and Sara looked down and saw she held an acceptance letter from the California Institute of the Arts. Sara heard the woman laugh, and the image shifted.

Sara stood in the same apartment, moonlight casting a silvery light on the coffee table and illuminating a strange assortment of tools neatly laid out on top of it: a hammer, a syringe, different size scalpels, medical gloves, and two empty jars. A whimper came from somewhere to her left. Sara turned to the sound. Pain blossomed at the back of her head. Her world turned black again.

The darkness was cold and quiet except for the consistent sound of water dripping from somewhere in front of her. Sara rubbed her face, her eyes finally adjusting to the darkness. Then she saw her.

The same blond woman lay on a mattress, legs splayed open with a bloody mess where her stomach should have been. Blood dripped from the bottom of the woman's foot onto the floor.

Drip. Drip. Drip.

Sara stepped closer and saw something carved into her body. Was that what she was supposed to see? She memorized the carving, a crude trident. It consisted of a single vertical line that cut from her sternum to her bellybutton with two additional diagonal lines that started a third of the way down the vertical line and cut through each breast. The line ended at the mess that was her stomach.

Bile rose up to her throat, and she turned away from the horrific scene, squeezing her eyes shut. She prayed that the next time she opened her eyes she would be in the ambulance. She focused all her attention on the memory of Johan's face as it hovered above hers. She felt his warm breath on her cheek, and heard the sound the ambulance sirens made. She put all of her energy to the scene. The sirens grew louder and louder.

Light filtered through her eyelids, and she opened them to Johan's face, just as she had imagined. She clutched him to her and sobbed into his shoulder. The EMT slid next to Johan.

"I need to take your vitals, Ma'am," the EMT explained.

The EMT pried her off Johan and shone a light into her eyes, checking her pupils for dilation.

"Are you dizzy? Do you know your name?" he asked in a clipped tone.

"Sara Caine. I'm not dizzy and I'm in an ambulance," she said, her voice trembling. She attempted to sit up, but the EMT pressed her back down.

"Please keep still, Ms. Caine. Your blood pressure is too low, and you WILL pass out again. We're almost there," he added and patted her on the shoulder. He nodded to Johan and took a seat at the end of the gurney.

"I want to go home. I don't know what's happening to me," Sara whispered to Johan as the siren gave one last moan and fell silent. Johan dipped his head to hers.

"You were out too long, Sara. You need to get checked out and, at the very least, get an MRI," he whispered. "Just in case."

"In case of what?" Her voice rose in anxiety.

"I'm here for whatever happens, Sara," he said as the ambulance slowed.

The EMT threw open the back doors, jumped down and waved ER personnel over as he unlatched the locks to the gurney. Sara got dizzy from all the commotion and closed her eyes. They lifted the gurney up and out of the ambulance. Johan called out to her, but she couldn't make out what he was saying. The gurney moved, and the sounds of shouts and machines replaced Johan's voice.

Lou Fairbanks listened to the recording of the séance Fredrick had made. At first, he resisted giving it to her, but he was so worried about Sara Caine that she wore him down without too much effort.

Even though her research of successful séances mentioned ghosts presented themselves through recorded sound, this recording only contained static. Frowning, she took the headphones off and checked on Dads. He was still seated at their small table, having not moved since breakfast.

"I'm not hearing any voices on here, Dads, and no other sounds," she said and put the small mp3 player on the table between them.

Dads shrugged and turned to her.

"I don't know, I was certain I'd hear something. She said no one was there, but I don't believe her. Did you see her face? Her eyes were moving rapidly in their sockets, and that's how other mediums look when they make contact," she explained and took a sip of her tea, grimacing at the bitter taste. "Something attacked you." Her face crinkled and stood up abruptly. "I forgot your pills," she said and bustled over to grab them from the counter. Lou counted out two pills, poured him a glass of water and placed them in his hand. He stared at them then at her.

"You need to take them, Dads. It helps you remember," she said. He grimaced.

"Take them!" She pushed his hand toward him. He narrowed his eyes and threw them in his mouth, taking a sip of water.

"That wasn't too hard, was it?" Lou asked, smiling again.

13
Kindererziehungslager
Bruczków, Poland
DECEMBER 20, 1942

Szymon shivered under the blanket and didn't understand why the women, wearing the same brown uniforms every day, had to keep the windows open. It was freezing outside. He overheard the meanest woman tell one of the other boys that the cold would make them stronger.

They had given them a good dinner though: potatoes, roast chicken and warm soup. They even had small cakes for dessert. He hadn't eaten that well since Papa went to heaven, and he couldn't remember the last time he had dessert.

He rolled over to his side and peered into the darkness.

None of the four boys in the room with him were from his town. He'd always been the tallest boy in his class, but the other boys were as big as he was, and they all had blond hair and blue eyes just like him. They all could have been brothers. All the kids he saw in the lobby looked like him too. Szymon heard a snore from across the room and pulled his knees up to his chest. He closed his eyes, and his mama's face appeared. She smiled at him, and he felt sleepy again. Am I going to be OK, Mama?

Szymon woke up to one of the brown women distributing a bundle of clothes to each of the boys. "Wake up! It's time to get dressed. If you want breakfast, you will stay quiet," she warned. Szymon glanced at the uniformed bad man in the doorway, jumped out of bed, and got dressed. This place wasn't too bad, he thought. The clothes were some of the best he'd ever worn.

"Follow me," the woman said. The boys formed a line behind her and all trooped out and down the long, white hallway. He peeked into the open doorways, and saw doctors in white coats and uniformed men measuring the kids he'd seen in the lobby yesterday.

The line stopped abruptly, and he bumped into the boy in front of him. "Sorry," he muttered under his breath. The boy never looked back. The woman gestured to one of the rooms, and the boys went inside. Three doctors in white coats and a uniformed bad man waited for them. Szymon kept his chin up as Papa always said to do.

The tallest doctor stepped forward. "Please take off all your clothes and stand against the wall." The doctor nodded to the nearest wall, and the boys obeyed. The tall doctor took out a ruler with two long teeth along one end. He came up to Szymon and opened the teeth wide enough to span his head. One of the other doctors stood next to him holding a pen and notebook.

The doctor said something in the language that all the bad men spoke. His mama had called it German. The doctor adjusted the ruler teeth and measured the other side of his head. Szymon did his best to stand as still as possible. Out of the corner of his eye, he saw the remaining doctor start on the boy next to him.

The tall doctor measured his nose, checked his hair, and observed his nails. He even touched his privates. After each measurement, he said something to the doctor next to him. They seemed pleased with him.

He didn't flinch when they touched him down there either. Not like the short boy near the door. He saw him flinch and noticed that the boy was led out of the room. They must have not liked him, he thought, and made sure to stand even taller, his chin up.

Szymon, belly full of oatmeal, sat in front of another man at a low table in a tiny room. The man placed several puzzles in front of him. He had always been good at puzzles. Like his papa. He finished each one very fast because they were easy. The man smiled, patted him on the head and placed a harder puzzle in front of him. He would finish this one faster than the last one, he promised himself, and turned his full concentration to it. If he was good then maybe he wouldn't go to heaven like his Mama and Papa.

14
Investigations
FEBRUARY 21, 2005 - DAY 6

Diane Lawrence sat in a small interrogation room across from Detective Murphy and Detective Larson, files scattered in front of them. When she'd decided to divulge the unusual amount of deaths at the Sunshine in recent months, she hadn't expected the ensuing interrogation. The detectives made her feel as if she had something to hide, and she didn't like it. Not one bit.

Because of her intense demeanor, Detective Murphy was the reason Diane was seated in the tiny room, sweating her ass off. Her partner couldn't have cared less.

"These are all the residents?" Detective Murphy shuffled through the files again.

"All of them. I've tagged the ones who died from heart attacks," Diane repeated herself. Her stomach churned in response. She should have eaten before she came.

"That's ten people in the last three months?" Detective Murphy arched her eyebrow. Diane nodded. She had nothing to hide and anyone in her position would have made the same call.

"That's right. I'd like to remind you again, this is an assisted living home. People come to us to die and that's what they do. They die."

"The coroner has deemed the last two deaths suspicious," Detective Larson said, his eyes boring into hers. Diane ignored him. He had mean, beady, black eyes and smelled cheap. His blue, cotton, button-down shirt looked as if it had gone through twenty years of rough washing and his brown slacks were two sizes too big. Who was he to judge her?

Diane's eyes rested on the gun on his right hip. Her face flushed. She sat back in her seat and put as much distance between her and them as she could. She didn't like him, his gun or his attitude.

"Where were you during the hours of four to six the night before last?" Larson asked, getting into her face.

"You can't possibly think that I killed her?" She shouldn't have come. Dammit, she should never have called.

"You seem upset by the routine questions. Are you keeping something back?" Detective Larson smiled like a piranha.

"I was asleep like everyone else." Diane smiled back, not giving him an inch.

"Alone?" He kept his tone even. Diane smiled and nodded. At least, he thought she still had it.

"According to your security tapes, no one came in or out of the facility that night. Either they were doctored, or the killer is still at the facility,"

Detective Murphy said in a kinder tone. "We're going to have to talk to all the residents."

"That's fine. Everyone loved Lauren and if there's a killer at the Sunshine…" Her voice trailed away. Someone at the Sunshine was killing people. She'd known it, but didn't want to face it. If she had done something sooner, Lauren might still be alive. "How did she die? Was it the same way as Barbara? Did she suffer?" She directed the questions at Murphy.

"Do you have access to syringes?" Larson asked.

"No, why would I? I hate needles. I have a nurse and doctor who take care of that. I'm the administrator," Diane said to Murphy, ignoring Detective Larson. "Is that how she died?"

"Are syringes kept in the facility? What kind of access do the residents have to them? Who is your support staff?" Larson barked at her.

The man's voice made her head pound. She rubbed her forehead for some relief. "Like I just said, I don't know anything about syringes or medications. You need to talk to Dr. Jerris or Lou, Nurse Louise Fairbanks. I'm just the administrator," Diane snapped back at him. "How did a syringe cause a heart attack?" She directed the question back to Detective Murphy.

Detective Larson flipped through some photographs and pushed one forward.

"Can we use one of your rooms as an interview room? I'm assuming you'd prefer the residents to stay at the home," Detective Murphy said. They weren't going to tell her anything important.

"I can arrange that," Diane said, ignoring Detective Larson's tapping finger. He pushed the photo into her line of vision and gave her no choice but to look. She stared at the photo of two puncture holes in the crook of an arm.

"Your doctor didn't notice this when signing the death warrant," Larson said.

"Apparently not," Diane said. "Have you talked to her doctor yet?"

"Yes. He was sure that she had only one puncture wound when she left his office. His nurse agreed. That makes the second one suspicious," Detective Murphy said.

"But people at her age get blood taken out all the time. How does this prove that someone killed her?" she asked. "Was she poisoned?"

"The M.E. ruled her death suspicious. She died of an embolism. The coroner stated air in the vein could be a cause." Detective Larson stopped and let that sink in. "We have calls out to the owner of McGregor Holdings," he said. "Who is your Supervisor? We need to speak with him as well," Larson added. Diane hid her fear.

"Matt McCready is my direct supervisor. I'll call you with his number. I don't have it on me," she said. "Are we done? I've been away too long."

Murphy nodded. "Thank you for coming in. How does nine o'clock tomorrow morning sound? We can get your formal statement then and start the resident interviews."

"That should give me enough time to prepare," Diane said and stood up.

It was 10 am on Tuesday morning. The last place Diane Lawrence wanted to be was the Sunshine House cafeteria, the former Art Deco Cafe. A pall hung over the room. Many of the residents ate in silence. The wild bunch, the residents who caused her the most trouble, sat at one of the corner tables in complete silence, eyes everywhere but on each other.

Mary Ann, Barney, and Doreen were responsible for that ridiculous séance last night. The medium's collapse left McGregor Holdings open to a lawsuit and it was all on her. She wouldn't think about that now, though.

She leveled her gaze at Barney. He nodded at her. The man's behavior had caused her too many problems. The worst part was she agreed with Lou on something. The doors swung open and Detective Murphy and Detective Larson sauntered in like they owned the place. An irrational hatred made her want to scream at them. The residents faced the intruders together

"Can I please have your attention, everyone." Her voice rose and the few remaining heads who hadn't noticed their entrance turned. "Lauren Dolmar's death has been ruled suspicious as has Barbara Monroe's. Detectives Murphy and Larson will need to speak with each of you." She stopped and let the news sink in. The room erupted with questions. Detective Murphy stepped forward and took over. The room quieted down.

"We'll be holding interviews in Diane's office throughout the day. With your cooperation, we hope to discover what happened to Lauren and Barbara." Some residents stole glances around the room as others shifted in their seats.

"We'll do this in alphabetical order for ease and convenience," Detective Murphy continued as

Detective Larson pushed in front of Diane. Asshole, she thought and stepped away from the both of them as Nancy, a woman in her early nineties, rose up with a quiver.

"Will we need a lawyer?" Her voice came out stronger than her tiny, reedy body should allow.

"No, Nancy. You don't need a lawyer," Diane said and crossed the room to help get her back in her seat. Detective Murphy shot her partner a look and held her hand up for silence.

"No one is a suspect at this time. In order to establish a timeline of events, we will ask you for your movements on the days in question," she said to the now silent room.

"You think one of us did it, don't you?" An older man with close-cropped, white hair voiced what, she was sure, the others were thinking.

"That's not what Detective Murphy said," Detective Larson answered. Diane pursed her lips at his patronizing tone. His treatment of the seniors as children pissed Diane off and made her hate the man even more. She shot him a nasty look. If he noticed, he didn't show it.

Detective Larson picked the first name on the list Diane had provided for them.

"We'll start with Aaron, Doris. Doris Aaron." A murmur ran through the room. He scanned the crowd as a small, wizened woman got up from the far end of the cafe and made her way to the front.

"This way," he said and motioned for Doris to go in front of them. She obeyed, hobbling out, Larson and Murphy right behind her.

The din of voices reached a fever pitch as soon as the doors closed behind them. The only topics of conversation were gossip and speculation about the murders. Diane clapped her hands to get everyone's attention.

"Please, people. We need to be calm at a time like..." She trailed off when no one listened. Diane turned to go, a scowl on her face. Lou stepped through the swinging front doors, and was the last person Diane wanted to deal with. She frowned to dissuade her from starting a conversation. As per usual, it didn't stop her.

"What is going on here? I could hear the racket at the elevator banks," Lou said. Diane's hand fluttered to her forehead as a throb hummed above her right eye. Excellent. A headache. She rubbed at the spot.

"The police are interviewing everyone about Lauren and Barbara's deaths." Diane said and watched Lou sidle up to her.

"Really? How? I mean..." Lou asked, her curiosity revving up behind her eyes. Diane could see right through her. She was as bloodthirsty as the rest of them. Lou stepped in even closer, making Diane pull back. The woman had no concept of personal space.

"Yes, Barney was right after all. There is a murderer in our midst," Diane said, watching for any guilty twitches or strange movements. Lou stayed as still as stone, a smile frozen on her face.

"Have they ruled out an intruder? Surely the cameras picked someone up. The surveillance camera could pick up a ghost too? Has Russell Hall alerted you to any suspicious activity?" Lou asked, fiddling with the buttons of her cardigan.

"Ghosts don't handle syringes," Diane said. That made Lou's smile disappear.

"Syringe?" Lou stared at Diane, her gaze never faltering. Diane backed up, an irrational fear gripping her. Lou knew how to use a syringe and the deaths increased with her arrival.

"I have to go, Lou. You don't need to do your rounds today. Go be with Dads," Diane said, once more checking out the cafe. No one would be leaving there anytime soon which would keep them safe for now. Diane nodded at Lou and headed for the door. If she let the detectives know almost everyone would be in the cafeteria for the day, it would give her a good enough excuse to interrupt them.

Lou Fairbanks would not skip her rounds. Her patients needed her. For Diane to suggest such a thing was troublesome. Lou knocked on Room 437. "Ginny? You there?" she called out and knocked again. No answer. She pressed her ear to the door. Silence. She stooped to pick up her nurse's bag and the vertigo hit again.

Her anger had replaced her anxiety the last several days, but the anxiety was back with a vengeance. She straightened up and leaned against the wall. I'm alright. This too shall pass, she said to the empty hall and pressed on down the hall. She would have to work through it. "You will not win. I'm stronger than you," she said out loud to the empty hallway.

This patient wouldn't reject her, Lou thought, as she rapped twice on Room 801 and opened the door. "Good morning, Nancy. How are you today?" Lou said in a cheerful voice and smiled at the tiny granny ensconced in numerous blankets.

"Morning, Lou," she said and averted her eyes. Lou walked to the foot of her bed, uncovered a shriveled leg, and started to massage Nancy's ankle to get her blood flowing.

"You're awfully quiet today, Nancy," Lou said and moved up to the calf.

"Is it true, Lou?" Nancy asked, her voice taking on a childlike quality.

"What's true?" Lou's grip tightened on Nancy's calf. The woman winced.

"Sorry," Lou whispered and loosened her grasp. Nancy's eyes didn't stray from her hands, smoothing the blanket down on her lap.

"Never mind," Nancy said. Lou put her left leg down and started on the right.

"You can ask me anything," Lou prodded as she kneaded.

Nancy's eyes fixed back on hers. "Did you really do it?" she whispered.

"Do what?"

"Kill Lauren and Barbara?" Nancy blurted out. Lou stopped the massage and dropped her leg.

"You think I'm the killer?" Lou's voice shook. Nancy stared at her quilt as if it were the most beautiful thing she'd ever seen. "Is that what you're asking me?"

Nancy lifted her eyes to Lou's. "Yes, that's what I'm asking. Everyone is talking about it," Nancy whispered. Lou pursed her lips, afraid she'd give any emotions away. She perched on the edge of the bed and took Nancy's hand.

"Why would you believe that? Haven't I been good to you? Taken care of you?" Lou asked, making sure her voice was gentle and modulated low. "I've always been kind."

Nancy turned away from her without answering any of her questions. Nancy tried to pull her hand away but Lou held on. Nancy pulled her hand harder. Lou's grip tightened. When Lou saw the fear creep into Nancy's face, she let her go.

"I'm tired. I'm going to take a nap," Nancy said and faced the wall. Lou rose from the bed.

"I'll be back tomorrow," Lou's voice cracked and she cleared her throat. "I mean, I need to massage your legs every day so they don't atrophy," she said and grabbed her bag. "So, I'll see you tomorrow."

Lou walked into her apartment just as Dads was putting the kettle on the burner for tea. She dropped her nurse's bag and rushed to stop him.

"Dads, how many times have I told you not to turn the range on?" She pushed him off to the side and turned the burner off again.

"I can make tea. I'm... not... a... child," he said.

"That's true but you forget to turn it off. We don't want to burn the place down," she said as she picked up the kettle and pointed at its blackened bottom.

"Buy an electric kettle then," he said, startling her with his clarity. She couldn't remember the last time he'd strung a sentence together. She stared at him till he looked down.

"We don't have the money," she said and slumped down into her chair.

He joined her at the table. "Don't yell at me."

"They think I'm the one murdering everyone," Lou said, studying the bandage on his forearm. She kneeled in front of him. "Who did this to you?" She searched his face for an answer, but his eyes were already unfocused. Frustrated, she got back to her feet. "I need to find out who's setting me up." She stomped to the kitchenette.

Sara Caine woke up to Johan's head next to her arm. She closed her eyes and breathed in his scent. Salt and a muskiness that made her breathe in deeper. She sighed, opened her eyes again and heard him snore. He wore the same clothes as the night of the séance and Sara realized it was morning.

Sunlight streamed through the window and onto his head, catching the bluish highlights in his black hair. She fought the urge to run her fingers through it.

Instead, she shifted her arm to check her head. At least the headache was gone. Her movement startled Johan awake, and his eyes met hers. He stroked the damp hair off her forehead. She attempted a hello but the only sound that came out resembled a raspy croak.

"How are you feeling?" he asked as his smile dazzled in the sun and warmed her.

"How long have I been out?" she managed to get out.

"Twelve hours, give or take. The doctors say an unexplained coma. Has this ever happened before?" Johan asked. She shook her head. He looked dubious.

"I would have told you, Johan. I swear." Her voice gained strength.

"Let me get the doctor, they should check you out," he said. "I'll be back in a second." There went that smile again. He motioned to someone outside, and Sara closed her eyes.

The woman's mangled body flashed behind her eyelids, soon followed by the strange symbol carved into her belly. The flashback transported Sara back into the room. She heard the drip, drip, drip of the woman's blood onto the carpet. Then the whistling started right behind her.

Her scream caught in her throat.

The killer stood behind her, his hot breath on her neck. The blood dripped in slow motion from the dead woman's foot as Sara waited to die.

He whistled a tune she recognized but she couldn't place. The floorboard creaked behind her. A sharp pain exploded behind her eyes, plunging her back into the inky blackness.

Sara clawed her way back into consciousness. Her eyes flew open and she cried in relief she was back in the hospital room. The sun warmed her face as she wiped the tears off her cheeks. Johan stepped back in, joined by a doctor in a white coat. Reality. This was reality. The dead woman was a vision. It hadn't been real, she reminded herself as she read the doctor's name, Dr. Nadal. Sara met Dr. Nadal's brown eyes, warmth and caring radiating from them.

"Happy to see you awake, Sara," Dr Nadal said as she pushed the blood pressure cuff up Sara's arm. "I'm going to check where we're at with your vitals." She pumped it tight and read the results. "Your pressure is normal, great. I've ordered an MRI so we can make sure all's good in there. The length of time you were unconscious for is concerning. Mr. Luken said this has never happened to you before?"

Sara nodded. "That's correct. I've never blacked out for this long before."

"Have you been experiencing headaches?" Dr. Nadal asked as she shined a light into each eye.

"Nothing out of the ordinary," Sara said.

"Alright. Well, hopefully the scans will tell us something," Dr. Nadal said and checked her watch. "It should be another half an hour before the machine is ready for you. Are you clausterphobic?"

"No, not really," Sara said.

"A nurse will come with a solution for you to drink about ten minutes before it's your turn," Dr. Nadal explained. Turning to Johan, "she can have water right now." She squeezed her hand once more and left.

"I'm scared, Johan," Sara said as soon as the doctor was gone. She met his eyes. "The MRI isn't going to find anything, is it?"

"I don't know. What do you think happened, Sara?"

"We did make contact and the ghost entered my body, bringing her trauma with her. Other ghosts have tried this same tactic before, but I always managed to keep them at bay." She paused. "I saw a young woman murdered on a bed. I was there.

The killer got me too. I've never been in a victim's place like that before. The images come back each time I close my eyes. The power of her trauma knocked me out."

"I'm not convinced it was a ghost. Louise Fairbanks grabbed your arm right before you experienced your attack," he said. "Have you ever heard of empaths?"

"People who are sensitive to other's feelings?" she asked. She'd heard Fredrick use the term but had never met one personally.

"Among other things. And sensitivity is not the only gift empaths have," he said.

"I'm not an empath," Sara said.

"You sure? You get images from touching objects and buildings. It was just a matter of time before the same happened with a human being."

"The touch I use to see ghosts and memories from inanimate objects is totally different from being an empath, Johan. It's not the same energy. Or that's what you've always said."

"It could have been a precursor to this new gift, and the shock you got from the trauma opened you up to it," he explained.

"I don't buy it, Johan," she muttered as her doubt blossomed. Her eyes rested on his arm. If she touched him now, would she know his deepest secrets? His hand moved away from hers. "I've touched you before and never felt your emotions or your traumatic experiences."

He raised his eyes to hers. "I know but you aren't strong enough to see me trauma yet."

"I need water. Could you get me some?" Sara asked, changing the conversation. Johan got up, concern evident in his eyes. "Thank you for staying with me," she added.

"Always. Let me get you that water," he said and left.

Sara sank back into the pillows, not knowing what to believe. She trusted him explicitly when it came to the paranormal, but she didn't want to believe she had another gift to deal with. Seeing ghosts was scary enough, but experiencing people's most inner emotions horrified her.

She left her mind churning through the fearful thoughts and focused her attention on her breathing. Mindfulness meditation classes helped manage her gifts. Using the tools she learned in the classes, she built the mental walls necessary to quiet the paranormal noise and protect her form the unseen. The walls succeeded most of the time.

Today, though, her walls were crumbling. Even the ptsd that lurked deep down after surviving the car accident that killed her parents had resurfaced and hit her with brute force. She took a shaky breath, and the anxiety invaded her body. The hot flashes rolled in immediately. She pulled her attention to her breath, but the tidal wave of adrenaline hurling at her was too much. She gasped and clutched at the pillow and waited for the wave to crash. She closed her eyes and saw the dead woman. That wouldn't work. She opened them again and locked her eyes on the view through the window.

Johan came back with the glass of water in time to see her pant, the last remnants of her anxiety attack. He handed her the water. All she could do was nod in thanks, praying he wouldn't notice the crazy look in her eyes.

"I don't want you on this case, Sara. It feels off," Johan said as she sipped the water.

"I can't do that, Johan."

"Why not?"

"I need the images out of my head. If I help then, maybe they'll recede. I also don't want to give up on Barbara. We need to help her pass," she said knowing she sounded unstable.

"You're not safe," he said. Sara focused on the window and the everlasting blue sky of Los Angeles. "Let's suppose it is a ghost. What happens when the ghost takes you over again? And in your weakened state? You might not wake up."

"If I'm going to keep investigating the paranormal, don't I need to do this. Find out how everything has changed? I can't be constantly worried I'll black out the next time I make contact. Please help me find out what's going on."

"That was going to be my next request. I'm glad we're on the same page."

"I gotta get out of here first, Johan."

"First you do the MRI. We aren't leaving until we're sure you're okay up there." He tapped her head.

"Easier said than done." Sara quipped and crookedly smiled.

15
The Lebensborn Heimschulen
(Home for German Orphans)
FEBRUARY 10, 1943

Szymon marched with thirty other children singing the big anthem. He kept saying his new name to himself, just as Herr Gunther told him to, as he sang. Simon made sure to say his new name to himself at least twenty times. Maybe thirty. Simon Gerhard. Simon Gerhard. Simon Gerhard. He sang louder and with gusto.

> Es zittern die morschen Knochen,
> Der Welt vor dem großen Krieg,
> Wir haben den Schrecken gebrochen,
> Für uns war's ein großer Sieg.

Simon still only understood several words. The song said something about bones and Germany, hearing them talk and victory. The boy next to him named Kasper stopped singing and turned to his neighbor, Alexander.

"What's the next line?" Kasper asked. Alexander,

eyes growing wide, shook his head but Simon knew it was too late. Herr Felix had already heard. The boys stopped in mid-march, and the song died down.

"Halten SINGING!" Herr Felix roared, and the boys started up again.

> Wir werden weiter marschieren
> Wenn alles in Scherben fällt,
> Denn heute erhört uns Deutschland
> Und morgen die ganze Welt.

Simon belted the words out while watching Herr Felix kick Kasper in the stomach. Kasper fell to the ground with a small grunt.

Please don't cry. Please don't cry, Simon said to himself. Herr Felix kicked him again, and Kasper took it like he was supposed to. Maybe he wouldn't disappear tomorrow after all.

Simon made sure to never speak Polish anymore and memorized many German words. His German was getting better and better every day. Father was Vater, and Mother was Mutter, and he would have a new, better family soon. His real one.

Herr Gunther had said that he was a German orphan and he would get good, proper parents. German parents. Eine Familie. He would be a good Deutscher junge. He didn't want to go to heaven like Mama and Papa and like some of the other children already had.

Simon. He smiled when he remembered to think his new name. He would be smart and make sure he never got in trouble. Papa told him last year he was a very smart boy, and he would not disappoint his papa.

16

Interrogation
DAY 6

Barney Leonard kept the manila folder close to his chest as he opened the door to Diane's office. Detective Murphy and Detective Larson sat behind Diane's ornate cherrywood desk, paperwork spread out before them.

"Mr. Barney Leonard?" Detective Larson asked, and Barney nodded while taking the seat across from them. "Thank you for coming to talk to us."

"It's about time you people came. Last time I spoke with one of you, they said they'd send someone out the next day," he said and arched his eyebrow at the detective. "That was a month ago."

"Right. We'll get to that in a moment. But first, where were you the night of January twentieth?" the female detective interjected before he could continue.

"I was asleep like almost everyone else in the building. I'm not whom you want. I have called your precinct several times over the last three months as I said a second ago," Barney said and paused for effect. "None of you wanted to speak with me then. I got the distinct impression that whoever took my calls thought I was some crazy old coot." He patted the folder in his lap. "I have all my notes here."

He opened up the folder and slid four yellow lined sheets of paper to them. "The deaths started about two and a half months ago. March had an unusual amount of deaths by heart attack. We all joked about it being such an unlucky month. We're all old after all," he said before they could mention the obvious.

Detective Murphy nodded and picked up the top page. Detective Larson opened his mouth to say something, but Barney put his hand up to stop him.

"I'm not done yet, sonny. It's a fact we are old, but the people who died were healthy and had many good years ahead of them. Before she came, we had a death once every three months."

Detective Larson frowned. "Who came?"

"Louise Fairbanks. The nurse we call Lou. Since she's been here, there have been four deaths a month. The names and dates are on that list," Barney said and waited. Diane had laughed him out of her office when he'd told her of his suspicions, but he had high hopes these detectives were at least smarter than her.

"How can you be sure all these deaths weren't natural causes?" Detective Larson asked him. Apparently, they weren't the sharpest detectives either. Damnit, Barney thought.

"I knew these people. Everyone at Sunshine talks about their medical problems. It's the most popular topic of conversation. Most of them check their blood pressure every hour, blood sugar after every meal. Health is no secret around here."

"I find it hard to believe that none of these people on your list had heart troubles," Detective Larson countered. Barney shook his head.

"Check the records yourself," he said and noticed the woman glance at her partner. She must be the smarter of the two.

"Did you share your suspicions with anyone?" Detective Murphy asked in a modulated tone.

"Diane Lawrence. I told her."

"And?" she prompted.

"She didn't believe me," Barney said and crossed his arms in front of his chest. He leaned back in the chair.

"It's a serious accusation. Do you have any proof that Louise Fairbanks is the person responsible for these deaths?" she asked. "Maybe throwing the accusation at her is your way of deflecting attention from yourself."

"We've heard of your love triangle between two of the women here, Barbara Monroe, the deceased, and Mary Ann McClatch," Larson said and Barney stifled a laugh.

"Another thing you might not know about assisted living homes. Everyone sleeps with everyone else. We've got the time. That's no reason to kill anyone. Lots of women here and I never slept around on Barbara. She was the love of my life. I'm not sure what Ms. McClatch told you, but there was never any triangle."

"That gives Mary Ann McClatch a motive then, doesn't it?" Detective Larson asked. Barney's eyes dropped to his hands.

"No, it really doesn't. Mary Ann is many things, but she isn't a killer. And that doesn't explain Lauren. You need to look into Louise Fairbanks. There is something going on with that woman, and she needs to be stopped."

"You're not telling us everything," Detective Murphy said and studied Barney.

"I've told you everything. You have all my notes. I've even interviewed some of the residents about the nights in question. It's all in the summary." He gestured at the sheets in her hand. "All I know is in there." Barney waited for them to thank him. No one said anything of that nature. Seriously, Barney fumed to himself.

"We'll need to speak with you again after we've looked through your notes," Detective Larson said

"That's all you have to say?" Barney asked, standing up to leave. Neither detective answered. What a disappointing pair of detectives. They didn't have enough brains between them to stop her. Brains was what Nurse Louise had going for her. She was more intelligent than the lot of them.

"I'm not going anywhere, and their medical records will show you all you need to know," he reiterated and stomped out the door. He checked his fury as he thought over his other options. Maybe Sara Caine would help. He pulled the door open and found Doreen rushing away from the door.

"What are you doing, Doreen?" he asked and shut the door before either of the detectives could see her. If they weren't going to help the residents, then they didn't need to know all their secrets. He grabbed her by the arm.

"Did you hear everything?" he whispered.

"I didn't hear anything, Barney. I swear," Doreen stammered as her watery eyes went wide. Doreen was a busybody as she herself enjoyed telling people. Her blushing felt out of character, though. Was she embarrassed about something else.

"You need to be careful, Doreen. Protect yourself at all costs," he said and jagged his finger back at the office. "Those fools aren't going to help us. We're going to need to help ourselves."

"Whatever you say, Barney." She pulled her arm back and hurried away from him. He hadn't meant to scare her but, on second thought, maybe it was better this way. Everyone who lived at Sunshine needed to be terrified.

Lou Fairbanks wandered through the streets of Hollywood, unaware of the crowds of tourists, peddlers, and Scientologists that walking past her, and tried to remember the last time she'd left the Sunshine. Was it last week? The week before? She breathed in deep and sucked in enough car exhaust to bring on a fit of coughing. Even with all the smog, Lou was glad to be outside. The sun warmed her skin and made her smile.

Her job didn't permit her too much alone time, and her patients had all they needed at the home. Since all their meals were served in the cafeteria, food wasn't an issue, and anything else Lou needed she got once a month at the local 99c store. The Sunshine House had a small pharmacy on the bottom floor that took care of everything else. No need to ever leave the place. She closed her eyes and tilted her face to the sun. How can anything be bad on a day like this, she thought and walked past the Sunshine, not ready to go back inside. There wasn't much to see on the blocks past Ivar but she didn't care. The sun almost made her feel normal. Almost.

It was some time before she stepped back inside the gloomy lobby of the home and left the sun behind. Diane hovered in the shadows looking as if she was waiting for someone. Lou ignored her as she crossed the lobby. Diane waved to get her attention. With trepidation, Lou stopped to see what she wanted.

"The detectives need to speak with you," Diane said and gestured to her office. The dread Lou kept at bay all morning creeped back in as she closed the distance between them.

"We've been looking for you forever," Diane added.

"Sorry, I went outside for a walk," Lou explained, her cheeks burning.

"They're waiting inside." Diane gestured again and Lou proceeded into her office. The two detectives had commandeered Diane's desk, and Lou sat down in the chair opposite them. Lou wished she was back in the sun.

"This is Detective Larson, and my name is Detective Murphy. We're investigating the suspicious deaths of Lauren Dolmar and Barbara Monroe. We met you before, remember?"

Lou shook her head yes.

"Where were you two nights ago?" Murphy asked.

"Asleep."

"The entire night?" Murphy asked.

"No, I woke up around two thirty. Dads was having a bad night and it took me forever to get him back to sleep."

"And Dads is your father?" Lou nodded. "And your father will corroborate this?" Detective Larson demanded as he scrutinized her.

"I hope so," she said. "He has dementia, and his mind comes and goes. But that was a particularly bad night—"

"How so?" Murphy asked looked up from her notebook and smiled reassuringly at her.

"You've been told about the ghost we have here? Or the séance?" Lou asked. The detectives glanced at each other. No, they hadn't been told apparently. She knew she sounded certifiable but how could she explain Dads getting hurt and then Sara Caine collapsing without mentioning the séance? What had Barney and the others said about their whereabouts last night?

"No one mentioned the ghosts?" Her voice now uncertain. Detective Murphy's face told her all she needed to know. They'd all left her flapping in the breeze alone, she thought.

"The EMT's came and took the medium away in the middle of it. That was around nine thirty last night, but you can always check with the other participants. Diane knew about it. Barney Leonard, Mary Ann McClatch and Doreen Stevens were all there with us."

"What was this called again?" Detective Larson asked.

"You mean the séance? Contacting ghosts? I don't understand the question. I'm the only one brave enough to tell the truth, I guess. There's been lots of strange sounds, sobbing, whispering, and thumps."

"All those sounds could be rats in the walls or faulty pipes in a place this old," Detective Murphy suggested.

"That's what I thought as well but then..." She stopped. "Dads got attacked," she blurted out.

"What do you mean attacked?" Detective Murphy leaned in.

"Someone carved HELP ME into his arm."

"Carved?" Detective Larson asked.

"Like, scratched. With a sharp object or something. The ghost hunters were here that day and we filmed the hallway during the attack. No one came in or out of my apartment."

"Did you say ghost hunters?" Larson asked.

"I did. They wired cameras in the hallways trying to document Irene—"

"Who's Irene?" Detective Murphy cut in.

"She's the ghost. She died on the floor above me," Lou answered.

"Are you mental? You're a nurse for chrissakes," Larson asked, his face screwed into a look of disgust. Lou reddened. Her head spun with vertigo, making her clutch the arms of the chair for support. She prayed they hadn't noticed. If she showed them her panic, they'd misjudge her anxiety for guilt. Lou focused on her right hand, another technique she had to combat anxiety, courtesy of Dr. Jerris.

"We will need to talk to your father," Detective Murphy said, breaking the silence. She shoved her chair back with some force. "We should do that now." Larson followed her lead.

"He tends to be more lucid in the mornings," Lou offered as she took the lead.

Lou hovered near the door, afraid they would notice her shaking hands and cold sweat if she came too close. Detective Murphy sat next to Dads on his bed while Detective Larson, perched in Dads' chair, inspected his arm.

"These seem very shallow," Murphy remarked.

"They are. We got very lucky," Lou said. She left the safety of the door and drew closer. "I don't know whether he would have survived if they were any deeper. He doesn't have a good heart and the healing process...I don't know. The kind of stress he was under has set his mind back a lot. He's barely lucid anymore."

"Why didn't you report it?" Larson asked as she took a seat across the table from him.

"As you said, they were shallow and I've watched him like a hawk. I took care of it. He didn't need stitches—"

"But this qualifies as senior abuse—" Murphy interrupted her.

Lou froze. "I didn't— I don't abuse my father. How could you say—?"

"We aren't accusing you of hurting your father," Larson said. Under Larson's scrutiny, Lou jumped out of her chair and kneeled in front of Dads.

"I feel the exact opposite, officer," Lou said.

"It's detective, Ms. Fairbanks," Larson cut in.

"Dads, tell them how well I take care of you," Lou

urged him. Dads nodded and his blank, blue eyes rested on Murphy.

"My life is in her hands," he said.

Lou twisted around to look at the both of them. "I would never do anything to endanger him."

"We'll need to contact human services—" Larson began.

"Why?"

"He's in danger here," Murphy added in soft voice.

"It wasn't me. I didn't carve into his arm and have been trying to find out who did." Lou directed her pleas to Detective Murphy.

"It appears to us that your father is in danger here. What is his full name?"

"Gerald Fairbanks."

"If someone hurt Mr. Fairbanks, that someone could also be abusing others," Detective Murphy added and gave Lou a questioning look.

"How does calling human services on me get to the bottom of this? I'm here twenty-four hours a day. If other patients were getting abused, I would know about it and I would have raised a red flag," Lou argued. She rose, giving Dads a squeeze on his knee.

"You didn't alert anyone when your patients started to die," Larson pointed out. Lou's heart beat faster.

"That wasn't my call. It was Diane's," she said. "I have nothing to hide, and I didn't do this to Dads. You won't find any elder abuse, not on my watch. I do rounds every day checking in with my patients. I would have reported any signs immediately."

"Like you did with Dads?" Larson asked.

"What was I supposed to say? A ghost did it?" Lou shot back.

The detectives got to their feet. "Thank you for speaking with us, Dads," Murphy said and gave him a smile. She turned to Lou.

"You really believe that? About the ghost?" Murphy asked, her tone serious. Her partner suppressed a laugh, but Detective Murphy shook her head at him to stop.

"I don't know what to believe anymore. When I left him, he was fine. They hooked up the cameras in the hallway and turned them on within half an hour of arriving here. I have video of the entire time between then until I found him. No one came into this room. What other explanation is there?" Lou said and sat back down next to Dads.

"There is still a half hour unaccounted for," Larson said.

"The cuts were too fresh. They would have scabbed over if it had happened in that time frame," Lou explained.

"Don't leave town. We're going to need to speak with you again," Larson said without acknowledging her answer.

"This is my home. I'm not going anywhere," Lou said and stuck her chin up. The door clicked closed behind them, and Lou put her arm around Dads, resting her head on his shoulder.

"Can you believe any of this, Dads?" she asked. He turned his eyes back to the window and the Hollywood sign without saying a word.

The Sunshine House cafeteria hadn't been this hot in years, thought Doreen Stevens. No one had retired back to their rooms after dinner. Instead, the residents stayed to talk about the latest developments. Doreen loved being in the spotlight and had the full attention of her table. Ginny, Barney, Mary Ann, and even old Martin hung on her every word. She might have embellished the story a bit but when was she going to get another opportunity like this?

"She almost broke down my door. She's so strong," Doreen whispered for effect. Ginny shuddered at that and Doreen couldn't help but smile. She was such a gifted storyteller.

"Did you let her in?" Ginny asked.

"Are you kidding?" Doreen exclaimed and shook her head. She lowered her voice, making them all lean in to hear her. "I don't want to be her next victim."

"Do you really think it is her?" Ginny asked.

"Of course it's her," Barney cut in. Doreen scowled at him. He was always interrupting her flow. Just because he was the first one to make the connection between Lou and all the deaths didn't mean he always had to lead the conversation, she thought.

A hush fell over the entire cafeteria. Doreen glanced over to the door to see what everyone was staring at. Lou Fairbanks loomed in the doorway, scanning the room until her eyes fell on them. She stalked to their table.

"None of you mentioned the ghost to the police?" Lou hissed. Everyone at the table looked away except for Barney, who glared right back at her.

"Whatever are you talking about? What ghost?" he asked. Doreen's head snapped up. This was unexpected.

"Last night never happened? You're all going to deny it?" Lou yelled. How embarrassing, Doreen thought and averted her eyes. The rest of the table did the same. Except Barney, who leaned back in his chair, a grim smile marring his features. The entire cafeteria waited with bated breath for his answer.

"We should do a movie tonight," Barney said, ignoring Lou's outburst. Mary Ann lifted her eyes to his. Annoyance shot through Doreen at his grandstanding. He'd made her lose her spotlight, and he wasn't even going to engage?

"All about Eve. Let's all watch that," Martin piped up. Martin speaking at all was unusual, Doreen thought. Doreen checked in with all the others. They followed Barney's lead and ignored Lou, except for Ginny who nodded and stared into space. She appeared terrified. Doreen rolled her eyes at the thought. What a drama queen.

"Why would you lie about something like that? You were the one that started all this, Barney. You called her in. You did all this," she shouted, jabbing a finger at him.

Lou's expression changed, a realization hitting her. "Was this all to get me? Make me look unfit to work?" Lou said in a much softer tone. No one said a thing. Lou turned and raced out of the room, slamming the door behind her. The room erupted in sound.

"It's only a matter of time now," Barney said. "She's cracking."

"But doesn't that mean another murder? Isn't that what murderers do? They kill when they get backed into a corner?" Mary Ann asked. Doreen nodded in agreement.

"We've pushed her to the edge, so now what? You don't think she's going to just turn herself in, do you?" Doreen said, calculating how much time she had left in the day to call in a locksmith.

"She's right. Lou's going to come after us now, isn't she?" Mary Ann said with rising hysteria.

"We all have good locks on our doors. No way she's getting in. Why would she attempt anything when the police are here? This is what we wanted. Movement. Police listening to us. They'll catch her. No one can keep committing the perfect crime. She must have made mistakes. They'll find them," Barney added.

Doreen had enough run-ins with the police to not hold them in such high esteem. She'd been a flower child in the sixties, and she saw how incompetent the cops were then. They were just brutes and she'd never met a smart one yet.

"You're putting a lot of faith in the police," Doreen said but everyone's attention was still on Barney. She looked around the room and wondered who would fall dead next.

17

Auschwitz Concentration Camp
Block #10
Oświęcim, Poland
May 3, 1944

Simon held the hand of Herr Sigmund Schreiber, his new vater, and watched as a naked, very skinny woman was wheeled into the doctor's room. He had never seen a naked woman before and made sure to keep his eyes averted, as his real mama wouldn't want him to look.

Today was the first time Simon had come to work with his new father. His new mother said it would be good for him to see his papa work and Herr Schreiber agreed. Simon, however, was worried it was another test.

Herr Schrieber wanted Simon to call him Papa and Simon made sure to do so. But, he would never forget his real mama and papa and called his neue Familie by Herr und Frau Schreiber when he thought about them.

"So nice you could join us today, Männchen Simon Schreiber."

"Guten Morgen, Doktor Clauberg," Herr Schrieber said and pushed Simon in front of him. Simon nodded and shook the hand Doktor Clauberg offered him. He turned back to his patient. One of his helpers handed him a large syringe filled with a pale yellow liquid. Simon had never seen a needle that big.

"Papa, what is Doktor Clauberg going to do?" Simon whispered not taking his eyes off the giant needle.

"We have to make sure they can't make babies anymore, son. It's called sterilization," Herr Schrieber said. Simon's eyes grew wide as they met the terrified woman's.

18
The Searchers
Day 6

Johan Luken drove east down Santa Monica Boulevard with Sara ensconced in the passenger seat. He helped get her discharged from the hospital against his better judgment, and she made him doubt his decision more when she refused to go home. She argued that she had enough energy to face the ghost and that they should do it as soon as possible. Johan had a hard time saying no to her and found himself driving back to the Sunshine House. He focused on the road ahead of him.

The mauve light of Los Angeles' magic hour, unique to this spread out metropolis, washed over the grime of bodegas and one dollar stores on this seedier drag of Santa Monica Boulevard. The light snuck into their car and made Sara's translucent skin glow. He'd never seen her more beautiful or more fragile. She looked as if she'd break apart at any moment. She turned to him and smiled, and the look on her face did something funny to him.

"It's so beautiful, isn't it? The hills look almost purple in this light," she said.

"It's my favorite time," Johan agreed.

"Hmmm." She turned back to stare out the window. His thoughts returned to the case and his worry about what they had gotten themselves into. His gut was telling him to turn the car around and drive both of them home.

"We should stay out of this, Sara. This doesn't feel paranormal." He kept his eyes on the road, but checked his peripheral vision to see her reaction. She stared out the window.

"I see that poor woman every time I close my eyes, Johan. I need to understand what happened to her," she said.

He turned to her sharply. "You didn't tell me that."

"I did at the hospital. And I'm telling you now," she said. He gripped the wheel for support. A dark foreboding hit him.

"Do you want to go home and get changed?" he asked instead. Sara wouldn't let this go. She never had in the past. Her need for helping lost souls overriding her sense of danger. He'd stay by her side and offer whatever protection he could.

"No, let's go there first. The faster we get this over with, the faster I can sleep," she said as he turned onto Highland Ave and headed north, the pink hued Hollywood sign glowing like a beacon ahead of them.

"As you wish. Should we call, Barney Leonard?" Johan slowed the car as the orange-pinkish light gave way to the blue and neon of the Hollywood Boulevard skyline.

"No. I want to speak with the manager, Diane Lawrence. I'm hoping she'll give us permission to go to the eighth floor."

"Louise Fairbanks's room wasn't on the eighth floor," Johan said, slowed the car and pulled into a line of numerous red taillights. "Damn. I forgot the time," he said. The LA Basin emptied through four main arteries at four o'clock every weekday. One of the arteries was Highland Avenue, and its traffic wouldn't lessen until at least seven o'clock. "I should turn off."

"It's only a couple of blocks, Johan," she said. She rested her head against the back of the seat and closed her eyes. "Getting there once the sun has set is better anyway."

They slowed to a complete stop. Johan's thoughts turned to the night of the séance. He'd gone over the sequence of events numerous times and each time reached the same conclusion. Sara's blackout happened because Louise Fairbanks touched her. He was sure of it.

The traffic moved and the car lurched forward. Sara's eyes flew open.

"Sorry."

"We're almost there anyway," she said, sat up straighter and rubbed her face. The purple smudges under her eyes grew darker as she faced him.

"I met Diane Lawrence when Barney called in Fredrick to set up the cameras. We can use that to ingratiate ourselves to her. Say something like he forgot to take down one of the cameras and we need to go pick it up."

"Were there cameras on the eighth floor?"

"Yes, Fredrick set them up on that floor without telling me why. He took them down but so much has happened, I'm sure she won't remember that," Sara said. Johan had his doubts but didn't say anything. Maybe this Diane would do his work for him and not allow them back into the damn place. His pulse picked up as they turned onto Hollywood Boulevard.

The night crawlers slunk among the tourists on the sidewalks as Marilyn Monroe and Spiderman impersonators plied their trade. Johan stared out into the crowd as the hairs on his neck stood up in fear. The demon Luther's presence elicited this exact kind of response in Johan.

He focused back on driving, while scanning the crowd out of the corner of his eye. He was out there. The demon whose face was in perpetual motion, a smudge where the features of a face should be. The most powerful entity he'd ever encountered and one that almost destroyed him while killing the only family he'd ever had. The demon held such power over him that Johan hunted him for the last ten years. He'd not come close to him in over three years.

Johan's hand slipped off the steering wheel and grasped the door handle. Come get me, he heard in his head. Luther was out there, calling him.

Come to me.

Johan put the car in park and opened the driver's side door. His foot was out the door when Sara's voice pierced through Luther's madness.

"What are you doing? Johan, get back in the car!" Her hand grasped his collar and pulled him back.

"JOHAN!" He faced her, his eyes going in and out of focus.

Sara slapped him hard, and stars danced in his vision. He placed his palm against his cheek, using the sting to bring himself back. To Sara.

"Johan?" Her voice came out gentle and soft now. Her hand reached for his. "Come back to me." Johan fell back into his seat, and when he saw the fear in her eyes, crashed back into reality. "Was it Luther?"

Johan closed the car door to the honks increasing in volume behind them. Luther almost pulled him into oncoming traffic, Johan thought and shivered. He pressed on the gas pedal.

Her hand had found his again. "Are you OK?" she pressed him.

"I'm sorry. He slithered into my head," Johan said. He drove past the Bockerman in search of a meter. Her eyes stayed on his face, Johan couldn't show her his fear.

On the edge of a sea of grey cubicles sat Detective Eva Murphy deep in thought as cops wandered around getting coffee, checking email, and doing the mundane everyday tasks of the precinct. The office resembled any business except for the occasional uniformed policeman who wandered in and out with files. Larson threw himself down in the seat next to her and let out a massive groan.

"Nothing. I've found nothing," he sputtered. "They're ghosts."

Murphy took the file out of his hand. "Nothing before Palm Desert?" she asked as her eyes flicked over his notes. "How does a ghost get a nursing degree?"

Larson grimaced and she gave him the warmest smile she could. "We hit shelter. Income is next, right?"

"I know, I've been at this longer than you have. Don't condescend to me," Larson said. She frowned.

"I wasn't trying to be condescending. I was talking it out," Murphy said, hurt he jumped on her. He'd been way more moody recently. Larson kept his mean streak in check around her. Today, though, he targeted her. Well, screw him, she thought.

"Like I was saying, shelter, income, transportation, and social contact are the keys to finding ghosts," Murphy reiterated. All she got was a grunt. "Shelter dead ends. We have no idea of profession as he's always been the retired patient, but she needs nursing credentials." She turned back to her computer and brought up the database for Death Certificates, typed in Louise Fairbanks and hit search. It took less than five seconds to pull up three relevant people. She clicked on the third and found a record that matched. A woman by the name of Louise Fairbanks died on September 15, 1985.

Larson leaned over. "Hello, Nurse Louise."

"Yup. I'm assuming the social security number will match up with our dead nurse."

Murphy was already typing. It didn't take long to match up Nurse Lou's particulars to the dead woman.

"We're going to need her prints. DNA. Something to identify who she really is," Murphy said, turning away from her computer.

"She must be in the system."

"Not necessarily," Murphy said

"Well looks like she's hiding something," Larson said, the familiar sharpness back in his voice.

"How do these homes monitor their employees? This is an expensive assisted living home, I can't imagine they didn't do an extensive background check on all their perspective employees."

"You mean like the background check they did on Russell Hall and his neo-Nazi family?"

"Good point. Credit check is enough for them, I guess." She checked Google for any Louise Fairbanks or Gerald Fairbanks and came up short. "And they have no web imprint."

"They're ancient like me, apparently," Larson said and cast her a side-eyed glance. Not this crap again, she thought. He pushed out of his chair and stood over her as she opened up Lou Fairbanks' file again. She scanned to their earliest known address, another assisted living home. What was up with the Sunny and Sunshine naming anyway, she thought.

"Mr. Larry Jenkins of the Sunny Days Assisted Living Home, where are YOU located?" Murphy asked the computer screen.

"What did you find?" Larson asked.

"Someone who had to know these two some years back," Murphy closed the file.

"Field trip?" He rubbed his hands together.

"Your favorite." She cracked a grin, relieved at the change of conversation.

"Getting out of the city is always a dream."

Diane Lawrence wasn't in her office. They had snuck into the back staircase after finding her door locked. The back staircase of the Sunshine House needed much better lighting, Sara Caine thought, as she and Johan rested on the landing of the fourth floor. Standing there now, she wasn't entirely sure if her need to help the ghost was such a good idea. She smelled danger. Even with its rundown beauty, the Sunshine House gave her the creeps.

Many details in the staircase were original from the old hotel. The wooden balustrade was polished to a veneer that only hundreds of hands could have created over the many years of the hotel. Several lights illuminated each floor making the staircase resemble a film-set straight out of a classic black and white Hitchcock film. Like the staircase from Vertigo, she thought. She stopped and gulped down air. Her stay at the hospital destroyed any stamina she had. Her chest ached as they proceeded up the stairs.

She snuck a peak at Johan. Since the episode on Hollywood Boulevard, he'd said about four words. Luther's hold on him was enormous. He'd told her Luther went underground for years, but now, apparently, he was back.

"You ready?" His voice echoed in the empty staircase. She nodded and grabbed the balustrade. She would do four more flights, not a problem. She took a deep breath and took the next step.

Sara's chest exploded in pain as she took the last several stairs and made it to the eighth floor landing with her face burning and breath coming out in small gasps. Johan's arm supported her as she got her bearings. She was grateful that she wasn't tumbling down the stairs.

"We should have taken a break," he whispered.

"Harder to start up again," Sara gasped, doubled over. She slowed down her breathing. Sara breathed in deep and held it in. After a minute, she blew the air out. In and out, in and out. She staved off both exhaustion and fear.

"Wanna just leave?" Johan asked.

Sara pushed the door open in response. Johan followed her. She poked her head out of the doorway. The hallway was empty.

"You sure about this?" Johan asked. Sara stepped into the hallway, closed her eyes and listened to the sounds of the home. Sara dropped her first wall and waited.

"Anything?" he asked. She dropped her second wall as fear coursed through her. Sara exposed herself to any entity out there.

Sound pulsated in her ears but no one voice separated from the din.

"Maybe it's you," she said half-teased and walked down the hall, away from him. The temperature in the hallway dipped to freezing as her breath came out in little clouds in front of her. Classic haunting, she thought. She'd found Barbara.

Sara motioned to Johan to join her.

Her ears popped as the pressure dropped. Another sign. Ghosts gathered energy from their surroundings to present themselves in a solid form. Sara strained to see the ghost.

A woman materialized in front of her, wearing a yellow, flowered nightgown and small pink curlers covering her entire head. Her mouth opened forming a perfect circle. Her lips moved, but no sound came out.

"I can't hear you," Sara said. The woman's eyes widened, and her silent words came faster. Sara held up her hand to stop her.

"You need to focus your energy. Slow down," Sara instructed.

The ghost flickered and turned to something behind her. Sara couldn't see anything else in the hallway. The woman faced Sara again, her mouth open and eyes filled with terror. Her scream pierced through the silence, echoing through the hall. Sara clamped her hands over her ears. The air popped and the scream cut off. The ghost was gone

Sara uncovered her ears. Her body tingled from the ghost's tremendous power surge.

"I heard that scream," he said in wonder. "That ghost has so much power. The death is very recent. Was it the same entity from the séance?"

"The energy was different. I'm positive she was the murdered woman on this floor," Sara said, shivers making her teeth chatter.

"But not the entity that caused your blackout?" Johan asked.

"No. No. That was too different." She turned to Johan. "You're right. A ghost didn't cause my blackout," Sara said. Her head spun with the implication of yet another unwanted talent.

"You need to start wearing gloves, Sara. Just in case," Johan said. She blanched at his words.

"Should we talk to Nurse Lou Fairbanks?" Her voice filled with fear.

"No. That's not a good idea. Let's go home. You're

exhausted," he said and took her by the arm. Sara didn't want to interact with Lou Fairbanks, now or ever.

"Alright, let's go home," she said much to his surprise.

Larry Jenkins had been a manager of the Sunny Days assisted living home for the last eight years and loved every minute of it. He'd dreamt of helping people since he was a child but wasn't smart enough to make it to medical school. He had, however, managed to work in health care professions all his life.

He took great pride in how well he ran Sunny Days. Outside that one hiccup the first year on the job, it had been smooth sailing. None of the residents had left over that specific incident, and he received many letters and emails about how happy the families of his residents were during their stay at Sunny Days. He should have called the cops back then, but without any concrete evidence all he had was a hunch and no evidence.

Despite all of this, his face burned as the two detectives sat down opposite him in his bright yellow office. He had put that year behind him and tried to forget it ever happened. He was paying for that mistake now.

"What can you tell us about Louise Fairbanks and her father, Gerald Fairbanks, Mr. Jenkins?" The male detective started without a preamble as the woman detective smiled in encouragement. Sent. He'd never been interviewed by the police before, but he'd watched enough cop shows to recognize the good cop bad cop routine. Law & Order used it all the time.

"What do you want to know? And you can call me Larry, everyone does."

"Do you still have their file, Larry?" Detective Murphy cut in, in a kinder tone.

"It was almost eight years ago, correct? We don't keep employee files that long," Larry Jenkins said as sweat ran down his back.

"Do you remember any of her references?" She pressed on.

He shook his head. "Too long ago."

"Did they ever call each other by any other names?" The male detective asked. The man reminded him of a barking Chihuahua.

"Nurse Lou called him Dads. She never used his given name." His brow creased. "I never heard him use her name. That's odd, isn't it?" he asked.

"Did they have any close friends? Socialize often with anyone?" the man asked.

"I'm sorry, Detectives but it was so long ago."

"How many suspicious deaths happened at this home before you let them go?" The Chihuahua pounced.

All the air in the room disappeared. Larry gulped and wondered where all his saliva went. His mind raced back to that horrible year. A lump in his throat prevented him from speaking. How many residents had he lost? 9-10? He never investigated and wasn't entirely sure how many were natural and how many were suspicious. But, the Doc had noted his concerns on some of the files, hadn't he?

"I'm not sure what you mean by suspicious deaths, but Dr. Riley, our facility doctor, brought something odd to my attention." He paused and hoped this would be enough for them. "One of our older ladies, Julie Richardson, had an odd marking on her body. Her official cause of death was by brain embolism but the doc found a small needle mark in the crook of her arm. Her records didn't show any recent doctor appointments so she shouldn't have had any needle marks on her person."

"How many other deaths happened around that time period?" Detective Murphy asked.

"Huh?"

"Did your death rate increase while the Fairbanks were here?" The Chihuahua detective leaned in closer, and Larry could almost smell the man's breath. There it was, his worst nightmare. He clicked on the mouse to wake up his computer.

"In general or just that year?" Larry asked, pretending to be nonchalant as he screamed inside. He brought up the spreadsheet of the incoming and outgoing residents.

"Please bring up that year, 1994, I believe." Detective Murphy took out a notepad and waited for him. He found the year they asked for and opened it.

"We had 18 deaths in 1994," Larry said and looked up to see Detective Murphy scribbling in her notebook.

"What about the year before?" Detective Murphy asked.

Larry opened the file for 1993. "Nine." This was happening, really happening. He really should have called the cops, he thought for the hundredth time.

"What about 1995?" The Chihuahua said, excitement creeping into his voice. Larry noticed his right hand shake a bit as he clicked on the mouse and worried about his own heart.

"Eight," Larry whispered.

"And you didn't find this strange?" the Chihuahua barked at him. Detective Larson was his name, Larry finally remembered and looked the detective square in the eye. He imagined him frothing at the mouth.

"I did...I didn't. I mean, the residents complained about Nurse Lou and when she left..."

"Everything went back to normal?" Detective Murphy prompted, and he nodded. They stood up, and Detective Larson made it a point to get into his personal space.

"The doctor's phone number please," Detective Larson said. Larry pulled away from the man and found Dr. Riley's number. He handed them the card and didn't breathe until they had left his office. He'd made it to the other end and survived, he thought, and the weight that he'd been harboring all these years miraculously lifted.

Lou Fairbanks sat across from Diane and glared at the desk's vast lacquered surface. She hated that desk. It made Diane's entire office feel old and dated. The light didn't want to touch this space, she thought. Her claustrophobia intensified. Diane's puckered face showed Lou this conversation wouldn't be pleasant.

Diane cleared her throat. "I don't know how to even say this," Diane began without meeting her eyes. Lou's stomach went into free fall. This was it.

"I've gotten many complaints from the residents," Diane said.

"What kind of complaints?" Lou asked. She wouldn't let her off easy.

"We've loved having you here but..." Diane voice trailed off.

"But?" Lou prompted, a frozen smile on her face. She just had to keep smiling.

"As you know, everyone is terrified with these most recent," Diane said and paused, "deaths."

"Do the police have any suspects?" Lou asked, fearful of the answer but unable to stop herself from asking.

"They haven't mentioned anyone to me," Diane said.

Lou didn't believe a word of it. "What does any of this have to do with me?" Lou asked.

"You know why."

"I don't. I really have no idea," Lou said and took a deep breath. "Diane, are you sitting across from me and accusing me of murdering my patients?"

"Of course not, but the problem is that everyone is afraid of you," Diane said and shuffled through some papers in front of her, avoiding her eyes.

"Why me specifically though? Because Barney Leonard accused me of things I haven't done? Is that why?" Lou kept her voice measured.

"That's part of it," Diane conceded.

"So what are you going to do about that? That's slander. He has no proof. I've done nothing wrong and I've taken excellent care of these people, I might add," Lou said. Diane stopped playing around with the papers and stood up.

"The residents think you killed their friends, Lou," Diane blurted out.

"But I didn't. I haven't killed anyone. The cops haven't arrested me. What happened to innocent until proven guilty? Do I need to call a lawyer?" Lou raised herself from her seat, and the two women stood head to head, the desk between them.

"I don't see how you can do your job as a nurse if no one wants to come near you," Diane said.

"Have you told your supervisor about any of this yet?" Lou asked.

"I need to get a better handle on the situation before I let them know anything," Diane said and turned away from her.

"You're not sure either then. Give me the time, Diane. I will see what patients will see me, and I'll prove this was all his doing and clear my name. I deserve that at least," Lou pleaded and held out her hand. Diane stared at it for a moment and finally shook it, albeit with a certain amount of reluctance.

At least, she hadn't fired her on the spot, Lou thought, and left before Diane could change her mind.

Lou checked both ends of the hallway to make sure she was alone before pulling out a credit card from her pocket and sticking it into Barney Leonard's door frame. She pushed it up to where she thought the lock might start and got it stuck.

She wiggled it around some more, but the card wouldn't budge. She should have known the man would be paranoid enough to have deadbolts installed on his door and kicked the door in frustration. It was a stupid idea, she admitted to herself, but she had to start somewhere. The elevator dinged open some distance away and Lou walked down the hallway to the stairs. The last thing she needed was anyone seeing her at Barney's door.

19

Los Angeles, California USA
July 21, 1948

Simon Schreiber listened to the gleeful radioman reporting on a federal grand jury indicting eleven leaders of the Communist Party for conspiracy to overthrow the U.S Government. As this was Los Angeles radio and the center of the film industry, the radioman switched to lambasting the courts for not giving the "Hollywood Ten," mostly screenwriters, tougher sentences. Simon switched it off before his father heard it. He didn't need another rant coming from him about the evil of Communism and how it would destroy the world.

Herr Schreiber hated the Communists even more than he hated the Americans. If it hadn't been for his old buddy pulling him into his aeronautical research in 1944, Simon was sure he'd be in Nuremburg standing trial. Instead, Simon and his parents had been spirited away from Munich in the middle of the night by the State Department as part of a secret program called Operation Paperclip. The Americans would stop at nothing to get the Nazi technology. Even if it had been originally tested on human subjects.

The Communists were coming. All hands on deck, he said in explanation on switching sides. Simon scowled. Herr Schreiber wouldn't get away with it, not if Simon had anything to do with it.

He'd imagined killing the man in numerous ways the moment Frau died, but he hadn't done it yet. Patience was a virtue in all things, and he'd strike when the old man least expected it.

Oddly, the opportunity presented itself later that evening. The old man got sauced good and proper after hearing the news about the Communists, sweat dripping down his face in the summer heat. Simon sat across from him in their tiny living room and watched him snore.

"Papa, it's so hot. Let me run you a cooling bath to help you sleep," Simon said and watched Herr Schreiber stir awake.

"Thank you, Simon. Sie sind ein guter Sohn." Simon got up, smiling.

"I work hard to be a good son, Papa," Simon said.

Tonight would be the night, he decided.

He ran Herr Schrieber a lukewarm bath and watched as the tub filled with water, and shivered. It had been four years. He'd been clever and made all of them think he'd forgotten. But he hadn't. Not for a second. He dipped his hand into the water. It was perfect. He went to get the man he had to call Father in order to stay alive.

"Papa, the bath is ready," he said and shook the man awake. Herr Schreiber got to his feet with a grunt.

"Help me," he said and Simon took him under the arm. The man leaned against him, and they went to the bathroom. Simon helped him take his shirt off and held him up as he let his pants fall. Simon picked up the clothes and left him in the bathroom for some privacy. He threw the clothes into the hallway and waited to hear the splash. The old man groaned in pleasure, and Simon heard the water slosh up and above the tub.

It was time. Szymon Michalowski's time. Payback for the death of his mother. Payback for everything. He would start with him. He entered the bathroom.

"Simon. What are you doing..." The old man started to get out of the tub but Simon came on too quick. He was still only twelve but tall and strong enough. It helped that the bathtub was slippery. The old man hit his head on the way back down into the tub.

He held the old man under the water with all his might. The man thrashed around trying to get up, to get air and escape him. Simon held on tight, his entire body quivering with the effort. He made sure to stare right into the man's eyes.

The old man was no match against Simon's young body and the thrashing ended. The eyes stopped blinking and Simon watched death come to the man. He saw the eyes lose the light.

Die. Simon Schreiber.

Szymon Michalowski had never felt such great pleasure in his entire life.

20
Theories
Day 6

Lou Fairbanks stood behind Dads in their small bathroom and handed him a toothbrush set up with toothpaste.

"Brush, Dads," she said and pointed at the toothbrush. He stuck it in his mouth and went to work on his teeth as she watched his progress.

"Spit," she demanded after a minute and he complied. She washed his face with a washcloth and watched him stare back at her through the mirror. He did it every night and although his eyes stayed blank, it still unnerved her. She needed to make sure he was taking all of his pills, she thought, as she dropped the washcloth into the sink and pushed him to the door.

"We're done, Dads," she said following behind him. He shuffled out to his bed. "Do you want the warm jams or..." she said as she pulled out a well-worn pair of blue pajamas out of the drawer. "It's cold out." She frowned when she saw he'd not made a move to undress.

"Dads, it's bedtime," she reminded him and pointed at his sweatshirt. He lifted his arms up without a word, and she tugged it over his head. "Are you going to make me undress you again?" she asked and sighed. His eyes focused back on her.

"I can do it myself," he said and turned his back to her. Lou stepped into their kitchenette to prepare their nightly tea. What was going to be her next move? If she couldn't get into Barney's room, how else could she prove he was behind all of this?

The ghost. Her hand froze on the teakettle as her mind raced over all that had happened with the ghost. She had encountered something in the elevator but that could have been her anxiety. She never heard the sobbing or heard "Help Me" in the elevator or anywhere else other than this room. But the other residents heard it as well. Unless, they lied.

Where did the ghost sound the loudest? The last time she'd heard it, she was in bed. Lou closed her eyes and went back to that night. The sounds came from above her, hadn't they?

She dragged the chair over to the wall nearest her bed and clambered on top of it. Standing on tiptoe, she ran her fingers over the wall mullions. If no ghost existed, then the sound needed to come from somewhere. There had to be a speaker somewhere. Lou found no sound devices. She hopped off the chair and watched Dads get into bed.

"I'll tuck you in, Dads," she said and pulled the covers up to his chin. "Are you going to be fine with the lights on for a bit?" she asked. He shrugged and flipped onto his side. She went back into the middle of the room and closed her eyes.

Hadn't the sound swirl all around her? She called back the memory of that night and concentrated harder. The sobbing swirled all around her and then it stopped. Then water turned on. The sound of water ran along the floor.

Her eyes flew open, and she dropped down to her knees. Peering along the wooden floor, she found no crevices or cracks that even a tiny speaker could be jammed into.

She caught sight of the old, iron grate on the wall underneath her bed. Lou shoved the bed aside and kneeled back down, attempting to pull the grate off with her bare hands. The thing didn't budge. She dragged her desk lamp closer to get more light and saw that four screws held the grate to the wall. She needed a screwdriver.

Her kneecaps screamed in pain as she rose up and hobbled to her miscellaneous drawer. She rummaged through it until she found the screwdriver and held it up in triumph. Dads sat up in bed with a confused look on his face.

"What are you doing?" he asked softly.

"The sobbing and water came from somewhere. If there's no ghost, which I now don't believe there ever was, then there must be a speaker somewhere in here," she said over her shoulder as she dropped back down to the ground. Taking back control of the situation was the best thing Lou had done. She should have done it sooner, she thought as she grew emboldened.

A drip of sweat ran down her forehead as she struggled with the third screw. The first two had been brand-new, but this one was bald. She leveraged her entire body to get the screw to turn and sighed as it finally gave. The last one gave her no problems, and she pulled the grate off the wall.

The hole was thick with darkness. She did not want to stick her hand inside that wall, especially with all the recent talk of rats. Instead, Lou pointed her desk lamp into the recess instead and saw it.

"Son of a b," she said under her breath as she pulled out the small speaker hanging from a small wire. She tugged on the wire, but something above held it in place. Lou sat back on her heels. The apartment above was empty. Irene's apartment, Barney had told her. The supposedly haunted one. That's where the equipment must be.

"They tricked me, Dads. The ghost was never real," she said to him. "If none of it was real though, then who attacked you?" she asked, her eyes narrowing.

Barney Leonard stepped out of the elevator and watched Lou enter the fire stairs. He snuck up to her door and knocked. When no one answered, he opened the door. Dads sat on the bed alone, staring at his carved up arm.

"Dads—Hey Dads, can I talk to you?" Barney asked as he stepped inside. He crossed the small room and sat down next to him. Dads didn't utter a word.

"You've met me once. My name's Barney Leonard," he continued and held out his hand.

Dads didn't make a move to take it. Instead, his eyes lost focus and he turned to the window.

"We need your help. Is there anything—" Barney said and stopped when he heard a thump from upstairs. She was up in the empty apartment. Dads tugged on his shirt, and stuck his arm out, pointing to the carved words.

"Gillian," Dads mumbled.

"Gillian? Who's Gillian?" Barney said, pointing to a picture of him and Lou. "Is that Gillian? Did Lou do this to you?" Dads gestured to the ceiling. Dad's eyes bore into his with an intensity that took Barney aback.

"Help me," Dads said without breaking eye contact.

"I'll help you if you help us. You know there's no ghost?" Barney asked, and Dads nodded. Dads' eyes wandered down to his hands, and when he met Barney's eyes again, the intensity was gone.

"I'll be back, Dads, and with a more formal plan," Barney said. Dads sat blank and silent. Barney heard another thump overhead. Lou had found the speakers.

Lou Fairbanks crossed Irene's former apartment and squatted in front of the grate, screwdriver out. All the screws were brand-new. This time, she had no problems getting the grate off the wall. The grate fell to the ground with a thump, and she shined her flashlight into the opening.

"A-ha! Gotcha," she said. Barney duct-taped the recorder to the inside of the wall with a wire hanging down into the darkness.

She yanked the tape off and pulled the recorder out, examining the hi-tech piece of equipment. Barney made a mistake in using such high quality gear, she thought. The equipment pointed directly to him. Lou pressed play and the familiar weeping started up. She clicked the off button and smiled. Now, to debunk the incident with the window. When she figured out how Barney accomplished that trick, she'd bring her findings to Diane and show the rest of them what a fraud Barney was.

She had to give it to him though, the hand print on the outside of the window was a masterful stroke. Lou studied the windowsill closely and found holes drilled into the painted wood and long scrapes running along its entire length. The dust on the floor directly below the window had been disturbed with shoe prints from some sort of sneaker. She checked the bottom of her Dansko clogs and knew the footprints weren't hers.

An idea of how this could be achieved popped into her head that was almost crazy enough to be possible. One of her former patients, Roxane Newbury, had been an avid rock climber and had talked her ear off about her passion. One of Roxane's proudest accomplishments had been rappelling down the side of a skyscraper for a benefit. If someone here had a similar talent, it would be much easier to rappel down this building than a skyscraper. It was the only idea she could come up with on how that handprint got on her window. The drill holes on the windowsill were proof that Barney's accomplice, or Barney himself, used those rope pulleys to scale down the wall just like Roxane told her she had done.

What she didn't understand is why Barney had started this whole charade in the first place? She hadn't made the same mistakes as in those other places, she thought, and she had given them no reason to blame her for what was happening here at Sunshine, no reason at all.

She left Irene's apartment with only one thought running through her mind: Who had attacked Dads?

Lou pushed the door to the tenth floor open, her mind still churning when she saw Barney Leonard leaving her apartment.

"What are you doing?" she demanded, making him jump as he closed the door behind him. Lou stormed at him, her anger boiling over at his audacity, and he threw up his hands in protection while smiling menacingly.

"Go ahead, killer. Do it and see how fast you're out of here," he hissed. "That's what we all want anyway."

Lou froze in mid-strike, her mouth opening and closing. Barney was right. Lou snapped her mouth shut. He would not win. Her arms dropped to her side and she gave him some distance. Barney had all but admitted to orchestrating the harassment against her and now she knew why. Barney wanted to force her out, and she'd be damned if she would allow them to succeed.

"What business do you have in my apartment," she demanded, still keeping her distance. She wouldn't let him provoke her.

"I was visiting Dads, if you must know, which is

no business of yours. He's a grown man and can have his own visitors," he growled.

"He has severe dementia and is heavily medicated. Dads didn't invite you in for a visit. What did you do inside? Put in more fake ghost recordings?" she shot back.

"He was lucid enough when I saw him in the hall," He countered. Lou paled at that.

"When? When did you see him?"

"About twenty minutes ago. I helped him back into the room," Barney lied. Lou stared at him mouth agape. That couldn't be possible.

"I don't believe you," she whispered.

"Believe what you want," he said with a shrug.

"I found your recorder," she said, wanting to hit back at him in any way she could. Barney pressed into her personal space.

"You're seriously cracked, Lou. Deranged even. How you've been able to do your job is beyond me. Now, you're adding paranoia to your long list of issues?" He shook his head in amazement. "Why Diane hasn't fired you yet none of us know, but she will. You mark my words, she will!"

"I have proof it was you. Did you do that to Dads as well or did you get one of your cronies to do it?" Her spittle sprayed his face, but he made no move to wipe it off. He narrowed his eyes at her and leaned in closer.

"I know what you are," he hissed at her. She locked her eyes on his.

"And what am I, exactly?" she whispered, brimming with violence. She wanted to throttle the man.

"A murderer," Barney bit back. "You killed Babs. You killed them all and I'm going to prove it." She stepped back, coming back to her senses.

"How? I take care of all my patients. Not kill them."

"You're not getting away with it this time," he said and pushed past her, stomping to the elevators.

"YOU will be the one that has to leave here after Diane sees what I have on you," she shouted at his receding back. He kept walking.

Her anger evaporated, the moment he was gone. She gasped for breath. The vertigo hit her, then a wave of nausea. The blackness crept into the edge of her vision. I'm passing out, she thought, and stumbled inside the apartment. Relieved to see Dads fast asleep on his bed, she aimed for her own bed and collapsed.

Sara Caine argued about her decision to see Lou Fairbanks after all, the entire way up. When they arrived to the tenth floor, her confidence wavered. "Are you ready for this?" Johan asked, tired of the argument. They stood in front of Lou Fairbanks door.

"We might not get the chance again," she reminded him.

"Let's get this over with," Johan said.

"You will catch me if something weird happens again?" she asked.

"Sara," he warned.

"Joking, but I hope you're wrong about this empath business," Sara added.

"Why?" Johan said and frowned.

"You know my feelings about these gifts." Johan didn't respond to that.

"What if she kills us after I touch her?" Sara joked. "You have thought of that possibility, haven't you?"

"I don't think that's going to happen, Sara," Johan said as she knocked on the door.

"Here goes nothing," she said. Nurse Louise opened the door within seconds, wearing pajamas with yellow duckies on them. She looked as if a Mack truck had hit her. She had purple circles under her eyes, and Sara couldn't remember seeing anyone look as pale as she did. They stood silent for a moment, no one sure of what to say, when Sara stuck her hand out in greeting.

"I don't know whether you remember me, but I was the psychic at the sèance we had several days ago," Sara began and Lou Fairbanks nodded, staring at her with the haunted eyes of a trapped animal.

"Of course, I know who you are. How are you feeling, Ms. Caine?" she said and took Sara's hand in her own. At first, nothing happened. But then, Sara's grip on Lou Fairbanks hand tightened and she was plunged back into the visions.

The same gruesome images replayed in Sara's mind: the laughing blond woman, the death scene on the bed, the poor woman's stomach displayed in the same grotesque manner and that horrible symbol carved into her body splitting it in two. The trident.

The vision went further this time. Someone screamed behind her and fear crashed into her, sending acid gurgling into her stomach and spewing up into her esophagus. The burning feeling was excruciating, and she bent over, retching, while white static overtook the ghastly images in front of her and then faded into a dark black silence. She heard a whimper so quiet, she had to strain to hear it. Why was it so cold, she wondered.

"Don't hurt me. Please don't hurt me," the woman pleaded between sobs.

Sara came to in Johan's arms as Lou Fairbanks slammed the door on them. She smelled the sour fumes of vomit, and her throat burned. Lou howled on the other side of the door.

"You were right, she didn't kill us," Sara whispered to him. "That's always a plus," she added. Lame attempt at a joke, she knew, but she was afraid to say what scared her out loud.

"You were only out for a minute this time. The emergence of this new talent and the power of the connection must have caused the coma."

"I don't want to be an empath," she muttered as he helped her get to her feet. "Something's not right," she mumbled as she attempted to stand on her own. She swayed with dizziness and grabbed Johan's arm.

"What about her?" she asked as they heard the sobbing coming from the other side of the door.

"You first," Johan said. "We need to get out of here first, Sara. Stay with me," he said as he wrapped his arm around her waist. They hobbled together to the elevator.

"Can psychopaths feel fear? Fear infused that memory," she whispered as they entered the elevator bank. She was more unsure of what Louise Fairbanks was than ever.

"You know her greatest secret. That would cause anyone plenty of fear," Johan said and hit the down button.

"What's her secret then, Johan," Sara said. Her acute exhaustion grew. She pulled away to test her strength. No dizziness but she was exhausted. The elevator dinged open before Johan could respond.

21

Secrets

FEBRUARY 22, 2005 - DAY 7

Barney Leonard woke early the next morning and rushed through his morning ritual. After his run in with Lou, he'd snuck into Diane's office and peeked at Lou's job application. Diane hired her because she had come cheap and not due to her surprisingly sparse experience. But, he'd found the next step in his plan.

Mary Ann made the perfect accomplice. She ate breakfast at the crack of dawn, and he caught her before she made any other plans for the day. He hugged her hello.

"How about a romantic getaway to Palm Springs today?" he whispered in her ear. Mary Ann beamed as Barney slid into the chair next to her.

"I've found something on her," he said, keeping his voice at a low whisper. Annoyance flashed across Mary Ann's face, and he regretted giving away his intention so soon.

"Oh, really?" she asked, her voice flat and disinterested.

"I went and saw Dads last night," he said and watched Lou walk into the cafeteria. "I'll tell you later. Can you be ready in an hour?" Mary Ann nodded.

Barney jumped back up, adrenaline pumping through him. He shot Lou a sideways glance. She, on the other hand, looked as if she hadn't slept in a week. Good, he thought. First, he'd spooked her, next he'd implicate her in these murders.

"Aren't you going to eat breakfast?" Mary Ann called after him as he grabbed a blueberry muffin and a piece of bacon from the buffet. He waved the muffin behind him as he pushed the doors open with his shoulder, his mind already spinning about what he needed to fix on the old Volvo to make the trip.

Lou Fairbanks knocked on Doreen's door with force. "Please, Doreen. I just want to see the card."

Doreen's voice sounded muffled through the door. "Leave me alone." Lou grunted and used all her willpower not to kick the door.

"I will if you give me the card," Lou said through gritted teeth.

"I don't have it." Doreen sounded closer.

"Open the door, Doreen. I won't bother you again. I want that card," Lou cajoled. The door creaked open, and a liver spotted hand appeared with a card. Lou plucked it from her and the hand slithered back inside. The door slammed shut.

"Thank you, Doreen," Lou called out and hoped the woman heard her. Doreen stayed silent. Lou's shoulders drooped.

"Dammit," she muttered. The card wasn't for Sara Caine but for Ghost Hunters INC. with an address in Burbank. Sara Caine had come with them though, and maybe she was part of their outfit.

She had no idea how Sara Caine knew who she was but if she did…Lou felt the now daily occurrence of the nausea and vertigo start and got moving before she passed out again.

Lou put on her best smile for the young woman who sat manning the front desk at the bustling reality TV office. A banner with loud graphics exclaiming Ghost Hunters INC. hung above her. "I'm here to see Fredrick. He's expecting me," Lou explained.

"Fredrick is in the dregs," the woman said without looking up.

"Dregs?" Lou asked. The woman pointed to a door to her right.

"Go through that door and down the hall. Take a right and go all the way down that hall. It's the last door on the right."

Lou pushed through the door and moved fast before the woman called her back. The hall consisted of generic, white walls with cheap, grey carpet running down its length. The glaring fluorescent lights made her claustrophobia flare up. Her vision swam and her strides quickened more.

Lou took the right and ran to the last door. The buzzing of the fluorescent lights penetrated her brain and made her want to scream. Breathing heavily, she threw the door open to a large room filled with wires and hardware. Fredrick sat in the middle of it, tinkering with a microphone setup at a small desk.

"Fredrick?" she asked, pulling herself together the best she could, and closed the door behind her.

"That's my name. Not sure what you need from me though?" he asked, recognizing her.

"Like I said on the phone, I'd like all the footage from that night."

"Why?" he asked and studied her as if she were a bug under a microscope. Tears welled up in Lou's eyes. Why did no one want to help her?

"I need those tapes to show that I didn't attack my father."

"But everyone knows you were nowhere near the room."

"Diane Lawrence needs the proof."

"I'm sorry. I can't help you. The police have all the tapes from that night," Fredrick said. Lou swiped at her tears.

"There was no ghost in my room. I found Barney Leonard's speakers and sound equipment in the wall," she pushed on.

Fredrick put his small screwdriver down and gave her his full attention. "I don't know anything about that. There ARE ghosts at the Bockerman or Sunshine or whatever it's being called these days. Maybe not whatever ghost you were expecting to find but they are there and that's why we came. I'm sorry you didn't find what you were looking for. Now, I really should get back to this," he said and gestured at the mass of wires in front of him. Lou scanned the room for similar equipment she'd found in the apartment upstairs. When she didn't recognize any, Lou worked on him to speak with her.

"Did Barney put you up to it?"

"If you mean by calling us in, then yes. The Bockerman Hotel is one of the most famous and haunted buildings in Los Angeles. That's just a fact. I don't know anything about speakers or sound equipment. When Mr. Leonard called us, I jumped at the chance to get inside. That manager of yours is a dragon lady, you know that? We've tried setting up appointments to check it out repeatedly over the years. She never once returned our calls." He screwed a panel shut. Something in his voice made her believe him.

"Sara Caine is a real medium, isn't she?" Lou asked.

"Why?"

"Her episode during the séance. That was real."

"It was real. She's the real thing." He smiled with pride.

"I want to get in touch with her. Do you think you could connect me?"

He stared at her for a moment. "Why?"

"She can tell me who hurt Dads. He's the last piece of the puzzle."

"Didn't you tell me someone has been scaring you? You found sound equipment? That's not a real ghost. How can a medium help you with that?"

"Sara Caine came to my door today and touched me. She fainted again. This time she came to immediately. She saw something. I want to know what she saw," she stated.

"I'll call her and let her know you want to speak with her," he said and pulled out his cellphone. "What's your number? Sara can give you a call if she wants to."

"323-555-3859. Please tell her it's important," she added as he programmed it into his phone.

"Great. Now, I should get back to this," he said and Lou nodded.

"Thanks for your help, Fredrick," she said and closed the door behind her.

Barney Leonard and Mary Ann made record time to Palm Springs, and Barney's plan was going off without a hitch. They sat across from Jebediah Horvath, the director of the Palm Springs Happy Horizons assisted living home. Jebediah's leathery face made him look much older than his fifty years, Barney thought, and the paunch that pressed against his shirt was a heart attack waiting to happen.

"Our home is rated the best in Palm Springs, Mrs. Leonard," Jebediah said in his best salesman voice.

"The grounds are indeed gorgeous. Oh, I do love it so, Barney!" Mary Ann exclaimed as she squeezed Barney's arm. Jebediah beamed at her.

"How did you hear about us? Always good to know where our marketing dollars are working," Jebediah explained. Barney leaned in. He'd been waiting for that exact question.

"We heard about this place from a friend, Louise Fairbanks. I believe she used to work here?" Barney said. Jebediah's smile faltered and disappeared.

"You're friends with her?" Jebediah asked and cleared his throat.

"Did you have a problem with her here? Your tone implies you did," Barney said, and watched the man redden.

"You aren't here looking for a place, are you?" Jebediah asked. Barney shook his head.

"Reporters, then?" Jebediah demanded as he gestured to the door. "I don't know who put you up to this, but I want you both to leave. NOW." He was almost shouting. Barney's smile wavered as Mary Ann got up.

"Let's go, Barney," she said and tugged at his sleeve. Jebediah came up behind them and hustled them to the door. Jebediah put his hand on Mary Ann's back and she stiffened at his touch.

"Please don't shove me, Mr. Horvath," she hissed.

This woman had balls, Barney thought appreciatively. Jebediah stepped back and put his arms up in defensive.

"Sorry, I meant nothing by it," he muttered as they crossed the threshold. "Don't come back. I'll call the police if you trespass on these grounds again," he said and slammed the door on them.

"Now what?" Mary Ann asked as Barney guided her to the entrance.

"We wait, my dear," he said as they stepped out into the blinding light of the desert afternoon. They settled back into the small red Volvo.

"Glad I packed us a lunch," Mary Ann said wryly as she slid into the passenger seat.

"I don't think we'll have to wait too long," Barney said and pushed the driver's seat into a reclined position.

Barney and Mary Ann had just finished up their lunch when they saw a well-dressed couple walk out the front door of the home and head down the street.

"They seem like a nice couple," Mary Ann said as Barney started up the car.

"I think they'll do just fine," he said and followed them down Main Street. The couple stopped in front of the El Compadre restaurant, and Barney pulled into a parking spot.

"Feel like some Mexican?" Barney said.

"I'm always up for Mexican."

Barney approached the couple sitting on the veranda of the restaurant enjoying the sunshine. Mary Ann pushed in front of him, her smile wide.

"Hi, sorry to disturb you but we saw you coming out of Happy Horizons. We were checking it out as a potential place to move to and wanted to talk to some residents," Mary Ann said as a dark haired waitress placed margaritas in front of the couple.

"And here you are," Barney finished.

"My name's Marvin and this here is Judy," Marvin said and motioned at his wife. "Join us and have a drink." Barney pulled out the chair next to Marvin and Mary Ann sat down.

"Name's Barney. This here's Mary Ann," Barney said and gestured at the drinks to the waitress. "We'll have what they're having."

Several rounds later, Barney, nursing his own drink, noticed the couple was lubricated enough to talk. He nodded to Mary Ann and raised his round goblet of glorious, golden liquid, several limes floating on top, in front of him. "I wanna propose a toast. To new friends," he said. Marvin and Judy both raised their glasses, and Mary Ann clinked with Judy.

"To new friends!" Their voices rang out.

"How did you hear about Happy Horizons?" Marvin asked as he eyed Barney over his drink.

"A friend spoke very highly of it. She raved and raved, and we decided we'd have to check it out."

"What's your friend's name? We might know her. We've lived there for what..." He glanced at Judy. "Has it been five years?"

"Amazing how time goes by at this age," Judy said, nodding. She took a rather large gulp of margarita and coughed hard. Her face turned red as Marvin clapped her hard on the back.

"Louise Fairbanks," Mary Ann said as Barney watched their reactions. It would have been hard not to notice their shared grimace. Silence fell over the table.

"So you know her?" Barney said.

"Are you really friends with her?" Judy whispered to Mary Ann. Mary Ann looked to Barney for direction, and he gave her a small nod.

"Not even a little bit," she continued. "We weren't sure if you'd know her or were friends with her and we wanted to be careful, in case," Mary Ann explained.

"Thank God she left. I felt so bad for Dads though," Marvin said. Judy leaned away from her husband in astonishment.

"I didn't know that you thought that way about Dads. The man was a downright creep when he was lucid," she said.

"How could you say that about that nice man?" Marvin asked, putting down his drink. He looked shocked at his wife's sentiment.

"You knew I tried to get him taken away from her," Marvin said.

"Well yes, because people were dying and she was most likely responsible. Doesn't mean the man wasn't a creep," Judy countered.

Barney leaned in. "Did people start dying out of the blue?" he asked.

Marvin nodded. "Lots of healthy folks getting felled by heart attacks."

"Healthy folks," Judy repeated for emphasis.

"How did you get rid of her?" Mary Ann took another sip.

"Initially, we revolted," Judy said, "but that didn't work."

"So we made life miserable for her," Marvin said. "Enough for her not to be able to do her job."

"Thank God she left," Judy said to Mary Ann.

"Here's the best part though. Ole Jebediah gave her a good recommend to cover his ass. It was a full on cover-up in my opinion," Marvin said. "He was such a chicken shit. Still is."

"At first, she was so very nice," Judy continued, "but something was off with the BOTH of them."

"How do you know her?" Marvin asked. Barney took Mary Ann's hand in his.

"She's killing us off one by one, and no one believes us. We also tried to get rid of her, but it hasn't stuck," Barney said. Judy and Marvin exchanged a knowing look.

"We thought she was drugging him. He didn't have the typical symptoms for dementia, and

I should know because I've been around many dementia patients. And he was lucid. Too lucid sometimes," Marvin said.

"We figured it was a perfect cover. She lived with us because of Dads and had access to us at night. We were easy pickins," Judy added.

"I can't believe you thought Dads was creepy," Marvin cut in.

"I don't know. Maybe it was my imagination or that whole lucid versus dementia thing. I was just so happy when they left."

"Sorry to hear ya'll are plagued by her now," Marvin said.

"Not for long. We're going to put a stop to her, aren't we, Mary Ann?" Barney said. Mary Ann nodded in agreement, all gaiety gone.

Detective Eddie Larson watched Louise Fairbanks sweat in the smallest interrogation room he could find. He'd been cursing Murphy with saddling him with the rest of the paperwork when Louise Fairbanks all but delivered herself to him. He now had a chance to break the nurse, her cockamamie ghost stories notwithstanding.

"I've heard enough," he said and hit stop on the recorder she brought in. Sobbing on a tape was not what this interview would be about.

"It has to be Barney Leonard. He accused me of killing my patients. Barney's running a con to force Diane Lawrence to kick me out of my position and my home. He's always talking about ghosts," Lou said.

"Why would he accuse you of murder?" He kept his tone casual. She laughed and threw her hands up.

"As if I know. The man is dangerous. Have you checked him out as a suspect? And I'm not so sure that all these supposed deaths are really suspicious. What if they died of fright? My patients are not in the best of health and if he could fake haunt me, what if he did the same with Barbara? She could have died of the heart attack caused by stress and fright."

"Do people die of fright? That sounds like something out of a horror movie," he said and studied her face. "An old woman dies of a heart attack. No one is going to check for anything other than natural causes, are they?" he asked. "And you know that, don't you, Nurse Louise? They're close to death anyway. Why not give them release?" He flipped the Barbara Monroe file open.

After Murphy told him what Coroner Grimley disclosed about Angels of Death, he'd researched the phenomena himself. Medical practitioners killing their patients to help them lessen their pain was some jacked up shit. Some of the caught killers actually thought they had done nothing wrong. Playing God was powerful, he figured.

Time in the interrogation room expanded then contracted, flowed, and ebbed. Lou Fairbanks struggled to catch her breath. She squirmed in her seat.

"I didn't kill them, if that's what you're implying. I'm not under arrest, am I? You can't keep me here." Lou Fairbanks stood up, ready to go.

"I can put you under a twenty-four-hour hold. Why don't you just tell me the truth?"

Time was an interrogator's best friend, Larson thought. Patience was not his strongest quality, but he had a gift for how long to hold out until a perp talked. This one wasn't ready to crack yet, even though facial twitches were already appearing underneath her right eye and in her hairline.

It was just a matter of time. She was his collar and not Murphy's. Larson liked the sound of that.

Detective Eva Murphy gave the hard-assed receptionist her warmest smile and repeated the question. "Is Dr. Riley in today?" she asked, tapping her fingers on the polished wood of the barrier. Mrs. Doubleday eyed her fingers with annoyance. "Sorry, nervous habit," Murphy said and put her hand back in her pocket. "This is official police business. He'll want to see me."

"Your badge?" Mrs. Doubleday asked. Murphy kept her smile pasted on her face as she pulled out her badge and stuck it in the old bat's face. As she guessed, the woman wrote down her badge number. "This says you're LAPD. Not really your jurisdiction, is it?" Mrs. Doubleday said, raising her painted-on eyebrow at her. Great, another one who watched cop shows.

"Not entirely. However, I am investigating murders at assisted living facilities. I spoke with Mr. Jenkins, the manager of Sunny Days. The place on Route 12. Anyway, Mr Jenkins mentioned that Dr. Riley found something on one of the deaths some years back," Murphy said.

"Well, why didn't you say so? I thought you were here on that other thing." Her tone warmed up considerably.

"What other thing?" Murphy asked.

"Never you mind," Mrs. Doubleday said as she picked up the phone. "Doctor, there's a detective here to see you about the Sunny Days assisted living murders," she said and listened for a second. "I'll send her back," she said and rattled the phone back into its cradle. "It's the first door on the right," she said, motioning behind her.

"Thank you, Mrs. Doubleday. Much appreciated," Murphy said, and headed down the bright and cheerful hallway. A small, round man with snow white hair and round, tortoise shell spectacles stepped out into the hall, his hand outstretched. He reminded Murphy of Boss Hog, the villain from the Dukes of Hazzard, an old TV series from the 1980s.

He wore a serious expression on his face, his grasp was firm. "Thank you for taking the time to meet with me, Dr. Riley," Murphy said and smiled. "I'm Detective Murphy with the LAPD," she continued. He motioned for her to take a seat across from him.

"LAPD doesn't have jurisdiction up here, does it?" he asked and slid into a leather chair behind a massive, mahogany desk. Unlike the shabby exterior office, the doctor's inner office spoke of wealth.

"No, we don't. I'm investigating a series of murders at the Sunshine House down in Los Angeles, and we've found a possible connection to deaths up here," She explained. He was eager to talk.

"I told that man there was something wrong with Maybel's death. This is a small town so I double as coroner," he explained and paused. "Lots of deaths came out of that home but I could never find anything suspicious. I mean, sure, they had puncture marks in their arms but every single one of the victims had tests done at their doctor's offices within days of their deaths. Nothing conclusive, you understand. I did mark Maybel's a suspicious death because of that mark."

"What mark?" Murphy asked. Dr. Riley opened up a file and slid the picture over to her.

"I would have almost missed it. I had been so flummoxed by the number of deaths, I was on a mission to find something. Anything to show the deaths were suspicious," he said and pointed to a place on the photo.

A woman's hairline filled up most of the image. His finger obscured an odd looking mark, showing through the hairs. He pushed the photo over to her. She studied a vertical line with three diagonals coming out the top of it, almost like a child's crude drawing of a trident.

"What is it?" Murphy asked.

"An ink drawing. Most likely black ink from a ballpoint pen. I caught it before I washed her. Otherwise, I would have washed it off. When I brought it up to the police, they decided the old lady did it herself. I had no other proof the death was unnatural. She died of a heart attack, same as the others."

"Did any of the other bodies have this mark on them?" Murphy asked.

"I didn't check the others this closely. All of them were buried or cremated," he said, and bit his lip. "I think the killer drew that on her."

"I agree," Murphy said and stared hard at the photo. A deep memory twisted in her brain. A lost and forgotten fragment from some past case. "Can I take this photo with me?" she asked.

"You think it's the same guy?" Dr. Riley fished.

"Or woman. An Angel of Death," Murphy said.

"Have you found that mark on the other victims?" Dr. Riley asked.

"Not that I've seen in the files. But, no one was treating them as homicides at the beginning either," she said and stopped. Where had she seen that symbol? It seemed so familiar. "Thank you so much for your help, Dr. Riley," she said and stood up, placing the photo in her bag. "One more thing. How many deaths would you have labeled suspicious from that time?"

"22," he said without any hesitation.

"That's a lot. Are you sure?" Murphy asked, surprised.

"I go over those files every year. They keep me up at night. I should have found out what was happening sooner," Dr. Riley admitted, his lips set in a firm lane.

"Thank you," she said.

22

Rune
Day 7

Sara Caine knocked on Ritchie's door holding a bottle of Templeton Rye Whiskey in one hand and the drawing of a symbol in the other. Ritchie opened the door and smiled when he saw it was her.

"Is our case heating up?" he asked, motioning her inside.

"You could say that again," Sara said blinking against the darkness inside. She handed him the drawing of the tattoo from her visions. "Have you ever seen this before?"

"Looks like a rune."

"That was fast. You sure?"

Ritchie grinned back. "Let's scan it in and run it. My baby will find out what it is," Ritchie said. He opened up the scanner and put the drawing against the glass. Several keystrokes and a scan later, the image uploaded and the computer started to churn.

"I wrote a program that does a scan and recognition protocol, almost like facial or fingerprint matching. It hits all the main websites like Wikipedia, Google, and image banks to find the source," Ritchie explained as the Internet windows popped open with the results.

"You were right. It's a rune," Sara said, reading over his shoulder. "Known as the Algiz rune, it translates into the word for Elk. That's weird. Elk? Why would that be on a dead body?"

Ritchie scrolled down one of the pages. "The rune got pulled into Nazi occultism and was called the "life rune". Whoa, they used to put it on headstones for the birth date. That's wild!" Ritchie exclaimed.

"So what does that mean when scrawled on the belly of a dead woman," Sara said as another window popped up.

"Holy shit," Ritchie said and stared at the gruesome images on the computer screen.

"That's what I see when I close my eyes," Sara whispered unable to take her eyes off the screen.

"Is that her?" Ritchie asked. "Or her?" he asked a moment later as more images of victims surfaced.

"You're scanning police archives?"

"No. Just anything leaked online to journalists, online bloggers, those kinds of people," he said and clicked through the windows. "I remember reading about this case. It was massive. He was kind of like the Zodiac and never caught. Most people thought the killer died. The media called him The Jerry Killer." He stopped at a declassified FBI file. "The police connected him to over fifty murder cases all up and down the West Coast. Both men and women. You've heard of the Jerry Killer, haven't you?"

"Of course. Never understood why they called the murderer the Jerry Killer though," Sara said as Ritchie scanned more of the files.

"Ah, here it is. Guess it started in the seventies. Former German soldiers from World War II turned up dead with this tattoo on them. The allied forces, including the Americans and the British called the German soldiers Jerrys during the war. The murders span over forty years. The killer moved to women in the eighties."

Sara left Ritchie at the computers and sank into the couch. Nurse Lou Fairbanks couldn't be the Jerry killer. She was too young.

"Do the files say how he killed the victim's? His MO?" she asked and heard Ritchie clicking.

"Damn, the men were castrated and the women had hysterectomies post mortem. It says here a chemical combo was found in each victim's blood stream and, to top it off, some of them were shot in the head, execution style. The FBI thought some neo-Nazi group was involved because of the symbol found on each one of the bodies." Ritchie swiveled his chair to look at her. "Very gruesome."

"That's a strange theory. Why would they kill their own? I mean, the neo-Nazis."

"What do you mean?" Ritchie asked.

"Former German soldiers? All the women are blond, Germanic like."

"Is Lou Fairbanks blond?" Ritchie asked.

"No, she's not."

"She's too young, isn't she?" Ritchie asked.

"She appears to be in her late fifties. She'd have had to start killing at fifteen. Who was the first victim of the Jerry killer?"

"A Maxim Bauch. He was in his sixties. Burly looking guy," Ritchie said. Sara pushed into the couch. The detectives needed to know about the symbol, but how would she explain to them how she'd discovered the rune. Telling them it was in a vision wouldn't cut it.

Detective Murphy might listen though. She seemed more receptive than her partner.

She dialed Johan, hoping he'd already made contact with his detective friend. When he didn't answer, she left a voicemail.

"Johan, call me. I've found something and wanted to know whether you spoke with..." The electronic voice cut her off, asked if she was happy with her message, beeped and hung up.

"I have to go to the police," she said.

"If you break their case, you'll get more legitimacy," Ritchie said.

"I guess, but it will probably get me killed first. I'm going to see the nice detective to hand this off to her," Sara said, her mind made up. "You, as always, are amazing." Ritchie smiled and turned back to the computer.

"I'm going to do more research on this. Maybe I can find something that will connect your Louise Fairbanks to the Jerry Killer," he trailed off, his attention back on the files.

Nurse Lou Fairbanks opened the door to her apartment and gasped, her worst nightmare come true.

Dads left the room.

She ran into the bathroom, but he wasn't there either. With the amount of painkillers she'd given him, he shouldn't be able to walk down the hall. The only way he left the room was if he didn't take the pills.

Lou rushed over to a drawer filled with syringes. Only a sedative would subdue him. She'd been chickenshit about killing him, she thought. Today was the day.

Using a small mortar and pestle, she ground ten pills to a fine powder and added water to create a colorless solution. The needle of a syringe sucked up the liquid. The sedative was ready and a quick stab would do the trick.

With the filled syringe hidden in her pocket, Lou left the apartment. Dads could be anywhere in the building. Security wouldn't let him out the front door so he was somewhere in here. Lou decided to start on the topmost floor and sweep down. She would miss him if he rode up the elevator but that was the chance she had to take.

She ran down the corridor and climbed the stairs two at a time up to the eleventh floor.

Lou fought back tears as she walked the length of the corridor and peered down the old servant's staircase. He had to be here somewhere.

The entire eleventh floor was empty. Lou used the servant's staircase to get down to the tenth floor. Pacing up and down that hallway, she listened at the doors in case someone was entertaining him. When Lou found no sign of him, she headed down to the ninth floor.

This wasn't working, she thought. She needed a better plan. Another thought stopped her progress. What if he was with Barney? The man had gone and talked to Dads. He wanted Dads to turn against her. She laughed at the very thought. Let him try. He had no idea who he was dealing with. She wiped away her tears. Barney was a good place to check.

Barney was on the eighth floor. The old servant's stairs were the closest. She opened the door and stepped onto the gloomy landing. The light flickered.

"There are no ghosts," Lou said into the dark. She proceeded down the first several steps, her heart beating frantically.

"Stop it," she said, her fingers clutching the syringe.

Someone shuffled closer to her, coming from the darkness. Lou rushed down the stairs to get to the next landing.

Dads, his eyes blazing, stood on the small landing.

"Hello, Gillian. I've been looking for you," he said with a smile that stopped her cold.

23

San Francisco, California USA
September 13, 1990

Simon Michaels whistled an old tune as he washed the blood off his hands. He'd been worried that he wouldn't be able to overcome her, but it hadn't been an issue after all.

It felt good to be back.

He'd been lucky with good health, but it was time to change his strategy. There'd been few mistakes in over fifty years, but Simon knew he was weakening. He walked out of the bathroom and saw a brunette woman standing in the doorway of the bedroom, her back to him. Her shoulders heaved up and down. She was about to scream and would alert the neighbors.

He could use her. Some breakdown techniques would be necessary but that wouldn't be a problem for a man like him. Simon had learned from the best. He rushed her without making a sound.

She never saw him coming. Simon wrapped his left arm around her neck in a well-practiced sleeper hold. The crook of his left arm cradled her Adam's apple as his right arm pressed her head forward. She dropped in seconds.

Simon appraised his work one last time. The blond woman's mangled body lay spread eagle on the bed, his sign carved into her belly. The blood dripped onto the white shag carpet.

The scene was perfect.

Simon stared down at the woman at his feet.

She was a tiny thing, he thought as he pulled her body toward him. They'd make a great family.

24

Trust

FEBRUARY 23, 2005 - DAY 8

Sara Caine sat on the hard, plastic chair in the waiting area of the Hollywood Division precinct and waited. And then waited some more. She wished that Johan was here with her. She'd tried his cell several times, but he hadn't picked up. That meant one thing. He had gone after Luther. He couldn't resist for long, not after all the years he'd searched for him.

Sara checked the time. It'd been an hour since she had arrived. How long should she wait? The decision to speak with Detective Murphy was the correct one though. More people would die if the connection with the Jerry killer murders wasn't discovered.

She stood up to leave thinking she'd come back later when Detective Murphy walked through the doors. Sara tugged at her newly purchased black leather gloves, feeling conspicuous. Explaining her supposed new gift to the detective was the last thing she wanted to do.

The dead woman and the gruesome scene flashed in her mind. Sara rubbed her eyes to chase away the vision. It came to her even when Sara's eyes were open now. She faced Detective Murphy.

"I'm sorry to have kept you waiting so long," Detective Murphy said as she extended her hand to Sara.

Sara held up her gloved hands. "I'm ah— I get nervous touching people," she explained. Detective Murphy arched an eyebrow at her but thankfully stayed silent. Sara flushed. She needed a better cover story.

"We can speak in one of the interrogation rooms."

"An interrogation room?" Sara asked.

Detective Murphy placed a reassuring hand on her shoulder. "It's not like that. The rooms are wired for recording," she said. Sara followed her into a stark room consisting of a table with a tape recorder on top of it and three chairs. "Have a seat. Do you want coffee or tea?"

Sara shook her head.

"All right then." Detective Murphy motioned to the chair beside her and sat down.

"You have something to tell me?" Detective Murphy asked. Sara pulled the drawing of the rune out of her handbag.

"Have you seen this mark before? One of my colleagues found a link to the Jerry Killer. Have you heard of him?" Sara asked.

Murphy's eyes lit up, and she smiled. "I've been trying to figure out where I've seen this all day. Thank you!" Detective Murphy explained, her voice rising in excitement. "Where did you see this?"

"You won't believe me if I tell you."

"Try me," Detective Murphy said and cocked her head.

Sara hesitated. Would this woman laugh at her? People had died, she told herself, and plunged ahead.

"This sign was carved into a dead woman's body."

"Are you a witness to this murder?"

"Not the way you think. I, um, had an unsettling vision that put me in the hospital."

"Wait, I've heard about this. You're the psychic?" Detective Murphy's eyes narrowed. "Did you lead that séance with Louise Fairbanks and the others?" Detective Murphy asked. Sara nodded.

"This happened during the séance?" Detective Murphy asked and turned the tape recorder off. The skepticism was evident in her question. Sara flexed her hands in the hot gloves and took a breath. She'd come here herself. Now, she had to explain.

"No, not exactly," Sara said and held her hands up. "It's why I'm wearing the gloves these days. This whole thing snuck up on me as well."

"I don't understand. So you're not a psychic?"

"Let me try to explain. I touched someone and found myself in the middle of a murder scene. This event put me in a coma. You can call Cedar Sinai ER for confirmation on that."

"Help me understand this. You touched someone and saw this sign carved into a woman's body? Who did you touch?" Detective Murphy asked, and Sara's eyes dropped to her gloved hands. She didn't want to point the finger at someone without definite proof.

"I don't want to get this person in trouble. She isn't the killer," Sara said. The detective leaned in.

"Whose hand did you touch, Ms. Caine?"

"The vision was very confusing, and it was the first time it happened. I don't..."

"Sara, who did you touch?" Detective Murphy pressed her.

"You are going to think she did it." Sara stopped. Detective Murphy waited. The silence stretched out. "The nurse. I touched Louise Fairbanks. But, it doesn't mean she was the killer. The whole thing felt off. The view was wrong. What I mean is, it was the wrong point of view."

"So you touched her, and then you saw this symbol."

"Our hands touched, and I went somewhere... and saw a dead woman covered in so much blood. She was young and blond and had that symbol cut into her abdomen. The blood was everywhere..." Sara stopped and rubbed her eyes again.

Detective Murphy sat back in her chair. Sara kept still, waiting for the verdict. Sara wanted this woman to believe her. The two women sat staring at each other.

The detective broke the silence. "No one ever thought that a woman was the Jerry killer. Is she even the right age?" Detective Murphy asked, deep in thought. "You touched HER? Not someone else."

Sara nodded. "Is that why you didn't want to shake hands?" Detective Murphy asked.

"It's a precaution. This is new enough that I don't know what to expect. It's never happened before," Sara said.

"Never?"

"In the past, I could sometimes call ghosts or see echoes from touching objects, like a wall in a building. But, it never happened with people before," Sara explained.

"But you see ghosts," Detective Murphy asked. Ah, there was the doubt.

"Yes, but this wasn't a ghost. It's hard to describe really," was all Sara could say. "You don't have to believe me, but I felt it was my duty to let you know," Sara said and stood up. "Thank you for your time, Detective."

"Please sit, Ms. Caine. I didn't mean to make you defensive. It's a bit out there," Detective Murphy said. Sara slipped back into her seat.

"To be honest, I'm not taking it that well myself. I hate the images running through my mind. Each time I close my eyes, I see the dead woman. It took me years to get used to seeing ghosts. I've tried to make it useful, but I wish I had other more mainstream skills," Sara said with the emphasis on the mainstream.

"I can't even imagine what that would be like. Could the Jerry Killer really be a woman though? I don't remember the exact particulars of the Jerry case, but I remember it spanning many years going back to the late sixties," Detective Murphy said, her mind clearly elsewhere. "Thank you, Ms. Caine. For coming in and…" she said and they both got up. "Being brave enough to tell me about your abilities."

"I hope it helps somehow," Sara said.

"Can you find your own way out?" The detective paused at the door.

"Yes, of course." Sara smiled and gave the woman a small wave. She cursed herself for being so lame, turned away from her and got out of there.

Sara didn't breathe until she got into her car. She wasn't sure how well that went, but the detective hadn't laughed at her. That was a start. She checked her phone and found no messages from Johan. He'd be thrilled she went to the police, she knew, but would be angry at what she was about to do next. Barbara the ghost needed help to pass on and she deserved that peace. Sara would stay far away from the current murders and just focus on the room on the eighth floor. She buckled herself in and started the car.

Detective Eva Murphy waited at her desk for Larson, fingers tapping. She failed to access the police files on the Jerry killer in the computer database, because the case was too old and wasn't being currently investigated. Her best bet was to locate the original paper files. She'd called the murder library downtown and made sure the official file wasn't already checked out. The librarian also confirmed the case file was not yet digitized.

Unable to wait any longer, Murphy called Larson. When his phone went to voicemail, she left him a note on his desk to call her. Jittery with nervous energy about a potential break in the case, Murphy all but ran out of the precinct. Could they have stumbled upon a monster by accident? She'd heard of cold cases going down like this but never thought she'd participate in one.

After some two hundred pages of savage murder later, Murphy's eyes were bleary and her stomach churned. The Jerry killer had indeed proven to be as elusive as he was brutal.

The first murder recorded with his signature was of an Andreas Bauer in 1975, a seventy-year old man found castrated and shot in the head execution style. The press nicknamed the man the Jerry killer when the next three victims were all German men who had served in various positions in the Third Reich in WWII. They were all castrated as well and finished off with a bullet in their heads. The Jerry killer changed his modus operandi in the 1980s to include younger men and women, but they were still all blond Germanic named people. The women had their sexual organs removed, and the men castrated.

He shot all of them in the head.

He changed his M.O. in 1987 to starving his victims over months of captivity. Murphy closed the file. His starvation victims from the late 1980s all looked similar to the victims from the World War II camps. The detectives speculated he was connected with 65 deaths from Washington through Oregon to California. The ballistics from half of the murders came back to an old Parabellum Luger Mauser pistol dating from 1941. No police department ever recovered the gun. The killer switched over to the more popular Glock in 1985.

The last victim attributed to the Jerry killer was a woman in San Francisco, LuAnn Herrmann, in 1990. Her sister, Gillian Herrmann, was reported missing at the same time. Her body was never found, and she was presumed dead.

Murphy gasped when she saw the missing woman's face.

It was Louise Fairbanks.

She had never considered for a moment that Louise Fairbanks was a victim. And if she was the missing woman—and judging from the pic she had to be—then the man she called Dads was the Jerry Killer. He fit the age range from the timeline of murders.

The question was did he have dementia? And if so, why did Lou Fairbanks stay with him? Could she have become the Angel of Death killer from the stress of being a captive of a prolific serial killer? Or had the Jerry killer changed his M.O. again.

Murphy dialed for backup. "Larson, I found the infamous Jerry Killer. And Louise Fairbanks is in danger. Meet me at the Sunshine. I'm headed there now."

Detective Eva Murphy showed her badge to Russell Hall, still on duty at the Sunshine House. She was amazed he still held the job after the revelations about his family.

"Diane left for the day, and she didn't authorize me to let you in," he growled at her.

"I will call McGregor Holdings then. Go above her head. Do you think she'll be happy about that, Mr. Hall?" she asked. He grimaced.

"That's what I thought," said Murphy.

Murphy jumped from the loud bang behind her. It was Larson at the doors. "About time," she muttered.

"You gonna get that?" Russell asked. Murphy shot him a withering look and opened the door for Larson.

"Where the hell have you been?" she whispered as he stepped in.

"I'll tell you later. Gerald Fairbanks is the Jerry Killer?" he asked, skepticism written all over his face.

"Unless Louise Fairbanks is Gillian Herrmann's doppelgänger. But what are the chances? I saw the Jerry killer symbol on some Angel of Death victims from that other home I went to. It has to be him." They turned to Russell Hall. She waved her phone at him.

"Tenth. Louise Fairbanks is on the tenth. 1085," Russell stammered out. Murphy and Larson pushed passed him.

"The evidence you have is a photo?" Larson asked as they stepped into the elevator.

"I don't know who killed the victims here. Still could be Louise. The MO doesn't match the Jerry Killer's at all. I'm positive Louise Fairbanks is Gillian Herrmann, however. The photo is fifteen years old, but she hasn't changed."

"She's killing old people while taking care of her fake father, the Jerry killer? Besides being totally circumstantial, we have no evidence linking either of them to the deaths," he said. The elevator dinged as they traveled up the building.

"When you put it that way..." Murphy said. Neither spoke after that for the remainder of the ride. The elevator doors shuddered open on the tenth floor. Both of them unhooked their holsters and readied their guns as they walked down the hall.

"Overkill?" Murphy whispered.

"Eh, safer this way," he hissed back.

She rapped on the door twice.

"Louise Fairbanks, please open the door,"

Murphy said and banged harder. The door stayed closed. She placed her ear against it.

No sound.

Murphy nodded to Larson and pulled out her weapon. He followed suit. Murphy tested the knob and found it locked. "What time is it?"

Larson checked his watch. "Eleven. We're gonna need a warrant." He eyed the door. "Or do we have probable cause. Is she in danger?"

"I don't have a good feeling about this," Murphy said and dialed the precinct. Larson tugged on her shirt and grinned at her, pointing to the door.

"Magic. Door is open," he whispered, gun ready.

"What the hell were you thinking?"

"Louise Fairbanks is in danger," he replied.

They stepped inside the room. One of these days, he'd go too far and tank her career, she thought. An argument for another day, though.

The apartment was empty. No sign of Louise Fairbanks or Dads.

"Don't touch anything. We'll get the techs in here."

"On what grounds? They could be in the cafeteria, eating or out shopping or something. Let's get out of here," Murphy said but Larson stood his ground.

"There is proof in this room."

"It won't be admissible in court. You've heard of illegal search and seizure?" Murphy asked. "The Jerry killer isn't even our case."

They stepped back into the hallway.

"Let's go find them then and have a nice little chat about their previous residences," Larson said. "It must be past their bedtime. They have to be in here somewhere."

Sara Caine stood in the alleyway behind the Sunshine House, waiting for him to open the door. Cop cars crowded the front entrance and prevented her from entering that way. She shifted from foot to foot, wondering what took him so long. Unless the cop cars were there for him? No, he'd told her about them and still said he'd help her. So where was he? She checked her watch one last time. It was way past midnight.

"Sorry, I'm late. The cops are crawling everywhere," Barney said, his head poking out of the open door. Sara smiled, relieved.

"I'm so glad you showed up. I was worried that you might have..."

"Been killed?" He laughed. "I'm a strong, old bugger. Lou Fairbanks and Dads have disappeared though. My plan worked."

"They're gone?" Sara asked, surprised.

"Yup. That's why there are cops everywhere. They're looking for them," he said and motioned her inside. She stepped into the gloom of the back hallway.

"Do you really think that Nurse Louise killed Barbara?"

"Who else could it have been?" Barney asked.

"Maybe Dads?" Sara suggested.

"As long as they're gone," Barney said.

"Wait, if the cops are everywhere, how are we going to get to the eighth floor?"

"They've cleared that floor. I checked," Barney said, and headed to the back staircase. "Are you sure Barbara will be there?"

Sara nodded. "She's appeared every other time."

They started up the stairs, Sara taking her time

going up, making sure she conserved her energy. Barney noticed and slowed down.

"I know you're eager to speak with her," Sara said as an apology. Barney nodded.

"It's only a couple more flights." He held out his hand, and she took it gratefully. They climbed the rest of the way in silence. When they reached the eighth floor, Sara took several deep breaths and nodded. Barney opened the door to the hallway, and they both stepped out.

Silence. She closed her eyes and focused her concentration on her breathing.

In and out. In and out.

"What should I do?" His voice came from behind.

"Stay behind me," she whispered and focused on her breath until she felt the familiar cold on her skin. Her eyes fluttered open to find Barbara standing in front of her. The woman wore the same flowered robe and rollers in her hair as she'd seen the other times. Barbara gestured to the end of the hall and walked a few steps away from Sara and Barney.

"She wants us to follow her," Sara whispered, keeping her eyes fixed on Barbara.

"What are we waiting for then?" Barney said and stepped up next to her. Sara smiled at him as Barbara turned away and walked down the hall. Sara and Barney followed behind her. The ghost turned the corner and disappeared through a smaller door in the wall.

"What's behind there?" Sara pointed at the door.

"It's a staircase that goes between the seventh and eighth floors. This place was a hotel, and these smaller stairs were used by the servants," Barney explained.

Sara turned the knob, and the door creaked open. Barbara stood on the top stair, waiting for them. She beckoned and walked down the first flight. Barney followed right behind her.

"What is she doing now?" Barney asked.

Barbara dropped to her knees and pointed at a small door inset into the stairwell wall.

She screamed. Barney and Sara pressed into the back wall, hands over their ears. Her effort to communicate had depleted her energy and she disappeared, leaving Sara and Barney alone.

Barney looked at Sara. "That was her, wasn't it?"

"She's gone now," Sara added. "She wanted to show us this door." They both stared at it.

"We should get the police."

"We should," Barney replied. "Are you going to open it?" Sara squatted in front of it.

"Maybe there's a clue in there about where they disappeared to?"

"I guess," Barney said, not sounding hopeful. Sara grasped the knob and pulled it open in one fast motion. Screams shattered the silence. Sara's scream, Barney's scream and the ghost's. Sara's back hit Barney as they both scrambled away from the horror in the cupboard.

Louise Fairbanks' body was stuffed into the tiny space below the stairs, her neck twisted in such a way as to be staring right at them. The Jerry killer's mark, the crude trident, the life rune, was cut into her forehead.

Sara stumbled back up the stairs, pulling Barney along with her. "Police. We have to get the police," she managed to sputter out.

25
The Jerry Killer
JULY 21, 1948

Simon Schrieber cried when he called the police about his father's supposed suicide.

"He missed her so much. I just wasn't enough for him," he babbled when two uniformed LAPD officers came to investigate. He wiped his snot on the edge of his sleeve and let his shoulders droop.

"I'm sure that's not true," the older of the two police officers said, and Simon knew he was in the clear.

"What's going to happen to me now?" he asked as a knock on the door made all of them turn. It was Regina Michaels, a widow who lived three doors down and had been friends with Frau Schrieber. She stood in the open doorway, tears streaming down her cheeks. Just like that Simon had found his savior.

Regina welcomed him into her home and within months he'd taken her name. He became Simon

Michaels and worked hard to put his past behind him. Regina helped him in any way she could.

He never told her that the Schrieber's had kidnapped and brainwashed him into being their son, but she was perceptive enough to know that they weren't the happy family she once thought they were.

The nightmares that followed him out of the old country subsided gradually and with Regina's unconditional love, he blossomed in high school. He excelled in science and mathematics and had no difficulty in landing a spot at UC Berkeley to study medicine. Regina encouraged him to go, and he did.

Simon moved back down to Southern California twelve years later as a newly qualified Doctor at the UCLA Medical Center. He had only been in Santa Monica for two months when Regina died of sudden cardiac arrest.

Between sleepless nights in the ER and his grief over Regina's death, Simon's lust for blood grew as the nightmares of his past took over his daily life. He took the most mangled cases in the ER and worked hard to stitch them back together.

His sleep returned.

The blood washed away the terrors of Auschwitz. However, dreams of his mother plagued him in earnest.

His coldness and emotional distance didn't inspire warmth in his colleagues, but it made him a brilliant surgeon. He managed to keep his nasty blackness at bay for many years. No one questioned his bachelorhood since they understood his life was his work. And in truth, it was.

Until 1975, when Simon saw him.

Simon Michaels first encountered Andreas Bauer at a dive bar off Lincoln Boulevard after a twenty-four-hour shift. He had stopped in on a whim to quiet his mind from a hard day of catastrophes when he encountered Herr Schrieber's long lost buddy. Simon remembered Andreas and his vitriol towards everyone and everything in his new home country.

Simon swigged his whiskey when Andreas Bauer's still accented German voice rang out in the nearly empty bar.

"So the Polack told me not to come back. Claimed I didn't work fast enough," he snorted and threw back another vodka. "This whole town is crawling with the Jews, Commies, and Polacks." He glared at Simon who lifted up his drink to him. The old bastard didn't recognize him at all. The grizzled bartender nodded absently at him, not really paying attention. But, Bauer's words lit the nasty, black, and wondrous rage that hovered just below Simon's surface. The man hadn't changed in thirty years.

"I think it's time to leave, sir." The bartender took Andreas Bauer's empty glass and pointed to the door. Andreas Bauer grunted and slid off the stool. Simon finished his own drink and left a generous tip.

He followed Andreas out of the bar and watched as he took a left turn onto a smaller side street.

Simon ran to his car and followed Andreas Bauer to a ramshackle bungalow, its front yard overgrown with weeds. Simon memorized the number. He'd be back.

The murder of Andreas Bauer went off without a hitch. The old man was more than happy to let a fellow German into his home, however lame the excuse was, and never noticed the surgical gloves Simon wore. It took Simon a minute to overpower the old man, and he did it without disturbing anything but the rug.

He expertly used his scalpel to emasculate him and finished old Bauer with Herr Schrieber's Parabellum Luger Mauser pistol. Simon had kept it for this type of reason and thought its use poetic.

As he glanced around one last time, he found an old picture of Herr Schrieber's buddies. When he checked the back, he found all their names written neatly in the back. Germans were nothing if not precise and organized. He smiled. An idea formed, and his blackness blossomed.

After going through the men in the photo, six in all, he found that his blood lust was not satiated. It felt right to rid the world of the Nazi vermin, and he wanted to keep his good work going. The only problem was finding them. Israel had done an excellent job of hunting down many Nazi criminals and there just weren't that many around the States anymore. Simon stopped hunting for several years. His sleep never returned.

Simon's need wouldn't leave him. Each time he saw a blond woman with that look, the high cheekbones and the broad Germanic face, the nasty black would well up inside of him. He remembered the blond women with the brown uniforms in the children's home and their smiling faces as they led the less desirable children off to their deaths. He fed that rage and decided these women didn't deserve to live either. Their entire race didn't deserve life.

He did his due diligence in making sure the men and women he chose were of Germanic descent. Once he was sure, he did his good work and the sleep and calm came back to him.

Age was not kind to anyone, Simon thought. He made no mistakes in the forty years he hunted the vermin. Not until LuAnn and Gillian Herrmann. Simon hadn't prepared properly. Luck was what stood between him and failure that time.

Ever adaptable, Simon used Gillian to his advantage. He didn't want to kill her. She wasn't up to Germanic standards. She would have never been stolen, grabbed and brainwashed. Gillian would have been shot in the street. She was petite and a brunette and could have been Jewish. He decided to keep her. It was time to do something more befitting his age.

It took him three years to break Gillian down and transform her into Louise Pickford and himself into Dads Pickford. He believed it would only take several months, at most, but he hadn't taken Gillian's age into consideration. Most of the children brainwashed at the Kindererziehungslager were under ten years old and their malleable brains made breaking them so much easier. But, it worked out in the end and they landed at the Comfort Homes just as he had planned.

In his many years of living in California, Simon never encountered someone like his true self until he met Grazyna Nettlebaum at the Comfort Homes. Speaking Polish again was glorious. At first, he spoke rather haltingly but the more they talked the more his mother tongue came rushing back to him. He tamped down the nasty, black rage and focused instead on the Poland of his memories, his mother and Grazyna. He could have stayed that way if it wasn't for Jacques Fournier and his anti-Semitism. He saw Grazyna's tears and knew he would kill again.

Simon couldn't shoot Jacques since that would bring the cops running and wake up the entire home. Using his trusty scalpel would be too messy, and he couldn't take the risk of getting any blood on himself. It didn't take long for him to settle on air embolism, a way of death created by the Nazi's, and one that would fly entirely under the radar. If he was good enough, the death might even be ruled as a natural cause. He smiled at the very thought.

Simon had to give Gillian, otherwise known as Lou, credit. Her technique was ingenious. She started him at the lowest dosage and was patient enough to not raise it for months. She almost convinced him that he was in the middle of a descent into dementia and muddled his brain enough that he took the pills she gave him without question. If it hadn't been for the weeklong stomach flu that affected his dosage, his mind might have never cleared and Gillian would have gotten away with it.

But, luck was not on her side. He devised ways of hiding the pills and within several months he was back to his old self. He made sure to keep mindless anytime Gillian was around. It wasn't hard as she was devolving right before his eyes. All of Sunshine blamed her for the current spate of murders. Barney Leonard had even tried to see him several times. Simon figured it was time to get out from under Gillian's thumb. It barely hurt when he carved HELP ME into his own arm.

26
The Nightmare
FEBRUARY 24, 2005 - DAY 9

Sara Caine sat across from Detective Murphy and Detective Larson at the Hollywood precinct, a cup of steaming hot coffee in front of her. As far as Sara knew, no one had slept since Nurse Louise's body was found under the stairs. Sara was upfront about how she and Barney had found the body, but Detective Murphy felt that those details shouldn't be mentioned in the report. Sara took a sip of coffee and rubbed her bloodshot eyes.

"So Dads, whatever his name is, is the Jerry Killer?" Sara asked the detectives.

"We are working under that assumption."

"Nurse Louise had been drugging him to keep him in a state of dementia," Detective Larson said.

"Who was Nurse Louise then? Were they related?"

"She was the sister of one of his victims. We think that she was his slave for years. Severe Stockholm syndrome, our shrink says," Detective Murphy said, ignoring Detective Larson's discreet head shake. Sara guessed she wouldn't get too much more information.

"Did you hear Dads speak at the séance?" Detective Larson asked.

"I've told you all of what happened and Fredrick should have the tapes to back me up. I don't remember Dads ever saying a word."

"We do have the tapes, and he doesn't speak on them," Detective Murphy said.

"So what now?" Sara asked.

"A manhunt is underway. We'll be cataloguing their room for some time and are hopeful that forensics will find something we can use to track him. We've never had his fingerprints before."

"Why are you telling me all this?" Sara asked. Detective Murphy and Detective Larson exchanged a look.

"We're concerned you might be in danger. If he thinks you might have something on him..." Detective Murphy trailed off. Sara's already pale face turned translucent.

"But I don't know anything," Sara said.

"We're going to put a security detail on you for a couple of days until we're sure that he's left town," Detective Murphy said.

"He's an old man."

"Who can and has done a lot of damage," Detective Larson reminded her.

"But I don't know anything. He never spoke with me, and I had barely any contact with him." She looked from one to the other. "That doesn't matter, does it?"

"You'll be safe with us," Detective Murphy said. Sara didn't feel safe at all but decided to keep that to herself.

"Can I go home? I can hardly keep my eyes open."

Both of the detectives nodded. "Just know that we're watching you," Detective Murphy said as Sara got to her feet. "Will you be OK to drive?"

Sara nodded.

"I'll give you a call later today to check in on you," Detective Murphy said and Sara nodded again.

Sara walked out of the precinct and blinked against the bright sunlight. She'd been wrong about Louise Fairbanks, and the visions had made her point the finger at an innocent woman. All she wanted to do was sleep and forget.

Sara entered the elevator in her loft building, pressed the button for the fourth floor, leaned against the wall, and closed her eyes. She'd failed. The guilt swarmed in her belly like snakes curling around her intestines. The elevator doors slid open, and Sara stepped out onto her floor. She squinted against the harsh afternoon light filling the hallway. Pain stabbed behind her bleary eyes and made it hard for her to focus.

She rubbed her eyes and squinted down the hall. A figure stood at her door. Was that Johan? She shielded her eyes from the glare, but all she could make out was a shape.

The elevator dinged closed. That had to be Johan. No one else visited her at home. She stepped forward cautiously. What if it was someone else?

"Johan, is that you?" she called out, and the figure turned to her without answering. Mr. Jacobs from down the hall might need something, she thought, but took her cell out anyway. It would be good to call the cops, tell them she got home.

Cell in hand, she dug around in her purse for her keys. The man walked to her, his face obscured by the light streaming in from the window behind him.

"Do you need help with something?" She shielded her hands against the light and heard the elevator ding open again. She turned to the sound and felt the man's body slam into hers, pain exploding in her head.

Images of death flashed through her mind. Feelings followed closely after them and made her tremble in fear. Rage, fury, lust, and then pleasure. Sick, twisted pleasure. The blood was everywhere, and there were so many bodies.

And then just blackness.

27

Dead Ends
MARCH 28, 2005 - DAY 32

Johan Luken glowered at Detective Murphy and Detective Larson and crossed his hands over his chest, making no effort to mask his fury. They could give up, but he never would. By the look on the woman's face, he knew his reaction didn't surprise her. She opened her mouth to say something but closed it again.

"So that's it?" Johan asked, his voice shaking. The police were calling off the search for Sara. He and Ritchie needed to take over. He stood up.

"It's been a month. The possibility of her still being alive with a monster like the Jerry Killer…" Detective Murphy trailed off, avoiding his eyes.

"Right. As you've said. Nothing I say will change your mind so I'd best be going."

"Many family members feel the way you do but that doesn't change the facts. A serial killer took your friend. He never kept his victims alive for long. His name remains a mystery, and we don't know anything more than the previous investigations uncovered," Detective Murphy explained.

"He kept Louise Fairbanks for years. He could do the same with Sara," Johan said.

"To be frank, the FBI has taken over the entire case. We're still treating her abduction as a priority in conjunction with them, but we wanted to temper your expectations," Detective Larson cut in. Detective Murphy elbowed him into silence.

"You don't have the case anymore?" Johan froze at the door.

"Something like that, yes. There's a task force but..." Murphy stopped again.

"Who do I need to speak with at the FBI?"

The detectives looked at each other.

"We're very sorry, Mr. Luken," Detective Murphy said.

"So the FBI is also assuming she's dead?" He read the truth on their faces. "That's what I thought." He yanked the door open and walked out.

The detectives surprised him with the phone call this morning. Johan assumed they'd be updating him on some sort of progress. But he had been wrong. The moment he sat down in the interrogation room, he knew what they would say. They informed him Sara was being declared dead.

He walked through the halls and out onto Wilcox Avenue, shielding his eyes from the afternoon sun. Ritchie Jones should be up by now. Johan had no idea how that man kept going on the amount of sleep he got daily, but he was thankful for his tireless effort in searching for Sara. He opened his car door.

"Mr. Luken. Johan Luken." He turned at the

sound of his name, Detective Murphy waved him down. "Mr. Luken," she said. "Glad…I caught you…" she gasped.

"What can I do for you, Detective Murphy?" he said, his voice cold. Sara had trusted the detective with her life and they were about to throw that responsibility away.

"I want to help you and Ms. Caine. Please believe me when I say that," she said.

"So help," Johan said.

She nodded at his car. "Can we take a drive?"

He opened the passenger door for her. He didn't see how she could do much of anything, but he'd hear her out.

"You sure about this?" he asked when he was behind the wheel.

"Drive," she said.

Johan drove north to Sunset Boulevard and took a right, waiting for her cue. It took some minutes before she spoke again.

"Once the FBI steps in, they take over. This case is high profile enough that my hands are tied. They talk cooperation, but this case will make careers and we've been effectively locked out. But, they've hit a dead end as well. Special Agent Richardson, who is the head of the investigation, is certain she is dead and demanded we call you in."

"So why are you here?"

"I know you are running your own investigation. Are you working on any leads?"

"Why would I tell you?"

"Because I want to help you."

"Why?"

"I don't think she's dead either. Sara could be Gillian Herrmann's replacement."

"Why aren't the FBI following that lead?"

"I'm not privy to the details they are working with," Murphy said bitterly. She took a deep breath before speaking again. "I know you've found something, I can see it in your demeanor." He sized her up. He would use her anger at the FBI to his benefit.

He nodded. "What's the most important thing we don't know about the Jerry Killer?"

"His real name," she said without hesitation.

"Which is what my friend and I have been attempting to discover for the last month."

"And?"

"We have some leads but no name yet," Johan said. "She's alive."

"Can I meet with the both of you tonight? I want to help in any way I can. Off the record."

"Why?"

"She was under our protection. We failed. I want to help."

Johan raised an eyebrow at her. "Alright," he said and rummaged in his backpack in the backseat. He pulled out a silver cigarette case and handed it to her. "Call me after your shift. My number is on one of those." She took a card out of the case and tucked it into her pocket.

"We will find her," she said.

"Yes. Yes, we will," he said and drove her back to the station.

#

A voice whispered to her out of the darkness. "Wake up, Sara, wake up."

Sara Caine struggled against her drowsiness and strained to open her eyes. Forcing her eyes to open was the hardest thing she'd ever done.

"Wake up. Wake up, Sara." The voice sounded like her mother's. Her consciousness swam to the surface of the drug induced slumber.

"You have to wake up now," whispered the voice. Sara blinked her eyes open and attempted to pull her arms back to her body. The pain jolted her back to reality. Handcuffs circled her wrists and were attached to an industrial looking headboard. She pulled harder and flinched as the metal ate into her skin.

She lifted her head. She was in the same room she had woken up in before. He hadn't moved her yet.

Dust lazily floated in the rays of the afternoon sun struggling through the closed blinds. She recognized the look and feel of a Southern California afternoon, and relief washed over her. She was still in Los Angeles, at least. Sara had been unable to track her time there. She could have been abducted yesterday or a year ago. Either would be possible.

Her mind slid to the man who kept her captive. He had told her to call him Dads the first time he came to free her so she could use the bathroom. She refused to call him that the first time and every time since. He came three times a day to feed her and let her relieve herself.

A key turned in the lock, and the old man shuffled in, his eyes a brilliant blue. She'd never seen eyes more alive and more frightening.

Johan Luken stood next to Detective Murphy outside Ritchie's door and questioned his decision on bringing her here. Since he'd picked her up, she avoided all eye contact and said barely four words to him. He was either stepping into some trap set up by the LAPD, or she was putting her job in jeopardy by being there.

"Who is this partner of yours?" was the first thing she asked.

"He's a friend of Sara's and a damn good hacker," Johan said and was about to talk Ritchie up more when he opened the door. Detective Murphy stepped back in surprise.

Johan cracked a grin. When Johan called Ritchie a hacker, he was sure Murphy imagined a thin, pasty looking guy with no social skills. Instead, Ritchie was a dead ringer for Brad Pitt in Troy.

He gestured to the detective next to him. "Ritchie, this is Detective Murphy," he said.

She held out her hand. "It's Murphy. Just Murphy," she said. Ritchie pumped her hand with a grin and waved them in. "As Johan told you, we've been trying to find addresses going back further than what's in all the files you and the FBI have," Ritchie explained and pointed to the leather couch in front of his bank of monitors. Johan and Murphy sat down.

"You've found something new," Johan said. He recognized the current of excitement in Ritchie's voice. But first, Ritchie would walk them through his process.

"We hit several walls immediately," Ritchie explained.

"Like we did. No usable fingerprints and no other way to identify him. We did find DNA, but no match to anyone we have in the system," Murphy said.

"I also found those fingerprints," Ritchie said and turned back to his monitors. After a furious amount of clicking, close-ups of smudgy fingerprints appeared on the screen. "Like you, I hit a dead end with them."

Murphy leaned in, all business. Her reticence was gone.

"Older people's fingerprints get smudgy when they put any pressure on them. Something to do with moisture in the skin or age or something," Murphy explained. Ritchie swiveled in his chair and nodded at her.

"Right. So anyway, the next step was to find where they both surfaced together," Ritchie explained. He'd found it, Johan was sure of it.

"I found another address before the ones in Palm Springs. Under a different name, of course."

Murphy leaned in. "How do you know it's them?"

"Fairbanks was the name of a famous silent film star. Douglas Fairbanks. I ran different combinations of other silent film star names and found a nurse named Louise Pickford at an address in San Francisco with a father named Dads who had dementia. A place called Comfort Homes of San Francisco," Johan said.

"You found them. Good work. So where does that leave us?" Johan asked.

"I checked Louise's driver's license," Ritchie said anticipating their doubts. He hit a couple of keys and pulled up a California Driver's License, with an unsmiling Lou staring out from a badly lit picture.

"Is it too late for a flight tonight?" Murphy checked the time on an antique watch. Surprising for a cop, thought Johan.

'Too late, we can go first thing tomorrow," Johan said.

"I don't fly," Ritchie added. "Plus, you want me in front of the monitors. I can get more information that way. The man had a name once, and I will find it," Ritchie said. "Oh, and another thing, the place was also managed by McGregor Investments."

"That's an interesting connection," Johan said.

"That could simply be a coincidence. They own properties all over the States, all of them assisted living homes. At some point, it's a numbers game. I tried calling them today but since the Sunshine is getting so much press, they're on major shutdown. No one's answering any questions," Ritchie said. "Can you use some of your LAPD muscle to get them to talk?"

"I took a personal leave of absence. I'm here unofficially," Murphy explained.

"What's the point of bringing a cop along if you can't use their influence?" Ritchie asked Johan.

Murphy cut in. "I'll influence in any way I can. I have my methods."

Ritchie turned back to his computers and numerous screens popped up.

"OK, first flight available is JetBlue leaving at six in the morning. Sound good?"

"Perfect. Let me give you my—" Murphy started but Ritchie interrupted her.

"Already taken care of. I can expense it," he said, his attention back to the computers.

"Don't you need my info?"

"Already got that," he said. Murphy glanced at Johan with a crooked smile.

"I told you he was the best," Johan added.

28
Mothers
MARCH 29, 2005 - DAY 33

Sara Caine sat in the back of her parent's Jaguar and watched as her parents fell into an angry silence. She preferred their shouting to this. The mood in the car now felt a hundred times worse.

"Mom, are we there?" Sara leaned into the back of her mother's seat and whispered.

"Hush, honey. Not right now," her mother said without turning around.

She jutted out her chin in frustration. "Why not now? No one else is talking," she complained.

"Sara, enough," her father threatened. Sara sat back in her seat and folded her arms around her.

She recognized the familiar dream although this start was different. A massive argument had always started the dream off. What did this new silence mean? Her mother twisted in her seat, tears streaming down her face.

"It's time to wake up, Sara."

"I don't want to."

Her father smiled back at her reassuringly. "You have to wake up, Sara. Now. It's time," he said. Sara closed her eyes knowing the accident was about to happen. She'd stuck around only once to see her parents' death and that was enough. She focused her energy back on her breathing.

In the distance, she heard her parents' screams, the sharp sound of metal on metal, a sickening crunch, and then a high-pitched whistle. Those sounds haunted her every night. But, she wanted to stay here and not wake up.

"Wake up," a voice whispered.

She opened her eyes to a black nothingness, a void. Outside her breathing, there was no sound.

If she was asleep, then where was she in the dream cycle? She'd studied sleep disorders and sleep patterns because of her own nightmares, but she didn't recognize this stage. The phase of sleep where dreams existed was known as REM sleep, but this didn't feel like that.

This resembled the first phase, when the mind shut down to recharge. The only problem with that theory was that in that phase there was no awareness of self. She knew she was herself.

She closed her eyes and focused on the only sound she could hear. Her own breathing. Fall asleep, she thought. Sleep. To sleep was to then wake up. And when she'd wake up, she might not be in this void anymore but back in that small bedroom, held captive by a monster. That would be better than this.

"He's drugging you," said a woman's voice through the darkness. Sara strained to recognize the voice. She knew her mother's voice from the dream but had no idea if that was what she really sounded like. She had no recordings of either of her parents, and the accident was all so long ago. She scattered photos of them around her house to make sure to remember them, but it never felt as if it was enough.

"Wake up," the voice said. It sounded as though it came from right in front of her. She opened her eyes and stepped toward the sound and opened her eyes..

"Say something. Let me use your voice to come to you," Sara said.

"You're almost there. It's only a couple of more steps. You need to wake up," the voice said. Sara stepped forward and detected the woman's Germanic accent with its hard, nasal sound.

"Am I getting closer? Can you see me?" Sara asked.

"Can you see the pin of light?" said the voice as it faded off into the distance.

"No, I don't. It's all black and you're fading," Sara cried, her anxiety rising. Becoming hysterical would not get her out of here, she thought. Calm yourself. She relaxed her body.

"I don't see it," she called out. When she got no response, she rushed forward.

"Please say something. Hello? Are you still there?"

Sara sprinted ahead. She felt the movement forward but her body stayed in place. She pushed herself to run faster.

She finally saw it. The pinpoint of light. She used whatever energy she had left and directed her body at it. She sobbed in relief as the pinpoint enlarged, became a circle and grew bigger until the light surrounded her.

Sara gasped awake and was momentarily thrilled to see the sun and her prison. As reality pushed her relief back into terror, she listened for sounds of her captor. Instead, she heard music playing somewhere in the house, a jazzy ballad that sounded like something from the 1940s.

The room she was held in transformed into a clean, sparse bedroom with a chest of drawers and a chair next to it. A colorful rug sat on top of newish, wood flooring.

Sara closed her eyes and opened them again. She recognized the shift as a vision and thought she could be in the 1940s.

An argument rose over the sound of the music, and it took her a second to register that the voices weren't in English but in German.

As Sara strained to make out the second voice, the light streaming from the window coalesced into a shape of a woman cowering at the door. The woman gained such a vivid, sharpness that Sara realized she probably died in this very room. The woman's dress cemented her thinking it was the 1940s, and she would be old enough to be her captor's mother.

The ghost cracked the door open and the shouting grew louder. The woman closed the door against the sound and sobbed. The intensity of her crying drew energy away from her corporality and made her translucent. She turned to face Sara, tears streaming down her face.

"All my fault. We made him," she wailed and

vanished. Sara stared out into the empty room and knew then she needed an escape plan. She would not get out of this alive if she didn't. He would not set her free.

·285·

29
The Past
DAY 33

Johan Luken paced back and forth in the lobby of the Comfort Homes of San Francisco and checked his watch for the thousandth time. Randall Atkins, the executive director of the home, had kept them waiting for the last hour. He glanced over at Murphy who was lost in her own thoughts.

Johan stopped his pacing. "We should check in with him."

Murphy got up and nodded. "Guess we can't be nice with this one," she said. She strode past him to the closed door and tapped on the door. The man's assistant poked her head out. Murphy smiled.

"Get him now or I'll call the media. They haven't found out that the Jerry Killer had a field day killing your residents here. YET. Would you like your face all over the news, dear?" Color left the woman's cheeks.

"Let me get him," she said and shut the door on Murphy.

"Let's hope that works," he said.

A grey haired, scowling man opened the door.

"Guess it did," Sara said.

"Why are you brutalizing my assistant?" he demanded.

"Interesting choice of words," Johan observed. The man grunted in response.

"Mr. Randall Atkins, I presume." Murphy stepped in, authority changing the timbre of her voice.

"Do you have a warrant?" Randall asked.

"I don't need one to ask you questions. I would think that as a representative of the McGregor Corporation and as someone who is in charge of these people's welfare, you'd want to talk to me about Louise Pickford and her father, Dads, the Jerry Killer," Murphy said. Johan gauged the man's reaction but Randall made his face stoic and unreadable.

"I have nothing to say on that matter."

"Were you the manager when they lived here?" Murphy said and got into Randall's face. He stepped back.

"I was the coordinator here at that time," he said, conceding.

"But you're listed as a manager in 1996. Were you promoted even though many of your residents were dying under mysterious circumstances? You must have had an unusually high body count during their stay," Murphy prodded. Randall turned scarlet at the accusation.

"You better come into my office," he said and turned away from them. Johan and Murphy followed him into a large, book-lined office. He gestured to several seats in front of a massive, mahogany desk. Johan sat down but Murphy moved over to the books, keeping her back to them.

"Why didn't you come forward about them living here? You must have recognized Louise Pickford as Louise Fairbanks from all the news coverage. It's been all over the news for weeks," Murphy said, keeping her voice casual. Johan twisted in his chair and watched her inspect a book, not even looking at Randall. Interesting way of interrogating someone, Johan thought.

"Corporate said I didn't have to," Randall said.

"You went through the death records, saw the spike and still you did nothing?" Murphy asked.

"Is that a statement or a question? Which precinct did you say you were from again?" Randall asked, his eyes narrowing.

"I didn't. How many deaths did you find in those records, Mr. Atkins? Have you alerted the FBI?" Murphy pushed on.

"And why would I do that?" he shot back.

"It would be the right thing to do. Corporate absolved you from all your sins, didn't they? Or did they pay you off with a promotion to keep you quiet?" Murphy asked as she stalked to his desk and stood over him. Randall took a deep breath.

"I don't like what you're getting at."

"You got a promotion, didn't you?" Murphy kept on him.

"I think you should leave."

"I want to see Louise Pickford's records."

"I don't have them."

"Why not? Where are they?" Johan said.

"They destroyed them, didn't they?" Murphy cut in leaning across Randall's desk. Randall nodded.

"I hope you have an excellent memory, Mr. Atkins. We're not leaving until you give us a year by year play of their time here."

"I won't be able to do that. That was over ten years ago."

"What do you think the FBI will do when they hear that you were part of the cover-up? And what do you think Corporate will do? Protect you?" She let that sink in. "You have a chance to get yourself out of this mess."

The man wiped sweat off his brow. They sat silent waiting for his response.

Randall turned back to them. "Grace Nettlebaum. Louise's father befriended her. They're from the same country, I think. I walked by them once and heard them jabbering away in some Eastern European language. Couldn't tell you what it was but they were thick, those two. Louise resented their relationship though, and I'd catch her giving them dirty looks. Dads laughed so much with Grace. I wouldn't be surprised if they were lovers. When they left, Grace cried for several days." He cleared his throat. "That's all I remember. Louise was a good nurse. She didn't give me any problems."

That surprised Johan. "Why did you let her go then?" he asked.

"They left of their own accord. She quit," Randall said.

"When did you realize your death numbers were off?" Murphy asked.

"Several months after they left, one of the relatives of a man who'd died of a heart attack was convinced that his uncle had been poisoned. We had to look into it, and they had an investigator look at our death certificates. That's when it came out."

"And they covered it up?" Johan asked. Randall nodded. Johan stood up and joined Murphy at the door.

"Where is Mrs. Nettlebaum now?" Murphy asked.

"She's on the fifth floor," Randall said and checked his time. "But she'll be in the sunroom now. She enjoys her mornings in there." Randall had shrunk in size before their eyes. He rose from behind his desk and motioned for them to follow him.

"Thank you, Randall. I'll make sure to let the head of the FBI task force know of your cooperation," Murphy offered.

Randall managed a small smile and led them down a marbled corridor and into an octagonal sunroom, all glass, with several gray haired ladies sitting among the purple and yellow orchids. Randall pointed to the smaller of the ladies.

"That's Grace. We don't get along so I won't introduce you but let her know I gave you both permission to speak with her." He nodded once and scurried away like the rat he was. Johan watched his receding form and hoped when he was old he wouldn't be under the supervision of men like him.

Sara Caine woke up and stared into the blue eyes of her captor. She lunged at him but barely rose an inch out of a chair, new restraints holding her down.

"What do you want from me? I didn't do anything to you," Sara demanded. The man stared at her in interest. She tried another tactic.

"Dads, who was the woman in the room. The one I sleep in?" That got a reaction out of him. His eyes lost their intensity for a moment. Could he have dementia after all? Her escape plan would be more credible if he had some weakness she could exploit. She needed all the help she could get.

He was drugging her because of her difficulties with walking and balance. The last time she was in the bathroom, she checked herself for any injection holes from a syringe but didn't find any. The drugs had to be in her food and drink.

Now, she made sure to drink her fill at the faucet in the bathroom and kept her food intake to a minimum. She hadn't eaten the lunch that he'd brought her but had passed out anyway. Her hope was that the drugs would get out of her system enough to, at least, make her more mobile.

He'd never let her out of the room before, she realized and her heart skipped a beat. Could this be the day that she died?

"What do you want from me?" Her voice rose in hysteria.

She didn't want to die. Not like this.

Not like Lou or the blond woman on the bed.

She gripped the armrests of the chair for support.

He cocked his head to the right and stared at her. He would not get the best of her, she thought and glared back. If he made a mistake, she would strike. But he had to make one first.

"You can see her?" he asked, his voice soft and lightly accented. It didn't sound like the woman's voice from the room. His was not a Germanic accent.

"You knew who Lou was. I saw your shock," he

said and edged in closer to her. "I need your help. I'm at the end of my life and someone out there delivered you to me. A gift from the heavens you could say." He paused and smiled at her. She used every ounce of her being not to react. She'd read that serial killers enjoyed the fear of their victims, and she didn't want to give him the satisfaction.

"Who do you want to contact?" she asked instead.

"I want to speak with my mother," he stated. If she didn't know he'd killed hundreds of people and was her kidnapper, she would have felt sorry for him when he said mother. Sara cleared her throat.

"I've seen your mother in the bedroom that you're keeping me in. I saw her listening at the door while you argued in German with someone in here," she continued. He sprang up from his chair with the ease of a much younger man and spit on the floor.

"Not that conniving, scheming bitch. She ruined my life. She STOLE me," he screamed and twisted his body away from her. She cringed back into the chair as he got himself under control. She cursed herself for upsetting him and prayed he wouldn't attack her. Dads dropped to his knees in front of her, fully in control.

"How do you work? I saw Lou touch your hand, and you got jolted. Is that what I need to do? Touch your hand and you'll see my mother?" He peered at her as if her face would give him the answer.

"That's not how I contact the dead. I need something of theirs. If they want to speak, they'll come to me. Ghosts know who I am. Did your—" She stopped, unsure. "Did your other mother leave you…"

He shook his head before she could finish.

"All that is left of her is me," he said. He grasped

her hands in his. He'd pulled off her gloves and his touch plunged her back into the deep darkness of limbo.

Sara opened and closed her eyes and saw only blackness, the only sound she heard was her own breathing. He sent her back in the place of no dreams. She waved her now free hands in front of her face and couldn't see them either.

Why hadn't she seen murders like she'd seen with Lou? She was thankful for the reprieve but didn't understand what was happening. Johan had been her guide into the "extra" abilities that people displayed but he'd never spoken of a place like this. Was this a new ability or her mind protecting her?

She took a step forward and heard a tinkle somewhere in the distance. It sounded like a piano. Her pace quickened to it and a melody emerged out of the darkness, one she recognized. Chopin. Her mother had loved Chopin, the Preludes especially and this sounded like one of them.

The music grew louder as a small pinpoint of light floated in front of her face. The light grew larger and enveloped her as before. This time she stood on a wintery, foreign street. People of all ages, wearing patchwork overcoats with yellow stars, picked up dead bodies from the gutters as soldiers with SS on their lapels watched on, laughing.

Sara waved at a passerby, but he didn't see her. Could this be Dads' memory? It definitely was a European country during World War II. She gasped as one of the Nazi soldiers hit a young man in the head, and he fell to his knees. One of the guards said something in German and shot the man in the head.

None of the passersby looked up.

No one did a thing.

Sara pushed to the edge of the sidewalk, turning away from the ghastly scene, and caught sight of a boy, the now familiar electric blue eyes under a mop of white blond hair peeking out of a hat, holding the hand of an attractive, blond woman. This could be the killer named Dads.

The mother and child were bundled up in several layers of coats, each layer having a hole in a different place. The mother tweaked the boy's nose, and he giggled. The mom put her finger to her mouth and made a small shushing sound as she pointed at the guards milling in the street. The boy nodded to her and kept his gaze averted from the dead man in the gutter.

A German yell sounded from somewhere behind her. Sara turned to see the murderous guard pointing at the young woman and her child to another woman dressed in a brown uniform alongside of him. Sara didn't want to see anymore and squeezed her eyes shut, hoping to go back to the void. Maybe being in limbo wasn't so bad after all.

The sounds of the street did not diminish. She opened her eyes again and found herself still in the street. The young boy and his mom stood in front of the German guard and the woman in the brown uniform. She watched as the German guard swiped the boy's hat off. The mom froze, clutching her young son's hand. The German guard said something that Sara didn't understand to the uniformed woman, and she nodded.

The mom started shaking her head no and

the German guard put the gun to her head. Sara plunged back into the darkness then.

Simon Michaels sat back and watched as Sara convulsed in front of him. He worked the ties loose at her wrists. He didn't want her to hurt herself. He remembered the reaction she'd had when Lou touched her and hoped his touch rendered different results. He'd heard she'd been in a coma for some time.

He shook his ever-increasing vertigo off and knew his own death was closing in. Death was coming for her too.

He picked Sara up from the chair and laid her now silent body down on the leather couch. At least she hadn't swallowed her tongue, he thought and was still breathing.

She'd surprised the hell out of him when she spoke of seeing Frau Schrieber in the bedroom. He shouldn't have grasped her hands like that, and now he'd lost his only chance to apologize to his mama for ever looking up at the soldier.

He felt abject failure. The revenge he meted out on the Germans would never equal the evil they unleashed on the world.

Simon left the woman on the couch and sat directly across from her. Whatever Lou poisoned him with in these last few years still affected his memory. He couldn't really blame her, though. He would have done the same if he was in her position. In truth, he would have been more aggressive with the poison.

The woman stayed asleep. He didn't want to kill her. Simon hadn't wanted to kill Lou either. Well, maybe a little. Payback for the poisoning. But this woman interested him. It would be a shame to take such an interesting creature out of this dirty, dark world.

What good would her death bring? His own life was done, he understood that. Or close to it. But hers? He would wait another night to see whether she woke up and try again.

He didn't have anything of his mother's to give her like she wanted, and he hoped that wasn't the end of the line for him. Frau Schrieber died in that bedroom of cancer and using her logic, it made sense that she saw her.

The woman's chest rose up and down rhythmically.

Simon was exhausted. If he closed his eyes, would they all be there waiting for him? His project, his mission, his revenge. He scratched at the stubble that had grown in overnight. Did any of this really matter anymore?

It was time to die, and he needed to accept that.

Detective Eva Murphy touched Grace Nettlebaum on the shoulder. "Excuse me, Ma'am? We'd love to have a moment of your time," she said in a kind voice.

"Call me Grace. I don't like the implication of Ma'am, if you know what I mean?" Grace said and winked at Johan. She waved them over to two white, wicker chairs to her right. "You can pull those over. It's not often I enjoy the company of guests," she said, her voice booming. Murphy smiled at the lungs on the woman as Johan dragged the chairs over.

"My name's Eva Murphy. Everyone calls me Murphy," Murphy said. "This is my colleague, Johan Luken. We wanted to talk to you about a woman named Louise Pickford and her father, Dads."

"You're police, aren't you?" Grace directed her question at Murphy.

"I am."

"Good on you, Murphy. Good on you. I hope that fool didn't give you too many problems?"

"Which fool?" Johan asked with amusement. Grace jerked a thumb back to where Randall had been just moments ago.

"How that nitwit ever got that promotion is beyond me. He's dense and crafty all at the same time, if you can believe it. I wouldn't trust him if I were you," she said and arched an eyebrow at Murphy.

Murphy loved this woman.

"She steamrolled him very well. I can say it was a pleasure to watch," Johan added.

"Good on you. Good on you," Grace said and nodded again. "What do you want to know about her?"

"Randall mentioned that you knew her father, Dads, quite well?" Murphy said with a slight conspiratorial air. "He even mentioned some sort of relationship?"

Grace snorted in disbelief. "The man's a fool," she said and cackled at the thought. "Imagine me and Szymon. Ha." Murphy shot Johan a glance. A name. They had a name. Murphy kept her tone calm even as she was bursting inside.

"Szymon? That's unique," she said, holding her breath.

"It's Polish. My name was Grazyna, but I changed it to the English equivalent, Grace, after the war." Grace stared into the gardens right outside the sunroom. "Another life that was."

"Did you know each other in Poland?" Johan asked.

"Oh no. We met here but..." Her voice grew soft and quiet. "We shared a...history."

"Oh?" was all Murphy said. The best way to keep a witness talking was to listen and not interrupt. She pushed down her growing excitement and sat on her hands. Her nervous tic of flapping her hands in front of her when she got excited could throw Grace off, and she didn't want to give her any reason to stop talking.

Grace nodded with a faraway look. "Those were terrible times. Hell on earth. It was so nice to chat in Polish. I spoke Hebrew, of course, but my parents had been less religious than most and we really considered ourselves Polish. Szymon and I spoke in Polish every chance we could. Such a gift to have as the end of life looms ahead of you."

"Do you mean the Holocaust? Was Szymon Jewish as well?" Murphy watched as Johan took out a small Moleskine notebook and jotted down some notes.

"I do. I was in Auschwitz. The concentration camp. I don't think Szymon was Jewish though. He always said Polish. He spoke about his mother often and how they'd been separated. He told me she died in the streets. I could never get it out of him how he survived the war, but we all did things. Survival sometimes takes over entirely. We spoke of the happy times before the war," she said and lifted up her sleeve. Murphy's heart dropped at the sight of the faded tattoo of numbers. "He didn't have one of these, I checked," she added.

"Did you know his daughter well?" Murphy said after a moment.

"I never thought of her as his daughter, if you can imagine. She was a satisfactory nurse. Kept to herself. I'm not sure she liked me much. I never got the feeling she appreciated my talking to her father as much as I did. I thought she was jealous for a while, but her eyes looked so haunted. I don't know." She frowned at the memory. Murphy didn't have the heart to tell her who her old world buddy had been. It would have been too cruel.

"Did you ever hear from him again? After they left?" Murphy asked instead.

"You know, that was a funny thing. They left in the middle of the night and never said goodbye. Never heard another word from them. I missed him something terrible. He'd been a good friend, but troubled." She nodded to herself. "He couldn't let the past go. Sometimes, I wondered if he'd rather be there than the present. Oh, how he missed his mother," she said and nodded. "Horrible times. No one can understand how depraved those times were. Not unless you were there," she said and shuddered, tears forming in her eyes. She gazed out into the garden without saying another word.

Murphy wanted to ask another question but didn't want to disturb Grace's thoughts. Johan gave her an imperceptible nod and Murphy cleared her throat to get her attention.

"He never mentioned his last name to you, did he?" Murphy asked.

Grace shrugged. "I always assumed it was Pickford. He never said any other. All of us changed our names in some way, and he loved the silent pictures. Mary Pickford was a particular favorite of his," Grace said, the faraway look back in her eyes. Murphy knew that was all they were going to get from her.

She got up and touched the woman's shoulder. "Thank you for your help, Grace," she said.

"Another thing. He mentioned a German family had adopted him. The way he said adopted made me think it was something more...sinister. He told me they were the worst of people. I think they could have been Nazis." The woman's teary blue eyes looked up into hers. "He's done something terrible, hasn't he?"

All Murphy could do was nod.

"He had it in him. The rage. You don't fully survive that kind of experience. Not intact anyway," she said. Johan clasped her hand in his in farewell and joined Murphy at the door.

"We got it. A name. A place. This is it. This is the keystone that holds everything," Johan whispered. Murphy couldn't take her eyes off Grace, who had visibly shrunk in her seat.

"We should go. I'll call Ritchie on the way to the airport," Johan prodded gently. Murphy nodded and let him lead her out into the hallway.

She wasn't old enough to have any direct contact with World War II vets or Holocaust survivors. She'd never known her grandparents, and her parents never spoke of the past. It was hard to imagine being so haunted your entire life. The keys to the mystery of Szymon, the Jerry killer, lay back almost 60 years ago and in another part of the world.

Johan's voice penetrated her thoughts. "Murphy? You there?" he asked.

Murphy blinked at the hazy sunlight of early afternoon. "Yeah. Sorry. What did you say?"

"I just got off the phone with Ritchie. He got us plane tickets. We leave in an hour and a half."

"Did you give him..."

"First thing I did. He's on it."

30

The Bungalow
MARCH 30, 2005 - DAY 34

Johan Luken and Murphy didn't have to wait long for their ride. The moment they stepped out of the terminal, Ritchie was there with his four by four, fingers drumming impatiently on the steering wheel. He grinned wide when he saw them. The locks clicked open. Johan got in the back and Murphy took the passenger seat as Ritchie hit the gas. They sped away from the Los Angeles International Airport Arrivals terminal, Murphy clutching at the door.

"You found him," Johan said.

"How did you know?" Ritchie looked back at him.

"Watch the road, Ritchie!" Murphy pushed his face back to look forward.

"You're out of your loft, aren't you?" Johan asked. He had never seen Ritchie out in the world. Ritchie grinned.

"That woman gave you gold," he said as he took the exit for the 105 East. "I first started with the

Shoah Foundation and the Holocaust Survivors and Victim's Database but didn't find a name with the right age or name." Murphy gave a small yelp as Ritchie jerked the car into the right most lane heading to the 405 South. Ritchie continued. "So then I hit up the immigration records..."

"How did you..." Murphy asked with incredulity. Ritchie waved her off.

"And you'll never believe what I found." He waited for their reaction.

"What, Ritchie?" Johan's heart fluttered in his chest. They were going to find her alive.

"I found a secret government program."

"Come again?" Murphy interrupted.

"This is legit. I'm not some crazy conspiracy theorist, I swear. Reporters and a novelist got info on it through the Freedom of Information Act. It just got declassified. It was called Operation Paperclip and consisted of a bunch of Nazi doctors and scientists brought to America in secret to help our government create all sorts of bombs and bio warfare gear. Our government looked the other way about the fact that some of these doctors experimented on human beings in the extermination camps. I found the list of names and came across several here in Southern California. One stuck out, a Sigmund Schrieber with his wife and young son named Simon," Ritchie said. Johan sucked in his breath. It had to be him.

"The old man died in 1948 from an apparent suicide in his bathtub. The wife died the year before from cancer. I couldn't find any records for Simon Schrieber after that. Sounds fishy, right?"

"The English version of Szymon is Simon.

The time frame, the bad parents. It fits. So what happened to the house?" Murphy asked.

"It went into foreclosure some years back and was snapped up by a woman named Regina Ann Michaels."

"How do we know he'll be there?" Murphy asked, holding on for dear life as Ritchie peered over the dashboard.

"I did some checking on Regina Ann Michaels. I found a name of a woman who lived down the road from them by the name of Regina Michaels, but the strange thing was she died in 1960."

"So a ghost bought a house?" Murphy asked.

"It's the perfect hideaway," Ritchie said.

"You really found him," Johan said.

"Do we call in reinforcements?" Ritchie asked as he took the Manhattan Boulevard exit.

"Let's find out if this is the right place first. If there's some poor old woman named Regina Ann Michaels living there, I don't want to give her a heart attack when the SWAT team comes through her window," Murphy said.

"It's him. It all fits," Johan muttered under his breath. Sara, hang on. We're coming.

They flew by shopping centers and small bungalows before Ritchie slammed on the breaks to take a left onto Elm Avenue. The car crawled down the street until Ritchie found number 19782. They parked right in front.

"I'm going in alone. If this goes sideways, I'm police," Murphy said as she checked her gun in her holster.

"You aren't leaving me behind. I'm coming with you," Johan said. She looked back at him, and he shook his head. "I'm coming. I'll focus on Sara while you find the Jerry killer. All I care about is Sara."

"Fine. But I can't protect you."

"I can take care of myself," Johan said.

"I'll stay in the car. I might even duck," Ritchie offered and then grew serious. "Bring Sara back."

Johan nodded, and he and Murphy both got out of the car.

"How do you want to play this?" Johan asked.

"We knock on the door," she said and gave him a small smile. "And take it from there. Stay behind me though."

"Yes, Ma'am."

Murphy banged on the red door. They heard someone shuffling inside, and the curtain in the window shifted. Dads peered out at them and then disappeared behind the curtains.

Johan threw his body against the door. It didn't budge. He jumped back several steps and launched himself again. The door gave way with a loud crack. Flinching from the pain, Johan caught sight of Sara on the couch. He ran into the house. "Sara! Sara!"

"Johan, be careful!" He heard Murphy behind him.

"Go after him," he yelled. He dropped down to his knees in front of Sara and checked her pulse. She had one, but barely. "Sara. Wake up. Sara! SARA!" He shook her but got no response. He took out his phone and dialed 911.

"My friend needs medical attention. I can't wake her up. 19782 Elm Avenue, Manhattan Beach. Please." He lifted Sara into his arms and sobbed.

Detective Eva Murphy held her gun in front of her as she navigated through the house in search of the Jerry Killer. She heard Johan calling 911 in the other room as she walked down a small corridor. She opened the first door on the right. An older woman stood in the doorway.

"Ma'am, close the door and get into the closet," Murphy whispered. "I'm LAPD. Do you know where he went?" The older woman pointed to the last door in the hallway.

"My fault. This was my fault," the woman said in a thick, German accent and closed the door with a click.

Murphy readied her gun and stared down the hall. Was that jazz playing on the radio?

She took a deep breath and approached the door with great care, trying not to make a sound. The carpet softened the small creaks of her footsteps, but she worried they still gave her away. What the hell was she doing here without backup? How was she going to explain this to the bosses upstairs and the FBI?

"Not now, Murphy," she muttered and stopped when she heard the faucet turn. He had to be in there. The sound of water filled the hallway.

Why was the water on?

"Simon, we know you're in there. Come out with your hands up," she shouted as she pressed her back against the wall next to the doorway. She had no idea how many weapons he had inside, and she'd seen what he was capable of.

"We can do this nice, and easy, or I come in there shooting." Could the old man even hear anything over the sound of that water? Larson would have gone in there swinging and this felt like the to do exactly that.

She checked the handle. He'd left the door unlocked. She turned it and let the door swing open. Steam poured out of the bathroom as she swung her Glock in front of her.

"Get your hands up, where I can see them?" she demanded and peered into the small bathroom, waiting for the steam to dissipate.

Dads, Simon, Szymon, the Jerry Killer, stood in a bathtub filled with water holding an old fashioned blow dryer in his hand. His hair stood on end, and his eyes were maniacal and the brightest blue she'd ever seen.

"Put the hair dryer down, Simon," Murphy yelled over the running water. Simon cocked his head in response.

"It's time to die," he said. "I wanted to kill them all and in the end I became just like them. Funny how things end, don't you think?"

"Put it down!" Murphy yelled again as Simon switched the hairdryer on and dropped it into the water at his feet. Murphy shielded her eyes from the light flash. The stench of burning skin and ozone filled the small room. With her eyes still closed, she backed out of the room.

Sirens grew louder in the distance. The cavalry was coming. She'd found the killer and he'd died. She'd failed. He would never pay for what he did and who knew what would happen to her career. But, Sara was found alive. That's what mattered, she reminded herself as she went back to the living room.

ABOUT THE AUTHOR

Dominika Best is the author of the upcoming supernatural suspense series Ghosts of Los Angeles. She lives in magical Los Angeles with her family where ghosts dwell around every corner.

Never miss the next ghost!
Sign up at www.dominikabest.com/newsletter

Contact info:
www.dominikabest.com

www.ingramcontent.com/pod-product-compliance
Lightning Source LLC
Chambersburg PA
CBHW051641180726
48284CB00006B/1816